Jane's head pounded

She shouldn't accept him. She knew she shouldn't. This was just like Alex. Impulsive. Doing things he would later regret. He'd been like this all through their childhood. But Jane had no energy. No strength. No courage. The fear Stepmama would, somehow, force her to marry Pikeford was all consuming.

She had dwindled until she was a mere husk, and like a husk, she allowed herself to be carried on the wind. "Yes."

All she wanted was for all of this—and all of them— to go away. The duke, she could see, was uneasy. But Stepmama—oh, she was delighted! Not only was her nuisance of a stepdaughter finally off her hands at the advanced age of three-and-twenty, but the family would now be irrevocably connected to that of the Duke of Cheriton, one of the most powerful and influential men in the land.

Jane's conscience made a valiant late attempt at fairness, and she clutched Alex's hand.

"Alex! No... I should not have... I am not thinking straight... You need not..."

Her breathless protest died away as he held her gaze with those gorgeous golden-brown eyes of his. Alex grinned that old, reckless care-for-nothing grin that had stolen Jane's young heart years before. He pulled her close and put his lips to her ear.

"C'mon, Janey. It'll be all right. It'll be fun."

Author Note

The Beauchamp family saga concludes with Alexander—the younger son of Leo, Duke of Cheriton—but, as always, this book can be read as a standalone story.

Lord Alexander Beauchamp's relationship with his powerful father has always been difficult, but not even Alex understands why, or why he keeps his entire family at arm's length. All he knows is he wants to be left alone to breed and train his beloved horses, and if he never visits his childhood home, Cheriton Abbey, again, he will be a happy man.

So, of course, his story just has to begin at the Abbey—the first time the entire Beauchamp family has all been under one roof in four years.

Now, Alex suffers no illusions about himself—he would make a dreadful husband with his black moods, so he has vowed never to marry. Ever. But when Lady Jane Colebrooke—his neighbor and childhood playmate—is trapped in an impossible predicament, Alex finds himself offering marriage in an uncharacteristically quixotic gesture.

At least they are friends—that's a good start for any marriage, isn't it?

Except, quiet Jane is determined to help Alex face his demons, and Alex is equally determined to keep her at arm's length.

I hope you enjoy the clash as Alex and Jane learn that love and trust go hand in hand, and as Alex finally understands his long-standing hostility toward his own father.

JANICE PRESTON

—

Christmas with His Wallflower Wife

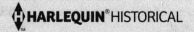

Recycling programs
for this product may
not exist in your area.

ISBN-13: 978-1-335-63553-2

Christmas with His Wallflower Wife

Copyright © 2019 by Janice Preston

Printed in U.S.A.

Janice Preston grew up in Wembley, North London, with a love of reading, writing stories and animals. In the past she has worked as a farmer, a police call handler and a university administrator. She now lives in the West Midlands with her husband and two cats and has a part-time job with a weight-management counselor—vainly trying to control her own weight despite her love of chocolate!

Books by Janice Preston

Harlequin Historical

Regency Christmas Wishes
"Awakening His Sleeping Beauty"

The Lochmore Legacy

His Convenient Highland Wedding

The Beauchamp Heirs

Lady Olivia and the Infamous Rake
Daring to Love the Duke's Heir
Christmas with His Wallflower Wife

The Beauchamp Betrothals

Cinderella and the Duke
Scandal and Miss Markham
Lady Cecily and the Mysterious Mr. Gray

The Governess Tales

The Governess's Secret Baby

Visit the Author Profile page
at Harlequin.com.

To all the readers and reviewers who have taken the Beauchamp family to their hearts.

Thank you for all your support and enthusiasm—I'm eternally grateful. xxx

Chapter One

Cheriton Abbey—early September 1817

Try as she might, Lady Jane Colebrooke couldn't quite suppress her quiver of excitement as her father's carriage passed through the gates of Cheriton Abbey, the Devonshire seat of their neighbour, the powerful Duke of Cheriton. It was Olivia, the Duke's daughter and Jane's childhood friend, who had told Jane that her brother, Lord Alexander Beauchamp, would be home for the first time in over four years and Jane's heart had twitched with the longing to see him again.

Not that him being there would make any difference. She'd long ago accepted he would never return her feelings. They'd last met in London in the spring. He'd even danced with her. And still he never seemed to notice her as a female, let alone a lady worthy of courting. No. To him, she was—as she had always been—good old Janey. She turned from the window and her heart shrivelled at seeing her stepmother's sharp gaze on her.

'Why the sour expression, Jane? You are going to a garden party, not a funeral.'

Jane bit the inside of her cheek, determined not to

retaliate. Defying her stepmother had never borne fruit and life, she had learned, was more tolerable if she allowed Lady Stowford's jibes to pass over her head.

'I hope you will at least be civil to Sir Denzil when you meet him,' Stepmama continued. 'He has been invited… I made a particular point of asking when I saw him at church last Sunday.'

Jane swallowed. Stepmama had been doing her utmost to pair Jane and Sir Denzil Pikeford ever since the man—another neighbour—had begun to show an interest in her. The fact Jane actively disliked the baronet made no difference—Stepmama was so eager to get her just-turned-twenty-three-year-old stepdaughter off her hands she had even persuaded Papa to add an extra one thousand pounds to her dowry.

One thing Jane knew for certain: if she ever *did* marry, she would not meekly accept whatever her husband decreed, as she accepted Stepmama's demands. She would stand up for herself. Right from the start. But it was hard to change the habits of a lifetime with the stepmother who had raised her from a baby and who ruled their household like an empress.

'You do not accuse me of incivility, I hope, ma'am?'

Papa stirred at her words. 'Jane is never rude to people, my dear.' Bless him for one of his sporadic attempts to support the daughter of his first marriage, no matter how unkind Stepmama might be. Jane couldn't blame him for intervening so rarely. Not when she, too, often chose to remain silent rather than setting the household on its ears for days on end.

'You know very well she needs to be *more* than polite, Stowford, if I am to bring Sir Denzil to the point. Really… have you forgotten our dear Miranda is to come out next year? How shameful if her older sister is *still* unwed!'

She raked her stepdaughter from head to toe while Miranda, the elder of Jane's two half-sisters, smirked.

'You had the perfect opportunity to marry—in your *debut year*, no less—when that nice Mr Romsley offered for you. Quite a coup for a girl as plain as you. But, oh, no! *He* was not good enough for *Lady Jane*. I begged you to accept him but, as ever, Lady Jane knows best! And since then, nary a sniff of a suitor until Sir Denzil. You are *such* a stubborn gel. I've always said so.'

It was hot in the carriage, with the family all squashed in together, and Lady Stowford, her face the shade of a beetroot following her outburst, collapsed back against the squabs, fanning herself furiously. Jane turned away, the all-too-familiar pain curling through her. It was so familiar she barely noticed it any more. The pain of unrequited love.

Ha! How naive had she been? In March 1813, the Beauchamp family had attended Olivia's wedding to Lord Hugo Alastair at the Abbey before all heading to London for the Season. It was Jane's debut year and she'd had such high hopes, certain Alex would finally see her as a young lady and not simply the annoying little neighbour who had dogged his footsteps throughout his boyhood.

He was two years her senior and her childhood hero. He'd taught her to ride and she'd willingly followed him into all sorts of adventures, often ending in trouble of one sort or another. But Alex always protected her from the worst of the blame and she'd marvelled at his bravery in the face of his father's formidable wrath.

But at the start of her first Season all her hopes crashed to the ground. London Alex treated her exactly as Devonshire Alex had always treated her—like another little sister. Her hero-worship of Alex might have matured over the years into love, but Alex clearly didn't see her in that way and who could blame him? His reputation as a skilled lover was legendary and unhappily married ladies of the *ton* vied for his attention. Why would he ever be interested in a plain, dull female like *good old Janey*?

Despite that inauspicious start, her love for him— buoyed by her blind hope that, one day, he would open his eyes and recognise her as his soulmate—had persisted and she had stubbornly refused Mr Romsley's offer, for how could she make her vows to another man when her heart belonged to Alex?

She had lived to regret her decision because she'd received no further offers in the intervening years and Alex had not returned to Devonshire since. The only time she saw him was in London during the Season each year and now she accepted he would never see her as anything other than his old playmate. *Now*, she would willingly marry. She longed to have her own household to run and to escape Stepmama and her constant barrage of criticism. But that would *never* be with Sir Denzil Pikeford. In his late thirties, he drank too much, his teeth were rotting, his manners were appalling and his conversation consisted mainly of boasting of his hunting exploits.

Even Stepmama was preferable to a lifetime with *that*.

The carriage drew to a halt. Jane looked up at the honey-eyed stone walls of the old Abbey... It had been like a second home to her throughout her childhood and the memories flooded back...happy childhood memories...

Grantham, the Duke's haughty butler, showed them straight through the huge hall and out to the extensive lawns at the rear of the Abbey, where a footman offered them glasses of punch or lemonade. There must have been fifty guests there already and Jane recognised many faces as her gaze swept the crowd, seeking...

Her heart leapt, then beat a tattoo in her chest. She

might have accepted her love would remain unrequited for ever, but still she could not deny it.

Lord Alexander Beauchamp—tall, broad-shouldered and impossibly handsome, with those strong Beauchamp features shared by all the men of the family: the strong jaw, aquiline nose, lean cheeks, beautifully sculptured mouth and arresting eyes under straight, dark brows. He stood with his older brother Dominic, Lord Avon, slightly apart from the crowd, and Jane recognised that Dominic was attempting to pacify his fiery-tempered brother.

They looked so alike, other than their colouring: Dominic shared the black hair and silvery-grey eyes of the Duke—as did Olivia—whereas Alex had the thick mahogany-brown hair and amber eyes of his late mother. In temperament, however, they were opposite. Dominic had always been the dutiful, responsible son. Alex had, for as long as Jane could remember, rebelled against his father—one of the reasons he hadn't been back to the Abbey for so long. The other, Jane knew, was the painful memory that haunted him whenever he returned...the memory of the day he'd found his mother's dead body in the summer house by the lake.

Alex had never spoken to Jane about that day—he'd been seven years old and he hadn't spoken at all for a year afterwards—but Olivia had long ago told Jane all about it and about the nightmares Alex suffered. Jane's young, tender heart had gone out to him, but she had never been able to penetrate the barriers behind which he retreated whenever anyone ventured too close to his memories of that day, or to his feelings about what had happened.

He kept everyone—family included—at arm's length.

While Dominic talked, Alex's restless gaze swept the crowd and Jane felt the physical jolt when his amber eyes— tiger's eyes, Dominic always called them—alighted on her. He grinned and beckoned her over. A blush heated her cheeks as she walked towards him and she schooled her expression, always afraid her feelings for him would shine from her eyes. A girl had to have some pride.

'Janey! How lovely to see you! You still game for a swim in the lake like we used to?'

'Alex!' Dominic hissed. 'For God's sake, think before you speak, will you? Would you say such a thing to any other young lady of your acquaintance?'

'I'd say it to Livvy.' Alex winked at Jane. 'Janey's just like one of us…she doesn't care about standing on ceremony, do you, Janey?'

Jane shook her head, stretching her lips in a smile. Defeat spread through her, settling like a lead weight in her stomach. There was the proof, as if she needed it, that Alex would never view her as anything other than his old childhood playmate.

'Of course I don't mind. After all, if I'm not accustomed to your teasing ways by now, Alex, I never shall be.'

Alex grinned again. 'There! What did I tell you, Dom?' He slung his arm around her shoulders and hugged her briefly into his side. 'How's the old witch?'

Dominic rolled his eyes. 'I'll leave you to it,' he said. 'Jane—please try to stop my reprehensible brother from upsetting anyone else. He's already enraged Lord Wagstaff by ripping up at him over the state of his horses and I really must go and see if Liberty needs help…she's been gone a long time.'

Liberty was Dominic's new bride—they had met earlier that year in London, fallen in love and married, despite Liberty not being the perfect society lady Dominic planned to wed. Jane had met her in London, where they had married in June, and thought she was, in fact, the perfect match for Dominic, helping him to take life, and himself, a little less seriously.

'Is there something amiss?' Jane wondered why Liberty might need help.

'That dog of hers,' said Dominic. 'Never have I known such a mischief-maker. He cannot keep his nose out of trouble for more than five minutes.'

'Romeo?' Liberty had rescued the dog as a stray in London earlier that year.

Dominic nodded. 'He sneaked into the kitchens again, knocked over a cream jug and helped himself to a crock of butter, just when the servants are run off their feet with preparations for today. Liberty's gone to catch him and shut him away. Why she insisted on bringing him here I'll never know!'

'You can't fool us, Dom. You dote on that dog as much as Liberty does,' said Alex, nudging his brother.

Dominic's jaw tightened. 'I do *not* dote on him. I merely tolerate him.'

'Is that why he was sprawled across your lap last night when I arrived? He was fondling Romeo's ears, Janey, and murmuring sweet nothings.'

'Rubbish! I was doing nothing of the sort. I'll see you both later.'

Alex watched Dominic stalk away, his mouth curved in a smile that managed to be both mischievous and satisfied at the same time, before switching his attention back to Jane. She tore her own gaze from his lips, that telltale heat building again in her cheeks.

'How does it feel being back after all this time?'

Alex's top lip curled. 'Same as ever. I arrive and then I can't wait to leave.'

'You can't mean that, Alex. It's years since you've been

home. And the entire family is here…surely you want to spend time with them?'

His eyes roamed across the crowd as Jane spoke and she noticed them pause as they reached his father, the Duke, his gaze turning wistful as it often did when he watched his father. She suspected he longed to have the same easy rapport Dominic had with their father, but that he simply did not know how to change—their relationship had been tetchy for as long as Jane had known him. That wistfulness didn't last long. His expression soon hardened.

'I do mean it. This is no longer my home. Foxbourne is. Let's not talk about that, Janey. Tell me, how is Pippin?'

Jane's throat tightened, aching at the mention of her beloved mare. 'She died, Alex. Last year.'

Genuine shock and sympathy played across Alex's features. '*Last year?* Why didn't you tell me?'

'When would I tell you? You are never here and, in London…it's not the same somehow.'

'But… Oh, God, Janey. I'm sorry. What are you riding now?'

Horses had always been their shared passion and they were the love of Alex's life. He bred and trained horses at Foxbourne Manor and had built a solid reputation for producing first-class riding and carriage horses.

'Sandy.'

'*Sandy?*' Alex burst out laughing, but quickly sobered. He searched Jane's expression, a frown knitting his brows. 'I thought you were joking, but you're not. How can a plod like old Sandy be a suitable mount for a rider of your quality?'

'Papa said it's not worth me having a new horse when Sandy is there doing nothing.'

'Your *father* said that? Now I know you're gammoning

me—he's always been so proud of your skill as a horse-woman. It was the old witch, wasn't it? What *is* her game?'

Jane burned with humiliation. Her stepmother's game was to make Jane's life so intolerable she would view marriage to Sir Denzil as preferable. But she wouldn't discuss such a subject with Alex of all people.

'Shall I have a word with your papa, Janey? I've got a filly at Foxbourne that would be perfect for you... I'd give him a good price. Half what she's worth.'

Alex hadn't changed. He'd always been ready and willing to take up cudgels on Jane's behalf whenever she was treated unfairly. To see that protective streak still in evidence infused her with a warm glow. She might not have Alex's love, but he did care for her. With that, she must be content.

'I would rather you said nothing, Alex. He'll only tell Stepmama and you know how cross she'll be if she thinks I've been complaining about my lot. It's not worth the upset, but I do appreciate the offer.'

'You're too forgiving, Janey. I've always said so. Look at the number of times you've forgiven me!' He winked at her and they both smiled at the shared memories. 'But I'll not say anything if you prefer me not to. Now, I really ought to mingle. Not that I want to, but I did promise Aunt Cecily and my stepmother I would be sociable.' Alex's father had remarried five years before. 'I'll see you later, I expect.'

Off he strode, leaving Jane deflated and with a headache pinching her forehead. She rubbed it absently. The thought of joining one of the loudly chattering groups clustered around the lawn held little appeal. Stepmama was talking to Sir Denzil Pikeford and Jane turned away before Stepmama could wave her over. She really couldn't face that bore with her emotions in such a raw state.

She slipped through a gate into the apple orchard next to the lawn and on into the copse beyond, on the far side of which was the Abbey lake where, it was said, the monks used to raise fish to supplement their diet. The fresher air by the water would hopefully help her headache. And no one would miss her.

Chapter Two

Tension gripped Alex as he made polite conversation with his father's guests. He didn't belong here. Even in this crowd, even among his family, he felt alone. Separate. For ever the outsider.

He hadn't been back to the Abbey since Olivia's wedding and was only here now because it was the first time in over four years the entire Beauchamp family had all been together under one roof. The rest had been here a month already and he had only finally agreed to attend the annual Abbey garden party because Dominic threatened to drive up to Foxbourne to fetch him. He'd arrived yesterday and fully intended to leave tomorrow.

An hour or more of small talk and sipping cider-apple punch was enough to try any man's patience and Alex had less than his fair share of that. When dealing with people, at least. Horses...now that was another matter. There, his patience knew no bounds. With a smile and a gesture towards the house, he extricated himself from an in-depth conversation about last year's appalling weather—still the main topic of conversation for country folk—and he slipped away, feeling his tension dissipate as he left the crowds behind. Once inside, he hurried through the library, and out on to the terrace that hugged the east wing of the Abbey. Down the steps, along the stone-flagged path that bisected the formal garden, through the arch cut into the beech hedge and out on to the path beyond. It took less than a minute to reach his goal: the small gate that opened into a copse of ornamental trees.

He closed the gate behind him.

Alone. As always. As he liked it.

Nothing but trees. No need to put on a charade. No need for polite conversation about trivialities.

He leaned back against the trunk of a copper beech and closed his eyes. It had been as painful as he feared, coming back. The family had all come out to greet him. Alex had tolerated hugs from his aunts and his sister, but when Father had come forward, his arms opening, Alex had thrust out his hand for a handshake, quashing his guilt at his father's sorrowful expression. He couldn't explain the aversion he felt for his father, but it was undeniable. Every time they met, Alex felt like a cat having its fur rubbed the wrong way and he couldn't wait to get away.

Then last night, in his old bedchamber, the dreams returned. Not as badly as in his childhood, but enough to unsettle him and for him to wake this morning with that old feeling of impending doom pressing down on him.

It was good to see the rest of the family, though. And dear Jane…his childhood playmate: the squire to his knight, the soldier to his general, the pirate to his captain. Shame about Pippin… God knew what her father was about, allowing that old witch to pick on poor Jane the way she did.

Alex pushed away from the tree and shrugged out of his jacket, then rolled up his shirtsleeves. Warm, dry days had been few and far between this summer—although it was still an improvement on last—but today was one of them: the sun high in a cloudless sky and insects humming. Alex wandered through the trees, his jacket hooked over his shoulder, absorbing the peace, disturbed only by the occasional burst of laughter from the garden party, taking little notice of where he was going. It was only when the sun reflecting off the surface of the lake dazzled him that he realised where he was. He stopped, his guts churning in that old familiar way.

He'd had no intention of coming here, to the place where it had happened. His mother's favourite place. And yet his feet had led him there. Unerringly. As they always did. The summer house overlooking the lake was no more— destroyed by his father after his mother died, a weeping willow planted in its place, in her memory.

The willow had grown in the years since he had last seen it, its fronds now sweeping the ground, and the sur- rounding trees and shrubs—also planted after her death— had matured, isolating the willow in a clearing bounded by woodland and water.

He stood, just looking, the dark memories close, claw- ing their way slowly, inexorably, out of the chasm of the past. His heart drummed in his chest, nausea rising to crowd his throat as he shoved those chilling memories of his childhood—of that day—back into the depths and slammed a mental lid on them. He'd had enough practice at keeping them at bay. Eighteen years of practice—he'd only been seven when his mother died...when she was killed.

He shoved harder, feeling sweat bead his forehead. He shouldn't have come here, should've stayed with the others, endured their chatter and their laughter, but it was the same every time he returned to his childhood home. No matter his best intentions, this spot drew him like a lodestone.

The sound of a scuffle and a scream, quickly cut off,

grabbed his attention. He scanned his surroundings, still shaken by the past that lurked, ready to catch him unawares. He saw no one, but a muffled cry and a grunted oath sounded from beyond a clump of rhododendrons. His heart thudded. Those sounds... The memories swirled, trying to form. He swore and strode into the copse, rounding the bushes. Whatever he saw would be preferable to the images hovering at the edge of his mind.

'No! Please! Stop!'

Breathless. Pleading. Scared.

No...*terrified*. Alex broke into a run, deeper into the trees, even as the sound of a slap rang out. He rounded another thicket.

Rage exploded through him—a starburst of fury that electrified every single nerve ending and muscle. He hauled the man off the woman beneath him and jerked him around, vaguely registering the stink of alcohol. His fist flew and he relished the satisfaction of the crunch of bone and the bright claret spurt of blood. He cast the man aside.

She was curled into a defensive ball, her back convulsing with silent sobs. Alex knew that feeling...he shoved again at the memory that threatened to burst free. The past needed to stay in the past. He fell to his knees and gathered the woman into his arms.

'Shh...shh. You're safe. He's gone.'

He'd recognised him. Sir Denzil Pikeford, a local landowner, who'd been well into his cups when Alex spoke to him earlier and now stumbled away through the trees, hands cupping his bloody nose. Pikeford would suffer the consequences for this, but he could wait.

He held the woman's head to his chest as he stroked down her back, soothing her, registering the bare skin, the ripped clothing. Her shuddering sobs gradually subsided. Her breathing hitched. Slowed. Hitched again.

'There now. You're safe.'

Alex looked down. And realised for the first time she was a lady…one of his father's guests then, not a maid, or an unwary farm girl caught off guard.

'Alex?'

A quiet, halting enquiry. She looked up, face blotchy with tears, one cheek stark red, eyes puffy, ringed by spiky wet eyelashes. Recognition thumped Alex square in the chest. He recalled the slap and another surge of fury rolled through him. How could anyone single out a girl as kind and inoffensive as Jane?

She pulled away from him with a gasp, frantic hands scrabbling to gather the tattered remnants of her gown to cover her exposed breasts. Then her eyes rounded with horror as voices called out. The sound of feet trampling the undergrowth came closer. Swiftly, Alex reached for his jacket—fallen nearby—and slung it around Jane before, still on his knees, twisting his torso to face her parents.

'By God, sir! What is this?'

Lord Stowford, Jane's father, was mottled with rage. Alex stood to face him, but before he could speak Jane's stepmother reached her husband's side.

'Oh! You *wicked, deceitful* girl! You are ruined!' She turned to her husband. 'Stowford! *Do* something!'

'Beauchamp! You shall answer—'

'Papa! No! Alex saved me. It was Sir D-Denzil.' Jane scrambled to her feet.

'I knew it!' Lady Stowford pressed one hand to her bosom and plied her fan vigorously with the other. 'As soon as I saw you sneaking off with him!'

Alex frowned, glancing down at Jane. Surely she knew better than to be so careless? But…he took in Lady Stowford's expression. The smug smile in her eyes. If she'd *seen*

Jane and Pikeford, why not follow them straight away, and intervene?

Jane swayed and Alex moved closer, cupped her elbow, supporting her. Shivers racked her body and tears rolled down her face. Alex stared in disgust at Jane's stepmother. Cold-hearted witch! What kind of a female...a *mother*... was she? Where was her concern for another female in distress, let alone one she had raised from a baby? But, then...she had always resented Jane.

'I didn't.' Jane was shaking her head in frantic denial. 'I *s-s-swear* it, Papa! I had the headache and hoped a walk by the water would help. He followed me. He *grabbed* me.'

'It matters not! You are ruined!' Lady Stowford's words rang with triumph. 'Stowford! Go and find Sir Denzil at once. He must make an honest woman of Jane. Then all will be well.' She eyed Jane with pitiless disdain. 'I will not allow your disgrace to taint your sisters.'

'Noooo!' Jane sagged against Alex as she uttered a low moan of despair.

'Have you no compassion?' Alex glared at Lady Stowford. A memory surfaced...of Her Ladyship trying hard to promote a match between Pikeford and Jane during last Season. And Jane's disgust at the idea. 'That foul drunkard *attacked* your daughter! He was forcing himself on her and you would have her *marry* him?'

Her haughty gaze raked Alex. 'I would, as would any responsible parent. At least she will have a husband at long last! She should be grateful.' She turned to her husband, his expression that of a man wishing he was a thousand miles away. 'Well, Stowford? Do not just stand there. Go and find Sir Denzil. You *must* see Jane *has* to be wed now she is no longer pure.'

'No! He didn't... I am still... Alex stopped him in time, Papa! *Please*, Papa!'

'Stowford! You must think of our other daughters. *Their* reputations are what is important now. Jane must be wed.'

'Then *I* shall marry her.' Alex released Jane's elbow and wrapped his arm around her waist, hauling her into his side.

'Alex?'

His heart plummeted at that voice. Behind the Stowfords three figures came into view: Alex's father in the lead of his uncles, Vernon and Zach. Father's eyes swept the group. Returned to linger on Jane, then levelled a searching look at Alex.

'What happened? Pikeford? We saw him stagger out of the copse just now.'

Grateful for his father's swift understanding, Alex nodded. He held that silver-grey gaze, his gut churning with the same mix of hopeless love and unwanted revulsion he always felt towards this man he so desperately longed to love unconditionally. Father walked forward, ranging himself alongside Alex and Jane.

'This matter can be contained, Stowford. No one will know but us. There is no need to force Jane to marry anyone.'

The swell of relief was brief. One look at Lady Stowford's expression—even as she was agreeing with his father—was enough to stir Alex's doubts. That old witch wouldn't rest until she had her wish—Jane married off, no matter the circumstances.

Jane was still trembling, like an injured bird…fragile… terrified.

'No,' he heard himself say. He slid his arm from around Jane's waist and grasped her shoulders, manoeuvring her so he could look straight into her swollen eyes. 'Lady Jane Colebrooke…will you do me the honour of being my wife?'

* * *

Jane's head pounded. She shouldn't accept him. She knew she shouldn't—this was just like Alex. Impulsive. Doing things he would later regret. He'd been like it all through their childhood. But Jane had no energy. No strength. No courage. The fear Stepmama would, somehow, force her to marry Pikeford was all-consuming.

She had dwindled until she was a mere husk and, like a husk, she allowed herself to be carried on the wind. 'Yes.'

All she wanted was for all of this—and all of them—to go away. The Duke, she could see, was uneasy. But Stepmama—oh, she was delighted! Not only was her nuisance of a stepdaughter finally off her hands, but the family would now be irrevocably connected to that of the Duke of Cheriton, one of the most powerful and influential men in the land.

Jane's conscience made a valiant late attempt at fairness and she clutched Alex's hand.

'Alex! No… I should not have… I am not thinking straight… You need not…'

Her breathless protest died away as he held her gaze with those gorgeous golden-brown eyes of his. Alex grinned that old reckless care-for-nothing grin that had stolen Jane's young heart years before. He pulled her close and put his lips to her ear.

'C'mon, Janey. It'll be all right. It'll be fun.'

The same words with which he had led her into devilment during their youth—he to prove he wouldn't be confined by rules; she, willing to do anything to escape Stepmama and to please her childhood hero. There had always been consequences, of course, but now—here was her chance to escape Stepmama for good. Never again would she have to bite her tongue as she endured one of Stepmama's diatribes about how plain and useless she was.

'Thank you.'

She caught the Duke's frown from the corner of her eye and quailed inside. But it seemed Alex had noticed, too, because his arm snaked around her waist again and he faced his father, chin jutting, head high, bringing to mind the defiant boy, full of bravado.

'Father?'

His challenge was unmistakable. A muscle leapt in the Duke's jaw, but he nodded.

'If it is your wish, then we will make the arrangements. Wait here.'

He turned on his heel and strode away and Jane felt the tension leach from Alex. She eyed those left in the clearing. Stepmama was already crowing to Papa about the connection and the splendid society wedding she would arrange. Alex's uncle, Lord Vernon Beauchamp, walked over to Alex and Jane, followed by Mr Graystoke—a half-Romany whose father was an earl, and who was married to Alex's Aunt Cecily, but refused to be called 'uncle'. Stepmama—for all she fawned over the Duke—held his brother-in-law in disdain and made no secret of the fact.

'Alex? What can I do to help?' Concern etched Lord Vernon's face as he gripped his nephew's shoulder.

'You can shut *her* up about lavish society weddings,' Alex growled. He looked down at Jane. 'Come and stay at the Abbey, Janey. Don't go back there and let her terrorise you into having what *she* wants. Unless…do you *want* a big wedding?'

Jane shook her head. She could think of nothing worse. 'Stepmama only wants one because she thinks it will help my sisters attract husbands.'

Mr Graystoke's lip curled. He strolled unhurriedly across to where Stepmama was still talking at Papa. Silence descended.

'The young couple prefer a quiet wedding. Family only,' he said.

Papa flushed red as Stepmama visibly bristled.

'Who do you think—?'

Her mouth shut with a snap as Lord Vernon joined them.

'And Lady Jane will stay at the Abbey until Alex obtains the licence,' he drawled. 'I foresee no objection from the Bishop and you may rest assured Jane will be well chaperoned in the meantime.'

'I shall come myself to collect her belongings,' Mr Graystoke added and Stepmama spluttered, spots of outrage colouring her cheeks. 'Shall we say in two hours? If you leave now, that should give you sufficient time to pack her belongings.'

The two men turned their backs on her parents and strolled back to Alex and Jane.

'*That* shut her up,' Lord Vernon said, with a wink.

Over his shoulder, Jane watched her parents leave, Stepmama gesticulating furiously. Even though she wanted them gone, it still hurt to see Papa walk away without a word.

'Maybe you should take her back to the house, Alex, and not wait for Leo,' said Mr Graystoke. 'She's had a shock.' He crouched slightly and tipped up her chin, holding her gaze with his dark eyes. 'All will be well, my dear. You are part of the family now. You are protected.'

The anxiety agitating her stomach settled and stilled. 'Thank you.' She glanced up at Alex, who was frowning at her. 'What is it?'

'You can't go back with your gown all torn like that. I—'

His jaw snapped shut and Jane followed his gaze. Alex's father, a gown draped over one arm, was approaching, the Duchess—Alex's stepmother—by his side.

'Vern, Zach, Alex…come. Let us return to our guests. Rosalind will help Jane. The fewer people who know what happened here, the better.'

'We'd better find a way to stop Lady Stowford from spewing her poison all over the district, then,' said Lord Vernon. 'I believe Zach and I *might* have contrived to upset her. Just a smidgeon, you understand. And *totally* without intention.' The twinkle in his eyes belied his apologetic tone.

'I have already helped the Stowfords to understand it is in their best interests to remain quiet,' said the Duke.

'We met them on their way back to the house,' added the Duchess, 'and Lady Stowford made the mistake of attempting to pull rank on Leo, claiming rights as the mother of the bride. I believe she now accepts it is what Alex and Jane want that is important. Now, off you go, you men, and leave me and Jane to make her respectable. Go on! Shoo!'

Chapter Three

Left alone with the Duchess, Jane found her voice again.

'I shouldn't have accepted Alex, Your Grace. I'm sorry. He doesn't want to marry me. I know he doesn't. Stepmama gave him no choice.' Suppressed tears thickened her voice. Why would anyone want to marry her? She wasn't pretty or even vivacious. Alex had been trapped. 'She *would* keep saying I was ruined and I must marry S-Sir Denzil.'

'Jane…you cannot possibly marry that villain after what he tried to do.' The Duchess took her hand. 'You and Alex have always been friends, have you not?'

Jane nodded.

'Then allow him to help his friend and…' The Duchess paused, a line stitched between her brows. Then her chin tilted. 'And, in return, you can be a friend to him. Alex *needs* someone like you in his life…' she nodded, emphasising her words '…although he would never admit it. Unless, of course, the thought of being wed to him truly repels you?'

Hazel eyes searched Jane's face. She shook her head. No. That thought did not repel her. Not at all.

'Good. Now, come, let us get this gown off you and

make you respectable. I have even brought a comb and hairpins. No one will guess what so nearly happened and Leo has already shut Sir Denzil in one of the outbuildings until he sobers up and can be…um…*"brought to fully appreciate the iniquity of his actions"* were, I believe, Leo's exact words.'

They were all being so kind, but Jane dreaded to think what they really thought of her. *She* knew Alex had stopped Pikeford in time, but did anyone else believe her? She shuddered at the memory of his hand painfully squeezing her breast…his fingers between her legs… Her stomach roiled, pushing the contents up. She ran to a nearby bush, bent double and vomited. Tears blurred her eyes. She could not stop retching, even after her stomach was empty and sore. Gradually, the heaving slowed and she became aware of hands supporting her, holding her hair back.

'Better now?'

'Yes. Thank you, Your Grace.'

'Then let us make you respectable again and return to the house.'

They avoided the lawn at the rear of the Abbey, where the garden party continued, by following the lake around until they met the grass path that wound up through the copse towards the formal gardens leading to the terrace and the library. The Duchess peered through the hedge into the gardens before smiling encouragingly at Jane.

'They're empty. When the Duke told me what had happened, I ordered bath water to be heated and a bedchamber prepared. You must be exhausted. Come.'

She slipped her arm around Jane's waist and they hurried through the gardens and up the steps to the terrace, where one of the French doors into the library stood open. Within minutes the Duchess had whisked Jane upstairs.

* * *

Father, as was his wont, moved swiftly to avert any scandal. Pikeford had already left for Plymouth, escorted by two footmen to ensure he took passage on the first ship bound for the Continent, thus thwarting Alex of the chance to thump the bastard again. But Father did not broach the subject of Alex's impending marriage until after dinner that evening, when he invited Alex to join him in his study.

Alex braced himself for the interrogation, every muscle locked tight, as though his body was preparing itself for physical battle.

'Well, Alex?'

Alex unclenched his jaw with an effort. 'Well… I hope you will wish us happy, sir.'

Father stared at him for several seconds, his eyes troubled, before pouring them both a glass of brandy. He handed one to Alex and gestured for him to sit in one of the pair of wingback chairs either side of the unlit hearth.

'You've had time to think this through, Son. Marriage is a big step—it is not something that should be rushed into on a whim.'

'It was *not* a whim.' As ever, he instinctively opposed Father.

One dark eyebrow flicked high. 'Did you know this morning you would propose to Lady Jane Colebrooke today?'

'Of course not! I—'

'Then it was a whim.'

As Alex opened his mouth to protest again, Father held up one hand. 'Hear me out, Alex, before you shoot me down again.'

Alex subsided. How he wished he could emulate Father's cool, calm control. Nothing ever seemed to rattle him whereas he… Alex…flew into the boughs at the slightest provocation. He must learn to control that tendency with a wife to consider.

His insides clenched. A wife! Marriage! He'd never, ever imagined marrying. He knew himself too well to believe he could ever make a good husband.

'It's not too late to change your mind, Alex. Once you exchange your vows, you will be together for life.'

'My mind is made up,' Alex muttered.

'Nevertheless you should listen to what I am about to say, not only for your own sake, but for Jane's, as well.'

'*Jane's* sake?'

Father didn't reply, but held Alex's gaze with his own.

'Jane will be happy to get away from that witch of a stepmother of hers.'

'Granted. But if I can guarantee you that Jane will never have to return to her father's house, will you reconsider your decision?'

Alex stared at his father. 'How?'

Hope warred with resentment inside. Hope, because marriage *was* irrevocable. His father was right, although Alex would never admit that aloud. Resentment because… well, resentment was his habitual reaction to everything his father said or did.

'I will undertake to find her a decent husband.'

He didn't like the sound of that. How could his father possibly know a man's character, or how he might change? Once Jane was wed, that would be it. She'd be bound for life to some stranger she didn't even know. Every fibre of his being rebelled against that idea… Jane was his friend. He'd always protected her, right from when they were children.

'You think I couldn't make her a decent husband? We've been friends a long time.'

'I am aware of that. But…you're only five-and-twenty, Alex. It's a young age for a man to take such a big step.'

'Dom is only a year older than me. He got married this year.'

'He thought it his duty. But then, thank goodness, he fell in love. Besides, you and Dominic are very different characters.'

Alex scowled, biting back the urge to rip up at his father. The truth hurt sometimes.

'*You* were only eighteen when you married my mother.'

'The circumstances were very different. My father was dying and fretting over the succession of the dukedom. I married for him.' Father thrust his hand through his hair. 'Alex…this is not wise… Allow me to find a good husband for Jane… Don't rush into this. You might both live to regret it.'

Alex drained his glass and rose to his feet. 'And we might not! This is *my* decision. I leave for Exeter first thing to obtain the licence.' He'd already arranged for Dominic to drive him in his curricle. 'The wedding will take place as soon as possible.'

Then he could leave this place with all its threatening memories and go home to Foxbourne where he was happiest.

'I intend to make the same offer to Jane tomorrow.' Father's voice was clipped. 'She deserves to know she has a choice.'

Alex's simmering temper boiled up at that. 'There is no need for you to involve yourself—I don't want you pressuring Jane just because you think you know what is best. You cannot manipulate us to your bidding like you manipulate everyone else. I bid you goodnight.'

His temper raged until he was halfway to his bedchamber when—as so often happened where his father was concerned—it cooled as suddenly as if doused in a bucket of icy water, leaving shame behind. He contemplated rejoining the family downstairs but couldn't face having to act the part of happy brother, nephew and son. Not to mention happy prospective bridegroom. He couldn't face his family. Couldn't face his father again. He continued on to his room, eyeing the bed with disfavour, already anticipating the restless night to come.

Why was life never straightforward?

He'd refused his father's offer, driven by that familiar but inexplicable defiance, but that didn't mean he knew exactly what he did want.

He was torn.

He'd been fully reconciled to life as a bachelor, with no need—or wish—to share his life with anyone. And as for marriage to Jane—she was like his little sister! No. She was more than that. She was, and always had been, his friend. But…marriage? Didn't that mean sharing his feelings and his innermost thoughts? That was unthinkable. He kept those to himself. Always had. He was an island— even when he was out with his friends, carousing, he was always separate, somehow, and that was how he liked it.

But, strangely, now he was faced with it, a part of him—a newly emerging, hesitant and hazy part of him— quite *liked* the idea of marriage. To Jane. At least she knew him and knew about his past. And at least she never looked at him with that infuriating mix of sympathy and pity he all too often identified in his family's expressions. He and Jane were friends—surely they could at least be comfortable together, as long as he learned to suppress his black moods. He could do it with the horses…when he worked with them it was as though nothing else existed. No past. No future. Just him and the horse. Could he learn to do the same for Jane?

And Jane loved horses as much as he did—he was sure she would be as happy at Foxbourne as he was.

It would be a better start than many couples experienced.

Jane must have slept right through to the next morning because she vaguely recalled waking at one point to find it was night-time, but now, as she propped herself up on her elbows, she could see daylight limning the curtains. Memories of the previous day loomed—Pikeford following her, his attack, his *strength*…so much more than she could have imagined. It was frighteningly impossible to fight him off and then, just as she despaired of ever stopping him, Alex had rescued her.

She flopped back on to the mattress, biting her lip against the hot sting of tears. How long had she dreamed of him seeing her as someone other than simply *good old Janey*, the girl next door? How many years had she fed her fantasies with images of him realising, at last, that he loved her…proposing to her…?

But not like this. *Never* like this!

Sick dread clogged her throat. She was in an impossible situation. If she protected Alex against his spontaneous, quixotic gesture then she must go home, to the stepmother who would not hesitate to marry her off to Sir Denzil Pikeford. And *he* would be perfectly willing…

She shuddered, rolling on to her side, curling into a ball, her arms wrapped around her torso. She would die rather than end up as Pikeford's wife. Her stomach roiled in disgust.

I cannot lie here for ever. I must face this some time.

She forced herself to rise, crossing to the window and pulling back the curtains. It was early, the sun still low in the sky. A movement caught her eye and she saw a curricle with two male occupants heading away from the Abbey.

She couldn't be sure, but she suspected the passenger was Alex and she recognised Dominic's matched bays. She frowned. Where were they off to so early? Would Alex leave in order to avoid her? He had run away rather than face unpleasant consequences when he was younger, but she couldn't believe Dominic would aid and abet him.

There's only one way to find out.

After dressing—a trunk containing her belongings had appeared as if by magic at the foot of her bed—she ventured downstairs only to find it was too early for the rest of the family to be up and about. She refused breakfast, too embarrassed to eat when none of the family was present. Ignoring her growling stomach, she selected a book from the library and settled in an armchair to pass the time until someone else appeared.

That someone, to her dismay, was the Duke of Cheriton. Jane shot to her feet, nerves churning her stomach. The Duke had never been anything but courteous to her, but he was a formidable and powerful man and some of Alex's feelings about his father had inevitably rubbed off on her over the years.

'Good morning, Jane.' The Duke gestured, indicating she should sit again. She perched on the edge of the chair. 'Grantham said I would find you in here. Are you well rested?'

'Yes, thank you, Your Grace.'

He pulled another chair across to sit opposite. 'You have a bruise on your face, I see. Did Pikeford injure you anywhere else?'

Jane shook her head, mortified at talking of such matters, nervy at being the sole focus of the Duke's attention.

His eyes narrowed and a groove appeared between his black brows. 'Unfortunately neither the Duchess nor my sister are awake, but I can send for a maid if you are un-comfortable being here alone with me.'

Her face flamed. How rude he must think her, when she had known him all her life.

'It is understandable you are still shaken after the events of yesterday.' He went to the door. She heard a murmur of voices, then he returned to sit again.

'I—I thought I saw Alex leaving,' Jane said.

A smile crinkled the Duke's eyes. 'He has not run off, you know. He outgrew that tendency a few years ago, I'm pleased to say. Dominic is driving him to Exeter, to obtain a marriage licence.'

She struggled to meet his gaze. But she must say this… she couldn't allow Alex to sacrifice himself for her. 'I will not hold him to his promise, Your Grace. I could not forgive myself if Alex married me only to regret it. *Please*. Can you tell him he need not marry me?'

'I have told him already and—'

He fell silent as the door opened and Jane breathed a sigh of relief when Olivia, her old friend and only eight months older than Jane, entered.

'Grantham said you needed me in here, Papa. Good morning, Jane.'

Olivia smiled, pulling a footstool over to sit close to Jane. She clasped her hand.

'Thank you, Livvy. Now, as I was about to say, Jane… Alex understands very well he is under no obligation to marry you and that, if he chooses not to proceed, I shall ensure you never have to return to your father's house. But I want you to understand—this offer I am about to make is for *your* benefit, Jane. Not Alexander's.' The Duke rose and crossed to the window, where the early morning sun lit his face, highlighting the silvering at his temples and the lines of stress around his eyes and mouth. 'You have known my son all your life and you know he is not always an easy man. My fear is that if he feels constrained to go ahead with your union—even by his own decision—then, later, he may well rebel against it. And you would bear the brunt of his resentment.

'You deserve to be happy in your marriage, Jane, and that is why I sought you out this morning…to make you the same offer I made to Alex. There is a third way and you may trust me when I say I shall find a way for you to be safe from both your stepmother and Pikeford.'

He returned to his chair, his silver-grey gaze on Jane's face. She swallowed. She should grab his offer with both hands. For Alex's sake. But the Duchess's words resounded in her head, keeping her silent. Alex *did* need a friend… not the friends with whom he spent his time on the town, but someone who would be there for him, day after day. Night after night. Someone to provide him with a safe anchor during those times the past came back to haunt him. Because haunt him it did. They all knew it. But no one had ever found the way to help him come to terms with the day he had discovered his mother's violated body.

And Jane, God help her, wanted to be that friend to him. If…

'What was Alex's answer to your offer, sir?'

The Duke exchanged a wry smile with his daughter. 'He threw it right back in my face and left for Exeter at first light. I believe his exact words were, "You cannot manipulate us to your bidding like you manipulate everyone else".'

Jane gasped and sympathy for the Duke buried her earlier nervousness. 'I am sorry. I don't understand—'

Olivia moved to perch on the arm of Jane's chair and hugged her. 'None of us understands my brother, Jane—there's no need for you to apologise for him. But you do need to think carefully about what *you* want. Papa will help you find a decent husband, if you decide against marrying Alex, and you mustn't be afraid the rest of us will hold it against you. You will still be our dear friend, whatever you decide.'

'Thank you, Livvy. That means a lot.' Jane pulled away from her friend's embrace, and stood up to face Alex's father. 'And thank you for your offer, Your Grace. I do appreciate it. But…as long as Alex does not change his mind and is still prepared to go ahead, I choose to marry Alex. I—I hope you do not mind? I—I…' She hauled in a breath. 'I cannot quite explain it, but…it feels right.' She laid her hand against her chest. 'In here. It feels right.'

Hot embarrassment flooded her. That was as good as a confession that she loved Alex, but she wanted to soothe any misgivings either the Duke or Olivia had about this marriage.

'I do not mind at all, Jane. In fact, I am delighted,' said the Duke. 'As I hope I made clear, my intervention was not due to any objection to either you or to the match, but merely to reassure you both that you need not feel trapped by what occurred yesterday.'

'And *I* say you are a brave woman to take Alex on,' said Olivia. 'But you know what he is like and you have always been friends. Perhaps you are just what he needs.'

She hugged Jane, and kissed her cheek. 'Welcome to the Beauchamp family.'

Chapter Four

Preparations for the wedding gained momentum throughout the day and Jane allowed herself to be swept along despite the unease that writhed in her stomach like a restless snake. She needed to speak to Alex. It was all very well the family assuming the matter was irrevocably settled but what if, now he'd had time to think, Alex had changed his mind?

All the frenetic activity infected the Beauchamps' dogs: the Duchess's wolfhound, Hector, Myrtle, a three-legged, bull-baiting type of terrier belonging to Mr Graystoke, and Liberty's Romeo. The three of them became increasingly excited, chasing one another around the house, in and out of the rooms, until Romeo darted in front of a footman carrying a tray of china and he went flying. The resulting crash brought everyone running.

'This is outside of enough!' The Duchess, her hair awry, shooed the dogs outside. 'The doors are to be kept shut and woe betide anyone who lets those animals back inside!'

Even that added to Jane's guilt. The entire household had been set on its ears just because she had foolishly decided to go for a walk alone.

* * *

The day wore on and, in the late afternoon, Jane found herself helping Alex's two aunts, Lady Cecily and Thea, Lady Vernon, to arrange flowers in three matching lead-crystal cut-glass vases to decorate the hall.

'These vases were made by Stour Crystal,' Lady Vernon said, her pride clear.

Jane knew Lord Vernon's wife came from a family of Worcestershire glassmakers. 'Is that your father's manufactory?'

'It is. Well, it belongs to my brother now. Papa died two years ago.'

'I am sorry to hear that…but you must be very proud. These are beautiful.'

'They are, aren't they? And yes, I…'

Her voice drifted into silence as the front door flew open and Alex and Dominic bowled in, laughing, the three banished dogs at their heels. Jane stilled, nerves erupting.

'Please leave the dogs outside,' Lady Cecily said to her nephews. 'Rosalind's orders. They are overexcited and have been causing mayhem, with everyone so busy. You're fortunate to have missed the worst of the chaos.'

She looked from Jane to Alex. 'Dominic?'

'Yes, Aunt Cecily?'

'Thea and I would appreciate your opinion on the seating arrangements if you will come to the dining room?'

The three disappeared, leaving Jane facing Alex, anxiety churning her stomach.

'Well, Honeybee, and how are you today?'

Honeybee…the affectionate nickname he had given her when, as a child, she was for ever buzzing around, like a bee around a flower. He sauntered over to the table and picked up one of the lilies still to be placed in the vases.

'I am well, thank you, Alex. You…you've been gone a long time.'

'Oh, I got the licence, all right and tight, if that's been plaguing you,' he said. 'But I must ask you—'

His jaw snapped shut as the Duke and Duchess came into the hall together and Jane's heart sank, knowing Alex wouldn't continue with his father present.

'Alex. You're back,' said the Duke.

'As you see.' Alex replaced the lily on the table, its petals now mangled, and withdrew a document from his pocket. 'With the licence.'

'So, you still wish to proceed?'

'Of course!' Alex took Jane's hand. 'As long as you aren't about to back out on me, Janey?'

She shook her head. Alex grinned, only slightly settling her nerves. She couldn't help but wonder exactly what was going on inside his head.

'We'll leave you in peace.' The Duchess linked her arm through her husband's and they disappeared into the drawing room.

'Sorry about that flower.' Alex nudged the stem of the lily he had destroyed. 'Shall I go and cut you another?'

'No. We already had more than sufficient. But thank you.'

He grinned again, flicked her nose and headed for the staircase. 'I must change my coat and boots. I'll see you later, Janey.'

'What was it you wanted to ask me, Alex? Before your father came in?'

He paused, then turned back to her. 'I just wanted to know if you have everything you need.'

'Yes, thank you.'

She doubted that had been his original question. She watched him bound up the stairs, hope and dread warring in her breast as she wondered what their future held.

* * *

Alex stood in the local church the next morning at eleven, waiting for his bride. He stared at the floor, Dominic by his side, still torn by what was about to happen. Every time his doubts had edged him close to backing out of this marriage, his father had said something that made him leap straight back into those slowly closing leg shackles. And besides…there was Jane to think about. Now she'd been compromised—and the whispers had already started—she must marry someone and quickly. And Alex could not condemn her to marriage with a stranger. That same boyhood instinct to protect her that had spurred him into that rash proposal made sure of that.

'This takes me back,' Dominic whispered. 'Waiting at the altar, fretting that Liberty might not show up, but mark my words…' he gripped Alex's shoulder, and squeezed it '…all your worry will fly away as soon as you set eyes on her.'

Except Dominic married Liberty for love.

Alex half-turned, eyeing the members of his family, sitting in the pews, waiting to witness his marriage to his childhood friend. The only one missing was Olivia, who was attending the bride. Lord Hugo Alastair, her husband, had his hands full coping with their two-year-old twins, Julius and Daisy, helped by Liberty. Alex's father and stepmother were there, with three-year-old Christabel and two-year-old Sebastian—his young half-sister and half-brother—and Susie, their adopted daughter. Further back were Uncle Vernon and Aunt Thea, with their three—Thomas, four, Sophie, two, and one-year-old George—and Aunt Cecily and Zach with three-year-old Florence.

Every one of them had married for love. But Alex, yet again, would be different.

Apart. Alone. Always the outsider.

Except you'll never be alone again. You'll have Jane.

And a whisper of…was that *hope*?…stirred in his heart. He forced down the doubts that clogged his throat, longing for that whisper of hope to be true.

The organ music changed and Alex turned to watch his bride walk up the aisle. Another lump filled his throat… not doubts this time, but concern. She looked desperately uncertain. A wave of protectiveness washed through him. Filled him. She was his responsibility now…her happiness depended on him and he would do all he could to stop her regretting their marriage.

Her gown was beautiful: peach-coloured silk that hugged her slim figure and complemented her mass of shiny conker-brown hair, held back with combs and interwoven with delicate white jasmine flowers, leaving loose tresses to wave down her back—and it was almost as though he were looking at her for the first time, which was absurd because he'd known her for ever. She was two years younger than him, his neighbour and his childhood playmate…he'd known her all her life. Taught her to ride. Led her into plenty of scrapes. And yet, here…now…he seemed to really *see* her. As his friend, Jane, yes…but also as a woman. An attractive woman. Not beautiful, maybe, but her figure was…mouth-watering.

And then all thought and conjecture ceased because she had reached his side and he turned to face the Reverend Padstow, his bride by his side, her sleeve brushing his.

Afterwards, he endured the congratulations and the backslapping outside the church, plastering a smile on his face. He felt like public property. This day couldn't be over soon enough for him. But he kept Jane close by his side, his hand resting at the small of her back. She was part of him now. They were a partnership. She was his wife. And when her father, stepmother and half-sisters approached and he felt her tense, he slid his arm around her waist and held her even closer.

'Well, Jane. This is a happy day indeed.' Lord Stowford thrust out his hand. 'You are a very welcome addition to our family, Alexander. You must visit us whenever you choose.'

Alex ignored the hand and inclined his head. 'I rarely visit Devonshire these days, sir, so you need not fear we will darken your doorstop with any regularity.'

We'll visit you over my dead body.

But it was his wedding day. He was the bridegroom. He must be polite to the guests, even when every nerve in his body craved solitude.

He nodded coolly at Lady Stowford and her daughters, and said to Jane, 'Come, my dear. Our wedding breakfast awaits and our guests must be hungry.'

'Thank you,' she whispered as they walked to the carriage waiting to drive them back to the Abbey. Alex handed Jane in and then collapsed on to the seat beside her, shutting his eyes.

'Are you finding this very trying, Alex?'

He cranked his eyelids open to find her watching him, her eyes filled with concern. They were lovely eyes, now he came to study them properly. Warm brown and thickly lashed and full not only of concern, but of kindness and understanding. And wasn't that typical of Jane? All her worry was for *him*. Even on her wedding day.

'A bit,' he replied.

He straightened. They would be home shortly...except he never thought of it as home any more. Foxbourne was his home now and had been for close on five years. His father had bought the estate, together with its breeding stock, five years before. Alex moved in later that year and, two years later—once he proved he could be trusted to run the place—his father signed it over to him. He loved Foxbourne and he couldn't wait to return. To go home.

He laid his hand against Jane's cheek, registering the softness of her skin.

'Shall you object if we leave here tomorrow? I cannot wait to show you Foxbourne Manor, although I fear it lacks a woman's touch at the moment.'

They would need more indoor staff—he'd led a bachelor's life until now, cared for by only his man, Drabble, and Mr and Mrs Kent, who ran the house.

'I have often longed to run my own household.' Her eyes glowed. 'And I cannot wait to settle into my new home, so I'm happy for us to leave tomorrow.' She smiled, then, and raised her eyebrows. 'And I know you well enough to know you'll be itching to leave here as soon as possible.'

He laughed. 'That I am.' He slipped his arm around her shoulders and hugged her. 'You are a brave woman, taking me on when you know what a moody wretch I can be at times.'

He kissed her cheek and the delicate scent of jasmine wreathed through his senses. Desire sparked through his veins, surprising him.

'Well—' Jane pulled back, capturing his gaze with a teasing smile '—in a straight choice between you and Pikeford I thought black moods a touch easier to cope with than drunkenness and r-r-r...'

Her lips quivered and his heart cracked. He pulled her close, nestled her head to his shoulder. 'Don't, Honeybee. Don't try to be brave and pretend it was nothing.'

She stayed there, trembling, for a few minutes. Then the carriage started to slow and she pulled away from him. Brushed a finger beneath each eye in turn and gave

a tiny sniff. Alex handed her his handkerchief without
a word.

'Thank you,' she whispered.

They both put on a decent show, Jane probably more
successfully than him. To watch her you would never believe anything troubled her, but Alex saw the effort she
was making all through that day.

Her family left early—to everyone's relief—and, watching Jane with the Beauchamps afterwards, Alex could see
she would fit right in. And why shouldn't she, when she had
known them for so long they were like a second family to her?

He watched over her, alert for any hint of distress. None
came. And, through the day, Aunt Cecily, too, kept her eye
on Jane and often drew her into conversations.

'She will need your patience, Alex.'

Zach joined Alex as the family gathered in the drawing
room after dinner that evening.

'I am aware of it.'

Zach turned his dark gaze on Alex. 'She is a woman
who was born to lavish care on those around her and she
will thrive, given love and care in return. You are a lucky
man. I feel you will be good for one another, but do not be
surprised if the path is bumpy in the beginning.'

Alex couldn't help grinning. 'Is that your Romany half
talking, Zach?'

Zach smiled. 'Perhaps.' He bent to fondle Myrtle's ears.
She rarely left his side. 'Or maybe it's more that I know
human nature and I know *you*, Alex.'

Alex sobered. Zach was right. He did know Alex—as
well as, if not better than, any other member of the family. Their mutual love for and understanding of horses had
fostered their friendship and respect. The rest of the family

were talented horse riders, but they did not share that natural *feel* for troubled animals, and for horses in particular, that Alex and Zach had in common. Edgecombe, Zach's estate in Hertfordshire, was less than thirty miles from Foxbourne and Zach regularly helped Alex with some of the challenging animals he was sent to 'cure'.

'I know it won't be easy.' He would need patience with Jane, but he suspected she would need even more with him. 'But I'm determined to be the good husband she deserves. We've always been friends. It is a good place to start.'

'Indeed it is.'

Alex noticed his father casting occasional pensive glances at him and Zach as they talked and his stomach clenched, aware Father wanted nothing more than to be as close to Alex as he was to Dominic. He turned away, allowing that same unhappy, unsettling mix of resentment and regret to subside. Why did he always feel that way? The rest of the family loved his father unequivocally and Alex—when he viewed him objectively—saw he was a good man. A good husband. A good father. A good employer. But no matter how he tried to overcome his unreasonable distrust with logic, his emotions always won.

He scanned the room for Jane. She sat with Aunt Thea, their heads together, chatting animatedly—well, Aunt Thea was *always* a veritable bundle of energy—and he wondered, for the first time, if his new wife might help him to change. *Could* he change? Was it possible? Could he, as he longed to do, learn to love his father unconditionally?

That thought unsettled him even more. Maybe he could, in time. But not yet. Now, all he wanted was to leave the Abbey and to return to Foxbourne, where it was safe. He no longer questioned that feeling of insecurity that assailed him at the Abbey. It simply was. It was how he had always felt.

'We are leaving tomorrow,' he said now to Zach.

Zach raised one dark brow. 'That is a pity when you have just arrived. The rest of us plan to remain a little longer—the children do so love to spend time with their cousins.'

'We'll all be sorry to see you go, Son.' Alex stiffened as his father interrupted them. 'But I guessed you would be keen to take Jane to Foxbourne as soon as possible. I've ordered your carriage for nine in the morning, but if you prefer to leave earlier, or later, just send word to the stables.'

'Thank you, Father.'

His father tipped his head to one side and smiled. 'Don't leave it so long to visit us next time.' He reached out and grasped Alex's upper arm. 'We miss you. *I* miss you.'

Alex swallowed, his throat constricted by a painful lump. 'I won't.'

But he knew he would.

He threw a smile at his father and Zach and moved away to join Jane and Aunt Thea on the sofa, wondering again if marriage and, in time, fatherhood might help him relax more around his father. He truly hoped so.

'I've been telling Jane about the children, Alex,' Aunt Thea said.

This was the first time Alex had met baby George, the youngest of Uncle Vernon and Aunt Thea's children. Thomas, with a mop of red curls like his mother's and busy creating havoc wherever he could, and Sophie, a little chestnut-haired poppet, had both grown since he'd last seen them and Alex felt a pang of remorse at missing so much of their childhood. At times like this, he could almost forget those feelings that kept him away. Kept him distant and alone. But then they would rear up, nipping and clawing at the edges of his memories, and he would retreat again, behind his barricades, to safety.

'They're all having such fun here together,' Aunt Thea continued, 'that Rosalind has invited us all to come again at Christmastide. I do hope you and Jane will come—we shall be here from a week before Christmas right up to Twelfth Night.' She looked at Alex hopefully. 'It would be lovely for the entire family to be together.'

'Oh, what a wonderful idea,' said Jane, before Alex could reply. 'I remember coming here at Christmas. How I loved all the old traditions—the Yule log, the Christmas Candle, decorating the house with greenery on Christmas Eve. Do you remember, Alex?' Her eyes turned wistful. 'The fun, the laughter, the games—so different to Christmas at Stowford Place. Stepmama never countenanced those old traditions. To her, Christmas is a religious observance and all about charity for the poor. We never even exchange family gifts, whether on St Nicholas's Day or on Christmas Day as your family did.'

'I remember. I'm sure we'll be able to come.' He said the words, but didn't mean them. Christmas was far too soon—he doubted he would be ready by then to stomach all that enforced gaiety.

Jane smiled happily at Alex. 'I shall look forward to it, especially as we won't be spending much time with you all now—assuming you still wish to leave tomorrow, Alex?'

'I do.' He averted his gaze, guilt at misleading her making him brusque, but there were months to go yet. Time enough to prepare her for disappointment. 'Father has ordered the carriage for nine so, if you'll excuse us, Aunt, I think it's time we retired.'

It was their wedding night. The perfect excuse to go to bed early…no one would question them doing so, especially with an early start in the morning. He stood, helping Jane to rise. Her hand trembled in his as they said their goodnights. If the circumstances had been different and if

Alex had been his brother, or his uncle, there would have been a few pointed, if not ribald, comments made. There were none. It was as though they'd been married for years: no teasing; no winks; no nudges.

He told himself he didn't care. He was used to being the outsider. He read the concern on every face in that room. Well, they needn't worry about him—he was determined he and Jane would be happy together. It wasn't until they were walking side by side up the stairs that it occurred to him the concern was for his bride. He squared his shoulders and hardened his heart. What did he care? He would be the very best husband he could possibly be to Jane. Surely her life with him couldn't be any worse than life with that old witch of a stepmother?

Chapter Five

Jane stared into the mirror. She was ready, clad in her best nightgown, trimmed with lace at the neckline and sleeves and fastened at the bodice with three pairs of blue ribbons. Her hair was loose around her shoulders and Peg, her maid, had brushed it until it shone. She pinched her cheeks and bit her lips to bring a little colour into them. Huge, troubled eyes stared back at her, revealing the dread coiling and writhing in the pit of her stomach. Dread at what was to come.

Eyes…the windows of the soul. What would Alex see in them? Would he even care if she was nervous?

She reached for the scent bottle on the dressing table and dabbed a spot above each collarbone and at her wrists, closing her eyes and breathing in the familiar scent that always calmed her.

Jasmine. Her mother's scent. Not that she remembered her mother but, after she died of childbed fever, Peg had transferred her devotion to Jane, ensuring she grew up knowing about her mother. Peg had even saved a half-used bottle of her mother's scent to give to Jane when she was old enough to understand and, since then, jasmine had infused her with a feeling of peace, even in her most troubled moments.

Except…now…tonight…peace evaded her. Her stomach still swarmed with nerves. She knew what must happen. And she desperately wanted to please Alex. She could not bear for him to regret this step they had taken. But, try as she might, she could not banish the memory of Pikeford.

The weight of him on her. His hands scrabbling at her body. The stink of spirits and of foul, hot breath and stale sweat.

Her stomach lurched and she pressed her fingers to her mouth, swallowing hard.

To give the newlyweds privacy, Jane had been allotted a room in the east wing of the Abbey with Alex in the adjacent bedchamber. The rest of the family slept in the main part of the house, apart from the children who occupied the nursery wing to the west. The quiet weighed on her… no distant murmur of voices, no doors opening and closing, no footsteps coming and going. She could almost believe she was entirely alone…until the sound of the door opening behind her set her pulse galloping.

She swallowed again and stood to face her new husband. Her nerves eased a little. This was Alex. He would not hurt her. As long as she kept her mind on tonight, and the present, and blocked all memories of the other day— surely she could manage that?—then she would cope.

She could hardly believe her long-held fantasy had come true as she gazed at him. He was still half-dressed, his shirt—open at the neck to reveal a tantalising glimpse of chest hair—tucked into his trousers. His thick mahogany brown hair was dishevelled and his amber eyes were fastened on hers, a look in them she had never seen before. She had dreamed of this moment, all those nights she had spent alone in her bed. If only… She thrust that thought away before it could take hold and spoil the night to come. Their wedding night. She clamped her teeth together, determined not to reveal her fear. She forced her lips into a smile as Alex stepped closer, scanning her from top to toe and back again.

'Your hair…it is beautiful. Before I saw you in church, I never imagined…' He lifted a lock that draped over her shoulder, allowing it to slide through his fingers. 'It is so soft, so silky.'

He tipped her chin, tilting her face to his, and his mouth covered hers. A gentle caress. She closed her eyes and concentrated on that. Only that. The warm smoothness of his lips as they moved over hers, unhurriedly. Soothingly. His thumb and forefinger still beneath her chin. No pressure. No force. Her heart lurched, and her breathing hitched.

'Shh…' A whisper of sound.

Concentrate. It's Alex. My love. My handsome hero. This is my dream.

His mouth moved, kissing and nibbling a path from her cheek to her ear. He nipped gently at her lobe, then caressed her neck with lips and tongue, and pleasure… anticipation…tiptoed through her. His arms came around her and tightened, bringing her close, and she relaxed into him. Into his hard body…his lean but muscular form shaping her softer flesh. Then his lips found hers again, moving gently. When his tongue probed her lips, she opened her mouth and let him in.

Alex. Her love. Her husband.

As he explored her mouth, she curled her arms around his waist and then slid her hands up his back, palms flat, learning the size and shape of him through his fine lawn shirt: the muscles either side of the dip of his spine, the wings of his shoulder blades, the broadness of his back, the width of his shoulders, the corded muscles in his arms. The strength of him. The maleness of him.

He murmured, deep in his throat. A sound of appreciation. And a strange, achy feeling gathered at the juncture of her thighs.

His hands wandered lightly over her back, shoulders and arms. Learning her, as she had learned him. They moved lower, cupping her bottom, kneading gently. Without volition, she pressed closer and the ridge of his erection pressed into her stomach. She could not prevent her whimper of distress, and pulled back. He released her bottom, but one hand at the small of her back stopped her moving away completely.

'Shhh, Honeybee. It's all right.'

His warm breath feathered over her lips and then he took her mouth again, deepening the kiss. Despite the anxiety building within her, she responded, kissing him back with fervour and when he again kissed and nibbled her neck, she tipped her head back, exposing it, giving him access, as she clutched at his biceps. She tensed as his lips dipped lower, tracing her collarbone, feeling increasingly helpless and at his mercy as he slowly bent her backwards over his supporting arms. He kissed the upper curve of her breast and then straightened her, soothing her with another kiss even as he played with the lace ruffle at her neckline.

'May I?' His fingers paused at the first of the bows securing the bodice of her nightgown.

She stared into his eyes.

Alex. It is Alex. He won't hurt me.

'Yes.'

She looked down, watching as he untied one bow after the other until all three were undone and her nightgown gaped at the neck, exposing the valley between her breasts. Alex's breath turned ragged, and Jane battled the fear that spiralled within her…the memory that sound evoked…the harsh rattle of Pikeford's breath in her ear as he—

She choked back her cry of distress.

Alex. Alex. It's only Alex.

'Alex… I don't…'

He smiled at her and, in one smooth movement, he pulled his shirt over his head. Distracted, she stared at his torso—the hair covering the curved muscles of his chest and narrowing into a thin line as it dipped below the waist of his trousers. Tentatively, she reached out and touched him. One finger at first, then all five and, finally, she flattened her palm against his warm flesh, the coarse hairs rough against her skin.

She'd be the death of him. When had Jane blossomed into this attractive and desirable woman?

Patience. Patience. We've got all night.

That glimpse of her bosoms was nearly his undoing. How he longed to dive in there and see…touch…taste. But he reined in his passion. A Herculean task when her hand splayed across his chest and her eyes darkened, her tongue flicking out to moisten her lips. He desperately tried to think of something else, to distract him from all that warm, sweet-smelling female flesh within his grasp, but it was nigh on impossible. He was an experienced lover, but this…this was different. It was erotic in a way that coupling with the most beautiful of partners had never been; partly due to her innocence and knowing he would be her first, but mainly—and this surprised him most of all—it was that she was his wife. It was new and it was scary, but it was sensual at the same time. He, who had always prided himself on his independence and his need for no one, was aroused by the bond that now linked them together for the rest of their lives.

A groan tore free from deep, deep within him—and he reached for her again, sliding his hands across her shoulders to hook his thumbs inside the neck of her nightgown.

Gently he slipped the bodice from her shoulders, exposing her breasts—so much fuller than he would have imagined given her slender figure—round and firm, with dusky
pink nipples at their peaks. He held the bunched fabric at
her waist as his other hand drifted over the soft curve of
her breast, his fingers closing around perfection, kneading gently.

'I didn't expect—' He fell silent as Jane tensed, even
more drastically than before. This time, she was as rigid
as a statue carved from stone. He released her breast and
lowered his hand. 'What is it, Janey?'

She shook her head, mute, but he could *feel* her distress.

'I won't hurt you. You know that, don't you?'

She nodded.

But she didn't believe it yet…he could tell. He reined
in his rampant desire, curbing his needs.

'Come. Let me warm you.' He tugged her nightgown up
to cover her again and then drew her into his arms, holding her until she stopped trembling.

'I'm sorry, Alex.' She stepped back, holding her nightgown close, covering her breasts.

'You have no need to fear me, Janey. I will never force
you to do anything until you are ready.'

She searched his face. 'I know. I am being foolish.'

He shook his head. 'You are not foolish.'

She held out her hand and he took it and followed when
she led him to the bed, her breaths short and sharp in the
silence. He did not fool himself it was passion that quickened her breathing. They lay down, side by side, and he
turned to her, resting his hand on her ribcage, beneath
her breasts. He leaned over and kissed her, ignoring the
clamour of his own body to possess her. To possess his
wife. He could be patient. There was no hurry.

He focused his mind and his senses on the pleasure of

kissing. Just kissing. He explored her mouth without haste, teasing responses from her until she was relaxed and following his lead, their tongues dancing, the occasional low moan vibrating in her throat. He stroked her face…her hair, neck, shoulders, arms…until she embraced him, her fingers threading through his hair. Still he held his passions on a tight rein, waiting for the right moment.

Her restless shift on the bed was his cue and he brushed the side of her breast. She turned slightly, pressing into his touch. Her breasts were still covered as he stroked and caressed, slowly nearing her nipple. He pinched lightly and she gasped into his mouth.

'Was that good?'

'Yes.'

She gasped again as he gently flicked, then moaned as he bent his head and licked her nipple through the fabric, turning it transparent, the darker areole visible when he raised his head to look.

'Beautiful,' he breathed.

A word he had never linked with Jane before. She had always been…Jane. But seeing her, lying beside him, a smile hovering around her parted lips and her eyelids heavy over passion-filled eyes…it was the exact word he needed. Of a sudden, his throat tightened and his heart skipped a beat.

Jane.

Beautiful. Sensual. And his *wife*.

But frightened, too.

The responsibility…his obligation to another human being…almost sent him fleeing from the bed. But then…

'Alex,' she breathed and pulled his head back to her breast, her fingers tangled in his hair.

And that fleeting moment of fear…of uncertainty… passed.

He tugged her nightgown down to expose her breasts again and took his time—licking, suckling and nibbling, smoothing and stroking her silken skin until she was moving restlessly and moaning softly. He moved so he half-covered her and gathered her nightgown at the hem, caressing her exposed leg, from shin to knee to thigh to hip. Again, he went slowly despite his throbbing desire to bury himself inside her. Again and again he returned to her thighs, stroking inwards and upwards, inch by tantalising inch. His fingers touched her intimate curls and played for a while, tugging gently and twirling. Then one finger slipped between her thighs, sliding along her cleft.

And she froze.

'Steady, sweetheart. It's all right.'

He went back to circling her lower belly. But as soon as he touched between her thighs again she stiffened, a tiny sound of distress escaping her. He'd expected it, but disappointment still coursed through him. He didn't snatch his hand away, but stroked from between her thighs, across her curls and on to her hip. He kissed her, taking his time, then turned her on to her side to face away from him, unwilling to push her any further tonight. He spooned his body into hers, gritting his teeth against the ache of unfulfilled arousal, and wrapped his arm around her waist, holding her close, knowing she would feel the hardness of his erection against her bottom, knowing she must eventually grow accustomed to him and to his body, hoping she would soon learn she had nothing to fear and that she could trust him to never force her or lose control.

'Sleep, my Honeybee. It's been a long day.'

'Alex?'

'Yes?'

'Aren't we going to…to…?'

'Not tonight. We have the rest of our lives together. There's no hurry.'

He willed himself not to drift off. He would wait until his wife slept and then he would go to his own room to sleep.

He'd thought he was done with those bad dreams that had haunted his childhood and his youth, but they had returned since his arrival at the Abbey. Last night's nightmare had been even worse—prompted, almost certainly, by Pikeford's attack. The vision of that animal ripping at Jane's gown haunted him, as did the sounds—Pikeford's grunts as she tried to fight him off, the ringing slap, her cries of distress.

But behind that memory lurked another.

Bigger. Blacker. Colder.

Waiting to catch him unawares.

Waiting for him to sleep.

Once the soft, even huff of her breathing told him Jane slept, he eased himself away from her warmth and returned to his cold bed to face his nightly ordeal.

Jane awoke with a start. She leant up one elbow, wondering what had disturbed her. The happenings of the day before…and the night…gradually surfaced. She reached behind her, feeling for Alex, but her hand met empty space. She sat bolt upright, throwing back the covers, at a shout. That was Alex's voice, she was sure. She scrabbled on the nightstand for the tinderbox and, with shaking fingers, lit the bedside candle in its silver holder.

She listened for any further disturbance, but heard nothing. She sat on the side of the bed, irresolute. Should she go and investigate? Was she overreacting? What if it was just a bad dream…? Surely Alex wouldn't thank her for disturbing him? And while all those thoughts rushed through her head one bigger, more important question hovered.

Why did Alex leave?

He must be so very disappointed in her, to wait until she slept and then creep away to his own bed. Yet he had been so sweet at the time…his care and consideration for her had filled her with trust and love, and she had vowed to overcome the trauma of Pikeford's attack and to become a wife to him in every way.

Another shout from the next room wrenched her from her thoughts. She shot to her feet, grabbed her shawl and flung it around her before hurrying to Alex's bedchamber. She hesitated outside the closed door, raising her candlestick to illuminate the dark passageway, her heart thumping at the low moans sounding from within the room. She tiptoed forward and opened the door, peering around it.

'No…don't.. no…no…stop…please…no…'

'Alex?' Her whisper threaded through his heartfelt pleas.

'No…no… No!'

She jumped at his final yell, her heart clenching at the sob that followed. She shut the door behind her, set the candle on a chest of drawers, then crossed the room to the bed. The blankets and sheet were pushed away, leaving Alex exposed. He lay on his side, shaking, curled into a ball, his arms bent over his face, his hands hooked over the top of his head.

Uncertainty clutched at Jane's throat. What should she do? Was it true one should never wake someone from a nightmare? What was happening to Alex in his dreams? She lowered herself on to the bed, swung her legs on to the mattress and then inched closer to him until her hip butted against his back. The entire time Alex emitted low, eerie moans that set the fine hairs on her arms on edge. Slowly, she eased over to face his back and—as he had done with her earlier that night—she nestled her body into his, like spoons in a canteen of cutlery.

'No…no… Mama…stop…no…'

His cries grew louder and, at the same time, more pitiful.

'Shhh…' Jane laid her hand on his arm. 'It's all right. I'm here.'

Her whispers were barely audible but, somehow, his trembling lessened and his ragged breathing steadied. She continued to soothe, stroking his arm and his shoulder and then, once he uncurled a little, his sweat-damp hair, as he relaxed and the nightmare loosened its grip. She tugged up the bedcovers and listened to his breathing, until she, too, fell asleep.

Chapter Six

'Janey?' A hand on her shoulder, shaking her. 'Janey?'

She stirred. As the voice came again, her eyes flew open. 'Alex!'

They were facing one another, in bed, his face close to hers.

'What are you doing here?'

His tousled hair revived the memory of the boy, but his unshaven cheeks and jaw were all man. Heat coiled deep in her stomach as his scent curled through her. Gradually, the events of the night before unravelled in her still-sleepy brain. She rubbed her eyes and yawned.

'I heard you cry out. You were having a bad dream. So I… So I…'

He was so close it was hard to concentrate on what she wanted to say. Warm pressure on her hip alerted her that his hand had moved there and the memory of his kisses sent hot tingles coursing down her spine.

His lips quirked. 'So you came to rescue me?' He pressed a kiss to her forehead. 'Thank you, Janey.'

'Alex? What were you…?'

'Shhh…don't think about last night. Not now.'

Their gazes fused. His tawny eyes darkened and lowered to her mouth. His hand skimmed up her side...settled at her back, splaying there, holding her still as his lips sought hers in a kiss to melt into. She sighed into his mouth, returning the gentle caress of lips and tongue.

The sound of the door opening ended the kiss. Alex lifted his head.

'Not now, Drabble.' Behind her, Jane heard the door click shut. 'Now. Where were we, Wife?'

Some time later—Jane couldn't quite swear to how long it had actually been—Alex lifted his head from her breast and smiled at her, a devilish glint in his eye.

'You're a bad influence, Janey. The carriage is ordered for nine. We'd better get moving if we're to leave on time.'

Already glowing, Jane felt a hot blush sweep her entire body until it burned in her cheeks. She felt so restless. She didn't want to move. She wanted more... Alex had woven such magic with his clever touch and with his lips, tongue and teeth that a hollow, yearning ache had taken up residence between her thighs. His kisses had awakened a fire in her, but she knew he was cautious for her sake. Not once had he attempted to touch her in her most intimate place, the place that was now in such need. Last night, one touch between her legs had sent her into a panic and she was grateful for his continued patience.

She watched him swing his legs out of the bed and rise. He was stark naked, standing with his back to her, rolling his shoulders back before stretching his arms above his head and she watched, fascinated by the slide of golden skin over flexing muscle and solid bone, the broad shoulders above a narrow waist. He had filled out since the times they had swum together in the lake. Then, he had been a boy. Now, he was definitely all man.

Her eyes lowered. To his buttocks. Firm and round. Her

mouth watered as she recalled touching them, squeezing them. His legs were straight and well shaped, dusted with dark hairs. They were beautiful. Paler than the skin on his back…did that mean he worked shirtless outside at times? Her heart kicked and her pulse raced. Would she ever get used to his chest?

He turned and her cheeks burned even hotter at being caught ogling her own husband and then scorched at the sight of his erection, standing proud. He grinned at her, totally unembarrassed.

'That was very enjoyable, Janey.' His smile faded. 'You will get over what happened, you know, and I will help you. There is no hurry and, in the meantime, you have discovered other pleasant activities we can enjoy, have you not?'

'Yes.' Jane's gaze clung to his face as she strove to ignore his chest and everything below his waist. She sat up, rearranging her nightgown and tying the ribbons into prim little bows, pulses of heat still sizzling through her from Alex's attention to her nipples. Her face scorched even hotter. My, that *had* been an education! 'I had better return to my room and dress if we are to leave on time. It won't do to keep the horses standing too long.'

'That's what I like about you, Janey. You love horses as much as I do. We'll make a good partnership.'

As declarations went, it was hardly romantic. But she didn't expect romance. Not from Alex. At least…maybe in time…? She cautioned herself not to hope for too much. Maybe. Maybe not. For now, she must be grateful she was here, with Alex, and not somewhere with Sir Denzil Pikeford. She suppressed a shudder, the events of two days before sending chills racing through her, effectively smothering those leftover frissons of pleasure.

Alex scooped Jane's dressing gown from the floor and

held it for her. She got up and, as he helped her into her robe, her roaming, random thoughts seemed to crystallise. Her eyes narrowed. She knew Alex of old—he was well practised in avoiding any discussion of subjects he found awkward and uncomfortable. In other words, any subject that threatened to delve too deep into his feelings. He retreated behind his barriers, keeping everyone at a distance, and pretending nothing mattered.

'Alex…?' She pivoted to face him. 'Your nightmare… Do you—?'

'Not now, Janey.' He spun away and crossed the room to tug the bell pull. 'Drabble and Peg'll be up with hot water in a minute. We'll talk later.'

Except they didn't. First there was breakfast and the goodbyes to the family, who all gathered to wave them off, amid hugs and kisses and promises to see them again soon. Jane's father was the sole member of her family to come and say goodbye, bringing with him Jane's beloved satinwood sewing box which had somehow been missed out of her trunk. He put his arms around her and hugged her close. 'I shall miss you, Jane.'

Jane hugged him back. 'I shall miss you, too, Papa.'

The exchange brought hot tears to her eyes and she ducked her head to hide her emotion, conscious Alex had completed his farewells and waited now to hand her into the carriage. 'Goodbye, Papa. You will write to me, won't you?'

'Of course I will, Jane.' He patted her shoulder. 'Hurry along now. You've a long way to travel. God speed.'

To give the newlyweds some privacy the Duke provided an additional carriage, for Drabble and Peg and the luggage and, as soon as they set off on the journey home to

Buckinghamshire, Alex settled back into a corner, crossed his arms over his chest and closed his eyes.

'You don't mind, do you, Janey? I'm tired as a dog.'

What could she say?

She had saved her questions for later, but Alex, it seemed, always had a plausible excuse for not delving too deep into the subject of his nightmares. But she knew they still plagued him, even though he reserved separate bedchambers at the inns they stayed in during their four-day journey. On the first night, when she heard him cry out, she went to his room only to find Drabble already there, tending to Alex.

'There is nothing you can do, milady,' Drabble had whispered as he ushered her away from the door. 'I am used to tending to him.'

Drabble had been with Alex for years and, before that, he was a footman in the Duke's household, since before Alex was born. If anyone knew what demons stalked Alex in his dreams, it was Drabble. All Jane could do was bide her time, until they reached Foxbourne Manor. And even on that—surely innocuous—subject, Alex was less than forthcoming. He fobbed off her questions about her new home, simply telling her to 'wait and see'.

The only subject he willingly discussed was his horses and, as it was a shared interest, they whiled away the journey by talking about how Jane could help by schooling some of the Foxbourne youngsters to side-saddle, to make perfect ladies' mounts. She was grateful for the distraction. Periods of silence inevitably resulted in Pikeford creeping into her brain and fear worming its way through her veins. She battled the memory with quiet determination. She refused to become a woman who trembled at shadows just as she had never allowed her stepmother to destroy her spirit.

* * *

Finally, the carriage turned through a wide entrance flanked by massive stone pillars, topped with eagles cast in iron. They followed a carriageway that passed through ancient woodland, in which Jane identified beech, elm and ash trees, before emerging into sunlight and continuing through parkland, much of it divided into paddocks in which horses grazed. Then the carriageway swept to the right and Jane caught her first glimpse of Foxbourne Manor, her new home. Her heart swelled with joy as she took in the many gabled, russet-bricked Tudor manor house, visible over a neatly clipped hedge. Sunlight reflected off the diamond-paned windows of the upper floor and, as the carriage drew to a halt before the front door, Jane turned to Alex in delight.

'I had no idea Foxbourne would be so beautiful! It looks steeped in history. I cannot wait to explore.'

He grinned at her reaction and hugged her. Other than kissing her—often very thoroughly—he'd barely touched her since their wedding night, telling her he would rather wait until they were home to try again, rather than consummate their marriage in a bed where who knew how many others had slept in the past. She had understood his logic, but the delay had done nothing to quell her nerves whenever she thought about the intimacies to come. She had found pleasure in his touch, but she couldn't help but be afraid she would freeze again if he touched her between her legs. Yet he must if she was ever to put what happened behind her. She was desperate not to ruin the experience for both of them and strove to hide her increasing fears about the night to come.

'I knew you'd like it, that's why I didn't tell you much,' Alex said. 'I wanted to see your face when you first saw it. I remember you always loved exploring the Abbey and

complained Stowford Place was modern and boring and
lacking in character. I only hope you won't find Foxbourne
too old-fashioned, though…it still has much of the original
wood panelling and dark beams in some of the ceilings. Or
too small. It has only six bedrooms plus a nursery suite—
nothing like the size of the Abbey or Stowford.'

That mention of the nursery suite sent hot and cold
flushes rolling in waves through Jane. She wanted children, which meant she must overcome her fear and put
aside her distaste for what Pikeford had attempted to do.
She loved Alex. He had already proved she could trust him
and that he understood how difficult it was for her. He, of
anyone, knew how memories of the past could rear up at
any time and cast ominous shadows over the present. At
least his memories of the past were contained, only visiting him in his sleep—proof, surely, it was possible to suppress horrific events with determination.

This—marriage to Alex Beauchamp—was her dream
come true, even though she would have preferred to win
him in a more conventional way. And she *would* make
him happy. Maybe he would never love her, but she had
enough love for both of them.

Jane loved everything about Foxbourne Manor, from
the minute she walked ahead of Alex into the spacious hall
with its gleaming panelling and wooden staircase that rose
to a half landing before turning back on itself. Alex had
sent word of his nuptials to the Kents, who looked after the
house, instructing them to hire in local help to prepare for
their arrival, and the house had been cleaned and polished
from top to bottom until it gleamed. It was dark, but not a
gloomy darkness—it had the warm, glowing richness of
well-cared-for and well-loved wood.

Alex's pride was clear as he showed Jane around the

L-shaped manor: the great hall, now an impressive draw-ing room, decorated in green and gold; the library, its bookcases crammed with books; the parlour, facing east to catch the morning sun; the dining room, with its pol-ished rosewood table large enough to seat six couples; and Alex's business room—remarkably tidy and organised and not at all what Jane had expected of the man whose public image tended towards that of a devil-may-care rebel. The kitchen, butler's pantry, larder, scullery and other offices were housed on the ground floor of the side wing.

Upstairs, as he had said, were six bedchambers, includ-ing a master bedchamber linked via an internal door to a feminine, if a little old-fashioned, bedchamber for the mistress of the house. The side wing housed a nursery suite, with accommodation for children, nursemaid and a governess's room. The servants occupied the attics, but Mr and Mrs Kent who had, until now, fulfilled the roles of butler-cum-footman and housekeeper-cum-cook, had a separate bedchamber on the first floor, reached via a spiral staircase leading up from the butler's pantry.

The Kents and Sally, a housemaid, had been at Fox-bourne from the time of Alex's predecessor. As well as hiring in temporary help to prepare the house for Jane, Alex had also instructed Kent to hire additional perma-nent staff in the form of a cook, a footman, a kitchen maid and a laundry maid. Alex's focus had always been on the business and ensuring he had enough grooms to care for and help train his horses, but he'd not once complained or quibbled over the need for a full complement of indoor servants now he was married and Jane couldn't wait to begin turning Foxbourne into a happy and comfortable home for them both.

'Now you have seen inside, would you care to visit the stable yard?'

Alex's attempt at nonchalance was not lost on Jane. What she really wanted, after travelling from nine that morning, was to enjoy a hot cup of tea. But, more than that, she wanted to please her new husband. And he, she could see, was eager to continue her tour of her new home.

'I would love to.'

Alex felt awkward and yet excited in equal measures. Never had he even contemplated sharing Foxbourne with anyone on a permanent basis, yet here he was, married. He suffered no illusions about himself and he'd had no time whatsoever to prepare for this change in his circumstances, but…Jane was his friend. If he had to choose a wife out of all the women he knew, she would always have been the most obvious choice to share his life and, to his surprise, he was more physically attracted to her by the day. How had he never noticed that Jane, the quiet little wallflower, was a flower waiting to burst into bloom?

He would make Jane happy to the best of his ability. He could offer her happiness, but he couldn't offer her love. Love meant letting down his guard…allowing another person closer than he'd ever allowed anyone…and the very thought terrified him.

No. He saved all his love for his horses and now, having shown Jane around the house, he couldn't wait to show her his real love: the stables, the horses, the schooling paddock where he worked with them.

He knew, instinctively, she would prefer to rest first and take refreshment, but… And there was his selfish streak. He had much to learn. He'd never had to consider anyone else's needs other than his own—*he* wanted to show her the stables and so that is what he had demanded.

He hauled in a deep breath and smiled ruefully.

'I'm sorry. You would prefer to rest first—I'll ask Mrs Kent to send a tea tray to the drawing room.'

'No!' She clutched his sleeve. 'No. Really. I am longing to see where you work your magic with the horses.'

And there was the difference between them. Him, selfish. Her, generosity itself. Always eager to please him. It had been the same when they were children. Jane had always given way to Alex's demands. A niggle of shame prompted him to say, 'They will still be there in an hour's time. Come...' he took her hand and led her to the stairs '...we'll have that cup of tea before we go outside', and was surprised by the sense of satisfaction he felt at putting her first.

Later, Jane took his arm as they walked the track leading to the barns and stables where Alex spent most of his time when at home. Jane was every bit as enthusiastic as he anticipated—their mutual love of horses had cemented their friendship long ago.

'She is beautiful,' Jane breathed, as they leant on a post and rail fence and watched an iron-grey filly with a light grey mane and tail float around a paddock at a trot. 'Was she born here?'

'Yes. She's three years old now and was one of the very first foals of my own breeding to be born here.'

'What is her name?'

'Whatever you would like it to be. If you like her, she's yours.' Her gasp of pleasure kindled a warm glow inside him. 'I thought how well she'd suit you when you told me about Pippin. She's already backed and we were about to start schooling her to a side-saddle. Would you like to help?'

'Oh! I'd love to.' Jane turned to him, her hands clasped in front of her chest, beaming. 'Thank you.'

The bright joy in her eyes drew him in and, without volition, he clasped her shoulders and pulled her close for a kiss. An unaccustomed emotion settled over him like a warm blanket and it took him a moment or two to identify it as contentment—surprising him. He'd always been self-sufficient, but now he wondered if his life had been missing something all along. Something he hadn't even known he needed. He'd always thought having Foxbourne was enough—the opportunity to take complete control if Father deemed him responsible had been the lure that saved him from the path of self-destruction in his youth. It had been a struggle to change his life but, despite a few hiccoughs, he had managed and Father had signed the estate and the business over to him three years ago.

That magnanimous gesture and vote of confidence from his father had still not been enough to banish the wariness and distrust he had always felt towards his sire, however. Thinking about his father prompted thoughts of the Abbey, and before he knew it he was puzzling yet again over the past and why his childhood home should still give him nightmares.

Jane pulled away from his embrace, her brown eyes searching his.

'What is it? Is something wrong?'

He knew her concern for him should make him feel good, but he couldn't quite dismiss his niggle of irritation. He might be reconciled to sharing his home and his life, but his thoughts were his and he never discussed those damnable nightmares. Not with anyone.

'Nothing's wrong. I was merely thinking of this place and how fortunate I am to have it. And how happy I am you are here to share it.'

It was no lie. It *was* what he had been thinking, it simply wasn't the whole.

'Oh. Well, that is good.'

Her robust response belied the expression in her eyes. He would have to take care with Jane—she was intuitive and, as she had just demonstrated, would soon pick up on any black moods if he allowed the past to gain a hold. It felt worryingly close to the surface at the moment—the visit to the Abbey had been bad enough, but that attack on Jane... Alex veered away from that line of thought with an inner curse. Not only must he lock that memory away for his sake but also, and more importantly, for Jane's. The sooner he could banish her memories of Pikeford, the sooner those shadows haunting her eyes would disappear.

'What will you call her?' The filly approached them, her head and neck stretched forward, nostrils quivering, as Jane extended her hand so the horse could take in her scent. 'She was black when she was born and her coat should continue to get lighter as she matures.'

'What have you called her until now?'

'Pearl.' He grinned as Jane turned laughing eyes on him.

'You named a black foal Pearl?'

He shrugged. 'We knew she would turn lighter and, besides, there are such things as black pearls, you know.'

'I do know. But, as it happens, I like Pearl so I shall keep it.'

They wandered back towards the barn where the stalls were. As they approached, Jane halted and clutched at Alex's sleeve.

'What is it?'

'Shhh. Can you hear it?'

Chapter Seven

Jane turned this way and that before setting off with purposeful strides towards a lean-to attached to the side of the barn, where sacks of oats and barley were stored.

Alex caught her up at the door. It was dark inside, but he, too, could now hear the pitiful mewling. 'Wait there,' he said and strode to the barn where there was always a tinderbox and lantern on a ledge beside the door. He lit the lantern and carried it to the lean-to. Eyes glowed, reflecting the light, and Jane stepped cautiously forward.

'It's a cat and kittens.' She crouched, crooning quietly. Then she looked back over her shoulder at Alex. 'She's very thin… I doubt she's producing enough milk for her babies. Poor things. They look hungry.'

Alex suppressed a sigh. He knew what this meant. Jane could never resist a creature in need. He squatted by her side and the lantern illuminated the cat.

'That's one of the stable cats.' He recognised its distinctive grey-and-white markings. Five kittens were at her belly, latching on to her teats and suckling for bare seconds before releasing the teat and trying another. 'She's one of the oldest—Lilley says she's been here since he first started work for Sir William.'

Sir William Rockbeare had owned and run Foxbourne before Alex's father bought it, and Lilley had stayed on as head groom.

'What do you want to do? The outside cats are not tame. I doubt she'll allow you—'

He fell silent. Jane had already made friends with the animal, stroking beneath her chin with one forefinger. He shouldn't be surprised. He resigned himself to the inevitable.

'Shall I find a basket for them?'

'Yes, please, if it's not too much trouble. I can feed the kittens with cow's milk—it's not ideal, but it's better than nothing and I shall give the mother some meat. She's very thin.' Alex rose to his feet and now Jane smiled up at him. 'Does she have a name?'

He snorted. 'Of course she doesn't have a name. She's not a pet.'

'She's purring at me, despite everything. I shall call her Dora.' She fixed him with a pointed look. 'Did you say something about a basket? I shall move her closer to the house where I can care for her better, if you don't object? There must be an outhouse or something I can use.'

He tweaked a lock of hair that had worked loose and now tumbled down her cheek. 'Of course I don't object. Anything to make you happy.'

She laughed. 'I shall remember that rash promise, Alex. You may very well regret making it.'

'Not me,' he said, airily. 'I'll be back shortly. You stay there.'

By the time they had carried Dora and her kittens up to the house and settled them into a disused storeroom off the courtyard at the back of the house, it was time to change for dinner.

* * *

The evening flew past and, almost before Jane knew it, it was time for bed. Her stomach roiled, but her determination to conquer her fear was fierce.

I love him. I know he won't hurt me. This *is what I want...what I've always dreamed of.*

They went together to check on Dora and to feed the kittens. Jane fed them with a small spoon, holding each kitten's head still as she dribbled milk into its mouth. She made sure they were satisfied before she left them for the night and left some finely chopped lamb and a saucer of milk for Dora. The entire time she was caring for the animals she was conscious of Alex watching her, his shoulders propped against the door frame, arms folded.

'All done?' he asked when she finally stood up.

She nodded, washing her hands in the bowl of water she'd put there for the purpose. Alex patted her hands dry with the towel, then raised them to his lips, pressing a kiss on first one, then the other. He held her gaze, fire banked in his amber eyes.

'Don't be scared, Janey. You will be in control... I'll do nothing you don't enjoy and I'll stop whenever you say the word. But *you* must tell *me*. If you tense up again, I will not stop. Not this time. Not unless you actually say *stop*.' He brushed a kiss to her forehead, then rubbed the pad of his thumb gently across her lower lip. 'Do you understand?'

It felt strange and embarrassing, discussing such intimate matters with him here, in this storeroom, but she understood why he chose to have this conversation away from the bedchamber. Away from the heat and the passion. Her blood stirred and her pulse quickened. She had already come a long way and Alex...she trusted him. Implicitly. She nodded again and, on impulse, rocked up on her toes and pressed a kiss to his mouth. A different feeling coiled in her stomach, thrumming and growing.

Anticipation. Desire. Excitement.

Her apprehension was still there, but it no longer overwhelmed her. She breathed in. Alex: familiar, loved, tasting of his after-dinner port. She cradled his face and traced the seam of his lips with her tongue, the way she had learned from him. A hum of approval vibrated through him. His lips parted and she deepened her kiss as his arms swept around her and hauled her close. Her body moulded to his and she revelled in his lean, hard-muscled form. Visions crowded her brain—his hair-covered chest…his ridged abdomen…those taut buttocks…his sinewy, hair-dusted forearms and gentle hands with those long, clever fingers—images that crowded out her fear.

She clutched his shoulders as their tongues tangled and their lips clung and that strange sensation once more gathered deep in her belly and in the feminine folds between her thighs. Another image arose—Alex, fully aroused. Very male. And hers! Her heart skipped a beat and her breath seized. Slowly, daringly, she reached down and stroked along the hard length of his erection, rejoicing in his groaned response. Alex swept her into his arms and strode for the stairs.

Once in Jane's bedchamber, Alex paused, his back against the closed door, Jane still cradled in his arms.

'The word is "stop", Honeybee. Not "no". I intend to have you screaming *no* many times before the night is out, but I will only stop if you say that word.'

'S-screaming?'

His eyes never left hers as a slow smile stretched his lips. 'Oh, yes. Screaming. With pleasure. In ecstasy.'

Then his lips found hers again and they were on the bed. Fully clothed still, but that did nothing to slow the explosion of desire that rocked her as Alex kissed, fondled and stroked every inch of her face, neck, shoulders and chest. He was too slow. Too cautious. She pushed him away and sat up.

'Help me,' she demanded as she tried to reach the buttons at the back of her gown.

He unbuttoned her and unlaced her corset. She pushed his jacket from his shoulders and tugged his shirt over his head, impatient to see that magnificent chest. When she was clad only in her shift and he in his breeches, Alex flung himself down on to the bed, smiled and beckoned, heat blazing in his eyes. About to join him, Jane hesitated. *You will be in control.* She caught her lip between her teeth, then slowly released it, rewarded by yet another flare of desire in those beautiful tawny eyes, and an impatient hand patting the mattress beside him.

Control.

Jane approached the bed slowly, holding Alex's gaze the entire time and then, slowly and deliberately, she slid her shift up to her thighs, lifted one leg across him and straddled his hips, her knees bent, hands splayed on his chest. He closed his eyes as though in pain, the planes of his face hardening, his eyebrows bunched.

'Alex?'

He opened his eyes at her whisper and their gazes fused again. The corner of his mouth quirked and he flicked his brows. He rested his hands on her knees, his thumbs rhythmically caressing her.

'Janey?'

'If you want me to stop, you must say the word.'

He burst out laughing. 'Janey—you are a tease!' Then he sobered, his chest rising and falling with his quickened breathing. 'Do your worst.'

She stroked across his chest, the hair crisp to her touch.

His nipples hardened and she bent to catch one between her teeth and gently nipped. His gasp encouraged her to explore further and she leaned forward, the tips of her breasts brushing against his hot skin as she kissed her way up his chest to his neck and his ear—the sensitive zones where the caress of Alex's mouth had provoked such shivers of anticipation. Her reward was a low moan of pleasure and a subtle tension that gripped the hard, male body beneath her.

When his hands settled on her hips, she protested. She wasn't done with exploring yet. But rather than lift her or move her aside, he held her still as he flexed his hips, the hard ridge of his erection pressing against her secret flesh. She tried desperately not to freeze, directing her thoughts to what she was feeling now and away from Pikeford, and before long all memory of his attack faded into insignificance as Alex moved her back and forth, rubbing her against his solid arousal.

When his grip eased, Jane kept moving of her own volition. A low moan hovered in the air. Realising it had come from her own lips, she opened her eyes and met his bright, tawny gaze. He smiled. Seductively. Her blood heated still further, her heart pounding. Alex. Her love. For ever. She reached for the hem of her chemise and, in one swift movement, stripped it off over her head. By the time she discarded it, Alex's mouth was on her breast and the tug on her nipple sent a ripple straight to her core. She pressed down on to his shaft, seeking to ease the need building deep inside her.

Slow, steady and languid turned to desperate. Hands squeezed and stroked…lips locked as tongues did battle… harsh pants filled the air, but now that sound drove her on. She thrust her fingers through Alex's hair and flattened her body to his, gasping into his mouth when he growled and flipped her over on to her back. He tore his lips from hers and stood, dragging his breeches down, kicking his feet free, his eyes pinning her in place. Jane shivered at the look in those tiger eyes…and held out her arms.

He lowered himself over her, and the seductive touch of skin on skin sent her temperature rocketing. Her thighs parted and he settled between them, kissing her, slow and deep. Her fingers dug into solid shoulder muscles as he kissed and licked his way to her breasts, and she shifted restlessly, moaning her impatience. She stilled when he explored her stomach with his mouth, dipping into the hollow of her navel, his body inching steadily down the bed. The first flick of his tongue between her thighs almost shot her off the mattress.

'Alex?'

Surely that can't be right? But… Oh… I want more…

'Shhh, my sweet.' Another lick. 'You taste so good. Like honey.' The words groaned out. Then his whole mouth was on her, kissing, sucking…tongue, probing…

Her body arched off the mattress and she reached for his head, clutching mindlessly at his hair, the muscles in her legs tensing as she pushed her yearning flesh against his mouth. His fingers replaced his mouth as he latched on to her nipple, working magic, driving her into a frenzy as she struggled to reach the unknown goal she sensed awaited her. The sensation of his fingers inside her…his tongue and teeth toying with her nipple…his thumb, circling, between her legs…ooooh…exquisite… She arched, helplessly, her fingers clutching blindly at anything within reach…higher…reaching…a sob gathered in her throat…

That sob shrieked from her and she flew into darkness spangled with a million sparkling stars, ecstasy rippling through her in waves. Gasps echoed around the room. Her gasps.

'Oh! Oh! Oh!'

She reached, found Alex and drew him up so she could kiss him.

'Ooh…' She sighed. 'Ooh.'

She felt his smile against her lips. 'You liked that, Honeybee?'

She nodded, unable to form coherent thoughts, let alone speech. Her eyes flew open then as Alex's weight settled between her legs, the head of his shaft at her entrance. She widened her thighs, welcoming him in. Propped on his elbows, he captured her gaze as he slowly, slowly pushed into her. She wanted him. She wanted more. She wanted hurry and urgency, not this slow, slow torture. She reached, finding his buttocks, tight with control, and she grabbed, pulling him in. A stab of pain, gone in an instant. He kept pushing, filling her, further and further until she couldn't take any more.

Then he smiled down at her. 'Do you want me to stop, sweetheart?'

Jane shook her head. 'Nooo…' The long-drawn-out sigh escaped her lips, like a plea. This felt so right.

He moved slowly at first and she soon caught the rhythm, and matched him, meeting each thrust, steady and controlled at first, but then faster and harder—driving her on, up and up, until she reached the edge again and threw herself over. Alex's roar of triumph mingled with her scream of joy as they soared high together. His weight slumped on to her before he rolled aside to lie on his back beside her, his hand seeking hers as, gradually, their breathing returned to normal. Then he turned to face her, propping himself up on one elbow, and stroked her cheek.

'Well, Janey?' His fingers sifted through the locks of hair tumbling across the pillow. 'Do you think you might eventually grow to enjoy such bed sport?'

She laughed at his teasing, gloriously happy, her confidence in herself as a woman as high as those stars. She kissed him, pouring her heart into it.

'Oh, yes. Although…' she tilted her head '…we might be compelled to practise. A lot.'

Alex laughed. 'I think we might manage that.'

He sat up, and swung his legs out of bed. Jane's stomach clenched. She touched his back, the skin warm and smooth beneath her fingers.

'Don't go, Alex. Please.'

'I don't want to disturb you, Janey. You know I have… that is, you know I'm a restless sleeper.'

This wasn't the time to discuss his nightmares so she let his comment pass, but she was determined to try to help him overcome his childhood demons. She was convinced talking about the past would help, but she knew how hard he would resist.

'I don't mind if you're restless. I would rather you stay— can we not at least try? I like having you here with me.'

'In that case, my sweet, I shall stay.' He lay back again, rolling over to face her. 'I like being here with you, too.' His lips curved into a wicked, teasing smile, his tawny eyes dancing. 'And I can think of no better way to start the day than waking up next to a beautiful woman.' He leaned across, seizing her lips in a slow, drugging kiss. 'Especially a beautiful woman who just happens to be my wife.'

Her heart swelled. Were they mere words, or did he truly think her beautiful? It was not how she had ever thought of herself: Stepmama had lamented her plainness often enough. But this was Alex—never a man to pay lip service—although she did recognise he meant all of her, not only her appearance. Even so, a warm glow of contentment radiated through her at the realisation he did, indeed, think her beautiful. She opened her arms and he snuggled into her, his breathing already softening and slowing as one hand drifted across to cup her breast and one leg settled between hers. He sighed. An upwelling of tenderness brought tears to Jane's eyes as she stroked his hair back and feathered a kiss to his forehead.

''Night, Janey,' he murmured.

Before long his limbs grew heavy and slack and he fell asleep. Jane's eyelids soon drifted shut and she, too, slept.

Chapter Eight

Alex roused, floating up from the depths of a long, dreamless sleep, his brain scrambling to catch up with his slowly awakening body. Gradually, the events of the night before formed coherent images and he smiled, a deep sense of satisfaction pervading him as he became aware his body was folded around another and his right hand loosely clasped a shapely breast.

Jane! His wife…and now they were married in every sense of the word.

He cranked open one eyelid and blinked, surprised by how light the room was, despite the drawn curtains. He frowned. Morning. It was morning. And he had slept right through. He tried hard to ignore the quickening of his blood and his growing arousal as he struggled to make sense of the time—what had happened to his nightmares? He searched his memory. No. There was no bad dream; no restless thrashing about to recall—merely a deep sense of peace and a burgeoning need to sink into his wife's welcoming heat. His arm tightened, drawing Jane closer to him, and he flexed his hips, pressing his erection against her bottom.

She stirred and murmured, her arm moving to lie over

his, her hand covering his, her fingers closing to encourage him to caress her breast.

'Mmm… Good morning, Husband.' She turned and pressed her mouth to his.

Maybe—and his spirits rose at this last coherent thought before passion took control—this was the answer to those nightmares that had plagued him ever since he had witnessed Pikeford's assault on Jane. Make love to his wife every night and sleep in her arms.

Some time later Alex relaxed back against the pillows, Jane sprawled across his chest. He sighed, tightening his hold. She raised her head, propped her chin on her clasped hands and fixed him with a direct look.

He bit back a smile…that look was very 'Jane'. People often thought because she was quiet, it meant she was shy, but Alex knew different. She was something of a rarity among females, in his experience—never one for small talk or gossip, but unafraid to speak her mind and, the more he thought about it, the more he realised he couldn't have picked a better wife if he'd tried. Jane, his best-ever female friend, who was revealing herself to be a far more sensual being than he could ever have imagined. He felt happier and more hopeful than he had for a very long time as he contemplated their future together.

'Thank you,' she said.

He frowned. 'For what?'

'For being patient with me.'

He laughed. 'Me? Patient? Hmm… My family and friends would stare to hear my name and that quality in the same breath.' He hooked his hands under her arms and slid her up his body so he could kiss her. 'But there's always a first time, I suppose. And don't they say patience has its own reward?'

He nipped her earlobe and nibbled his way down her neck.

'I think—' she tilted her head back to allow him better access '—the saying is "patience *is* its own reward"!'

Alex shrugged, distracted by the fluttering pulse in her throat.

'I like my version better,' he murmured, laving that pulse.

His hand wandered down her back to cup one delicious buttock. The blood rushed to his groin and, with reluctance, he rolled her off his chest.

'Alex...?'

The doubt in that one word was underlined by the worry in her lovely brown eyes. She might not be shy, but he knew only too well the toll her stepmother's constant criticism had taken on her self-confidence. He couldn't bear her to think he was rejecting her. He smiled reassuringly.

'You are new to this, my sweet—I don't want you to get sore. Besides...' he brushed her lips with his '...I need to recoup my strength.'

He reared up and flipped her over on to her back— making her giggle—before kissing her very thoroughly indeed.

'Now, my lady, it is time we got up.' He swung his legs out of bed before he could be tempted to take things further again. 'Have you an idea of what would you like to do today?' He stood up, turned to face her and bowed with a flourish. 'I am entirely at your service.'

She laughed up at him—a glint of mischief in her eyes—and reached out, but he stepped back before her hand could close around him.

'Good grief.' He shook his head at her. 'You *are* making it difficult to act the responsible and caring spouse, you wanton minx, you.'

She dimpled at him, her head tilted. 'You shouldn't be so hard to resist, you handsome devil.'

He laughed and grabbed her hands, hauling her from the bed and into his arms.

'Well? Would you like to make a start on Pearl's education?'

Her eyes lit up, but then a fine groove appeared between her eyebrows and she blushed. 'I think I might prefer to wait a day or so.'

He bit back his grin of pure male satisfaction. 'Of course,' he said gravely. 'Maybe later I will drive you around the area so you can get your bearings. Come on.' He released her, gave her a gentle push and swatted her backside playfully. 'Get moving. The day's half over already! I'll go to my room and get dressed and I'll see you in the parlour for breakfast.'

'Well?' Later, after they had eaten, Alex eyed Jane over the rim of his coffee cup. 'Have you any further thoughts about how we might spend the day? I'm completely at your disposal… I've already sent word to the stables I won't be available until tomorrow.'

'Well, first I must check on the kittens. Peg promised to feed them first thing this morning, but I can't expect her to take on the whole burden of caring for them. And I must consult with Mrs Kent on household matters and the new staff we need. And then—'

Alex held up his hand. 'Are you telling me you have no need of me today? You've had your wicked way with me and now I am *de trop* until it's bedtime?'

'No! Oh, Alex, I did not mean…' She stared at him, and pouted. 'You utter wretch! You are teasing me.'

'Of course I am, Janey.' He winked at her. 'Well, while you feed the kittens, and you and Mrs Kent make plans,

I dare say I ought to attend to my ledgers and correspondence. So I shall be in my business room should you have need of me.'

Jane pursed her mouth, shaking her head. 'Now I see why you were so keen to spend the day with me—anything is preferable to completing ledgers and writing letters.' She stood, and rounded the table. 'You never did care for studying and lessons, I recall.'

A dark shadow nudged at his memory. A time when he had skipped lessons with his tutor…the summer house by the lake… He thrust the memory away and forced a smile.

'You caught me out! But now, because my wife is too conscientious, I have no excuse.'

She laid her hand on his shoulder. 'Give me time to get accustomed to the routine of the house and I will help you. I always used to help Papa… I often wrote letters for him and ledgers hold no fears for me.'

Alex didn't need to force his smile this time. He shoved his chair back from the table, grabbed Jane around the waist and pulled her on to his knee.

'I knew I was right to marry you.' He nuzzled her ear. 'It is the best thing I have ever done. We will make a wonderful team.'

He believed every word. This marriage was going to work out far better than he could ever have hoped. After her reaction on their wedding night he'd wondered if Jane would find it hard to banish the memories of Pikeford, but she had surprised him with her determination to conquer her fear. Although…maybe he shouldn't be surprised, knowing Jane. She had never been one to buckle under one setback—she was a quietly determined soul who got things done.

Life looked rosy indeed, with Jane by his side.

'I'll be in the business room if you have need of me.' If

Jane was to help him in future he should at least present her with up-to-date records from the start. He pressed a light kiss to her mouth and lifted her from his knee as he stood up. 'I shall see you later.'

He left the parlour with a spring in his stride.

Later, while Jane changed her gown, Alex headed for the stable yard to collect his curricle and pair, ordered ready for two o'clock. Sure enough, the feisty pair of chestnuts were ready-harnessed.

'They're lively, milord,' Lilley remarked as Alex leapt into the vehicle.

'I'd be disappointed if they weren't. They'll soon settle once we get moving.'

He drove to the front door, where Jane waited for him, clad in a flattering cornflower-blue pelisse over a white carriage dress with deep blonde flounces and a matching broad-brimmed, feather-trimmed bonnet. The day was fresh and bright—a bit like the horses—and, as they set off at a spanking trot, Alex couldn't keep the proud smile from his face.

They drove to Malton, which boasted a church and the adjacent vicarage, an inn, a general store and post office, a bakery and a smithy. Alex had never mingled much with his neighbours, but today, when he saw a familiar face, he stopped to introduce Jane, accepting their hearty congratulations with a smile and a glow of pride. Mrs Phillips, the wife of the local vicar, was especially welcoming and she invited Jane to take tea with her one day. Jane accepted the invitation, her pleasure clear. As they drove on, Alex hid his happiness behind a grumble.

'No doubt we shall be plagued by a never-ending stream of visitors, all keen to make your better acquaintance and to invite us to all manner of entertainments.'

She tipped her head to one side. 'Should you object if we socialise with them?'

Would it be so bad? Getting wed had changed his outlook. Even though he'd never had any intention of leaving Foxbourne, somehow it seemed more settled…more *permanent*…now.

'I suppose not, if it makes you happy,' he muttered in a purposely grudging tone, then bit back his laugh when Jane's lips quirked into a knowing, but fond, smile. She could always tell when he was fudging the truth to hide his true feelings.

He saw they were about to pass the blacksmith's forge and reined the horses to a halt.

'I almost forgot; I have a message for the farrier from Lilley—one of the lads is bringing a horse down to be shod tomorrow. I warn you in advance, though—Benson does love to gossip.'

'Then I hope to learn even more about my new neighbours, but I am surprised you don't have your own farrier at Foxbourne.'

'Sir William always used Benson, so I carried on.' Alex handed her the reins. 'Are you happy holding the horses? They've had the fidgets worked out of them.'

'Of course.'

He jumped down as Benson emerged into the sunlight, wiping his glistening forehead with a grimy rag before tucking it behind the bib of his leather apron. His face creased in a smile as he recognised Alex and his eyes brightened when he noticed Jane seated in the curricle.

Alex relayed Lilley's message and then introduced Benson to Jane.

''Tis an honour to meet you, milady, so it is. We was all agog to hear His Lordship had wed—it's wonderful news, to be sure.'

Jane smiled at him but, before she could reply, Benson barrelled on, his eyes alight with the excitement of a juicy morsel of gossip.

'Have you heard the latest news, milord?'

Alex caught Jane's eye, saw laughter twinkling and he winked in response. It felt good to have someone to share a joke with.

'No. I'm afraid you have the advantage of me there, Benson. What news?'

Benson beamed. 'Halsdon Manor is let at last. You'll have new neighbours by All Hallow's Eve...my missus is hired on to help prepare the house.' He switched his gaze to Jane. 'It's been empty these five years, milady, so it has. And even then, Mr Lascelles only lived there a short while before he disappeared back overseas.'

That name left a sour taste in Alex's mouth—he'd almost forgotten Anthony Lascelles owned Halsdon Manor.

'Quite the mystery, so it was,' Benson continued. 'After all, why would a man buy an estate and then leave the country without a word? I never did—'

His jaw snapped shut as he caught Alex's expression.

'Sorry, milord. I was forgetting Mr Lascelles was a relation. You probably know more about it than me.'

'No. I don't.' Alex leapt into the curricle, taking the reins from Jane, but then paused, eyeing the blacksmith. 'Do you have any idea who has leased the Manor, Benson?'

'Nobody does, milord. We's hoping Mrs Benson'll find out more when she starts working up there.'

'No doubt we'll find out soon enough.' Alex nodded at Benson. 'Good day to you.'

As they drove out of the village, Jane said, 'Who is Mr Lascelles? I have never heard of him. *Is* he a relative of yours?'

'Black sheep of the family.' Alex chuckled as Jane's

eyebrows rose. 'And there was you, thinking *I* was the black sheep.'

'Is he from your mother's side?'

'No.' Alex's throat tightened, as it always did at any mention of his mother. 'Father's, on the distaff side.'

'He's illegitimate?'

'Yes. My great-uncle was the duke, but he never married. He had a long-standing affair with an actress and they had a son together.'

'Mr Lascelles.'

'Yes. And Great-Uncle still refused to contemplate an actress becoming Duchess of Cheriton so the title passed on to his brother, my grandfather, and then through him to my father.'

'So he's your father's cousin?'

'Yes. He hates Father, though. Uncle Vernon says he's eaten up with jealousy because he believed *he* should rightfully be the duke. He's…overseas now.' The story of why he had quit Halsdon Manor so suddenly could wait. 'He's actually lived overseas for most of his life. I only met him for the first time in London five years ago.'

'Perhaps he has returned and the house is being prepared for him?'

Lascelles would be a fool to return, given the way Alex's father felt about what he had done. But it was strange it was suddenly let after all this time. 'We shall soon find out, I have no doubt.'

Alex didn't give the potential occupant of Halsdon Manor another thought as he and Jane settled into married life. He would never have guessed he could experience such contentment; if ever he'd thought about it, he would have said he could never tolerate living cheek by jowl with any other person, but he found himself increasingly seeking Jane out during the day simply because he enjoyed her company. He also appreciated the calm and comfortable home she provided for him, he enjoyed sharing his life and ideas with her and, for the first few nights, he slept right through, dreamless, with his wife held close, waking refreshed and blessing the day they had wed.

The dreams began again after a week or so. In them, he was walking around the lake at the Abbey, towards the summer house. The sound of a scuffle from among the trees lured him into the wood before he reached it. He invariably awoke just as he hauled Pikeford off Jane and he would find himself in her arms, her cool fingers stroking his brow.

'Shh… It's a bad dream. I'm here. Sleep now.'

The images would disperse, leaving him thoroughly ashamed that Pikeford's attack was haunting him while Jane had put it behind her, so he denied recalling any details of those dreams even as he puzzled over why they included the long-demolished summer house. He also had the sense someone was walking with him, which was nonsense; he could only assume it was his brain muddling together different memories, as often happened in dreams.

He was grateful Jane's presence helped keep his old nightmares at bay and that he didn't dream every night. Surely they would eventually stop, as his nightmares had done in the past.

The days fell into a comfortable rhythm and their nights were filled with a passion and a depth of feeling Alex had never before experienced. Jane seemed happy and contented. She had gained so much confidence, now she was out of reach of that old witch with her constant disapproval. Jane even at times instigated their lovemaking. There was so much more to the woman he had always thought of as a little sister…how had he failed to recognise this treasure under his nose his entire life?

As time passed, his habitual guard gradually lowered as he allowed Jane closer than he had ever let anyone, but it seemed as though the more contented his life became, the more frequently dreams disturbed his nights. They took a dark turn, with odd images flashing through them—images that filled him with a deep foreboding. Those nights, he would waken with his heart thumping, but unable to make any sense of those fleeting images.

But Jane was always there to soothe and to comfort and although she often asked about his nightmare in the morning he continued to fob her off, determined not to remind her of Pikeford.

Chapter Nine

Jane was truly happy for almost the first time in her life, without her stepmother's criticisms to drag her down. The first weeks at Foxbourne were filled with fun and work, and gradually getting to know one another even better than before. They spent their evenings in comfortable companionship. If Jane took up her sewing—she was making and embroidering silk reticules as Christmas presents for the ladies of the family and monogrammed handkerchiefs for the men—Alex would read to her. Or they played cards, or draughts, or chess, although she feared she would never make Alex a worthy opponent. It seemed Alex could not do enough for his new wife and Jane's natural sunny nature began to reassert itself. Some evenings, she played the piano and they would sing together, Alex's rich baritone voice sending delicious shivers across her skin as his tiger eyes caressed her with the promise of the night to come.

His loving was sublime. Jane felt like a princess as he worshipped her body every night—and most mornings, too, because he continued to sleep the night in her bed. Her confidence in her allure as a woman grew—she enjoyed their intimacies and felt like the luckiest woman in the world.

Alex was changing. The man who had always been so guarded and self-contained relaxed as days turned into weeks, seeming more at peace with himself than she had ever known him, despite the return of his dreams.

To begin with, they occurred infrequently and seemed milder than before. He would toss and turn in his sleep and she would gather him close and soothe him until he slept again. In the morning he had no recollection of the dream and, because he seemed happy and content, Jane probed no further. Gradually, though, the dreams slid into nightmares until, one night, he shot upright in their bed shouting, 'No! Mama! No!'

Jane sat up and wrapped her arms around his shaking body.

'Shhh…shhh…'

He appeared to rouse, as he always did, but he soon settled back to sleep while Jane lay awake, wondering and worrying.

She waited until they were at breakfast.

'You dreamt again last night, Alex. Do you remember?'

'No. I never do. I've told you before, Janey.'

'You called out this time.'

His chin tilted higher. The planes of his face hardened. Jane recognised the signs—this was the old Alex who resented anyone probing too deeply. But she was his wife and she would not be intimidated into ignoring something that was troubling her husband.

'You shouted out. *"No! Mama! No!"'*

Alex thrust back his chair. 'I don't recall.'

But the way he avoided meeting her eyes suggested he did remember—he just refused to discuss it.

'Have you finished eating?'

She nodded.

'As have I.' He rose to his feet. 'I cannot tell you about something I don't remember. They're not important. I've always had them…they'll go soon enough.' He rounded the table to pull her to her feet. 'Now, tell me your plans for today. Shall we work on Pearl later?'

'I would like that.' She would get no further with him right now, but he'd given her an idea.

'Come to the stables at eleven.' Alex kissed her nose. 'And stop worrying about those silly dreams.'

As soon as Alex left for the stables, Jane went upstairs.

'Drabble—' Alex's valet was in his bedchamber '—might I ask you about His Lordship's nightmares?'

'What about them, milady? I thought they'd gone.'

'They did. At first. But they've come back and they seem to be worsening.'

Drabble frowned. 'That's bad news, but I'm not sure how I can help, milady.'

'I wondered…is it true His Lordship was free of them before he went down to the Abbey?'

'Yes. They disappeared completely when we moved here to Foxbourne, but even before that they were few and far between. He suffered much worse as a child.'

'Thank you, Drabble.'

Jane wandered downstairs, deep in thought. The maids were busy polishing and sweeping so, needing time alone to think, she set off for a walk. She'd had little time as yet to explore the estate, so she headed down the carriage-way, pondering Alex's nightmares. After last night, how could she doubt these latest dreams were linked to his mother's death?

She turned on to a winding path through a wood, still deep in thought. It wasn't until the canopy of the trees thickened, blocking out the sun, that her steps faltered. The outline of a thicket bordering the path ahead sent her heart racing and she was seized by an irresistible urge to look over her shoulder. She told herself not to be stupid, there was no one there, but fear still roiled in her belly. She retraced her steps, breathing easier as she emerged into the sunlight, but exasperated by her fearfulness.

Even when she was back on the carriageway that feeling of vulnerability persisted, so she headed back to the house, her thoughts tumbling. She'd worked so hard to banish Pikeford's memory, telling herself it could have ended so much worse, and she was angry he had undermined her confidence so badly she was too scared to walk on her own through a wood.

Determinedly, she diverted her thoughts to the subject of Alex's nightmares. According to Drabble they had gone away before, so why were they now getting worse? Could it be because Pikeford had attacked her so close to where Alex had found his mother? Had that somehow unlocked his memory of that day? Alex had never been able to remember finding his mother, according to Olivia, and his father had felt it was better for him that way.

How dreadful if the attack on Jane had somehow prompted him to remember it after all this time.

Eleven o'clock saw her at the stable yard and she pushed her worries aside as Alex lifted her up on to Pearl's saddle. When they had finished, they walked together up to the house and she gathered her courage.

'I have been thinking about your nightmares, Alex.'

'I don't want to discuss them, Janey. I told you.'

'But—'

'No!'

His brows lowered, his mouth set in a stubborn line. Jane frowned, considering. She'd had enough of biting her tongue for the sake of a quiet life with Stepmama. She recognised this *mind your own business* Alex of old… it was how he had always kept his family and friends at bay. She'd thought he was improving…that the barriers he erected against the world were slowly crumbling. This felt depressingly like a reversal.

As Alex's friend, Jane had never had the right to probe deeper. But…as his wife…

She grabbed his hand to pull him to a halt. 'Alex… please… I truly think it would help if you—'

'I said no.' He snatched his hand away. 'There's nothing to talk about.'

'But I wanted to tell you about…'

She watched him stalk away, back to the stables, frustration humming through her. They never spoke about Pikeford's attack—each protecting the other, she had no doubt—but she'd decided to tell him what happened in the woods earlier and also that the memory of that attack would sometimes catch her unawares; that the feelings she'd had at the time would burst upon her and it would almost be—just for a few seconds—as though it was happening all over again.

She'd hoped it might help him to confide in her. But he'd given her no chance.

The seething mass of his emotions drove Alex to seek solitude. He threw a saddle on Frost, his favourite gelding, and set off for the nearby hills where he could gallop his frustrations away. Except that didn't work. When they halted, breathless, on the brow of a hill, that cauldron of guilt, shame and resentment still bubbled away inside, making him feel sick.

Jane didn't deserve the way he had spoken to her. That was the guilt. But it wasn't powerful enough to persuade him she needed to know about his damned nightmares. How could he tell her, when they always began with Pikeford? She'd done so well to overcome the attack and it was his role as her husband to protect her not only from that memory, but also from the responsibility she would feel at being—as she would see it—the cause of his nightmares. Because that was Jane—she blamed herself and felt responsible even when the fault lay with other people.

Jane had made his life so sweet and he cared for her so very much…she had crept into his heart in the short time they had been wed and now he simply couldn't imagine his life without her. But that didn't mean he would willingly discuss his nightmares. Hell, he didn't fully understand them himself, so how could he explain them to anyone? Somehow, he must convince her to avoid the subject in future. They would both be happier, he was sure.

He slid from Frost's back and sat on a rock to think while the horse cropped grass.

He was honest enough—with himself—to admit shame at his own weakness also played its part in his reluctance to talk about the nightmares. He was ashamed that *he* had nightmares over that damned attack whereas Jane was not only strong enough to overcome her initial fear of love-making, but she also slept like the proverbial babe. Perhaps his family had been right all these years, seeing him as always troubled and needing their help and protection. He'd always resented it and now he was damned if he'd allow his wife to see him that way, too.

It was *his* place to be the strong one.

He swore to himself he would work doubly hard to make Jane happy. He would do anything for her. Anything except talk about his nightmares. They would disappear soon enough, as they did before.

Several days later, Alex strode in the direction of the stable yard, hurrying to beat the shower that threatened, his head full of last night's dream, determined to make sense of the few fragments he could recall in his efforts to banish his nightmares for good. He remembered the colour yellow…but how did that fit in? It made no sense.

Then a memory flared and his breath caught as he slammed to a halt with images filling his head—the lake at Cheriton Abbey, the sound of a scuffle, the image of Pikeford on top of Jane, as clear as the day it happened. But then…those memories were replaced with a vision—a swirl of yellow skirt, polished top boots, voices, low, angry, arguing, the words unclear. Almost as soon as it erupted into his consciousness, it scattered, leaving his heart slamming into his ribs and sweat breaking out on his brow.

He stumbled across to the fence and grabbed the top rail, his breaths ragged and urgent, a vice tight around his chest.

What the hell…?

His fingers thrust through his hair, dislodging his hat, then lingered at the back of his head, his nails digging into his skull as he struggled to recall exactly what that had been a memory of. His viewpoint…he must have been on the floor. But neither a carpet nor cool, smooth tiles. His eyes screwed shut. Another memory whispered—that of rough wooden planks against his cheek. He swallowed, lifting his chin to ease the action. Everything throbbed.

His head. His chest. His throat.

His brain.

Was it a memory…or a remnant of his dreams?

Slowly, steadily, the vice loosened its grip and his breathing eased. A drop of rain splattered on the back of his hand, still clutching the top rail. He tipped his face skyward, welcoming the cool rain on his heated skin. He swallowed again. Everything felt looser. Easier.

The distant recall of a dream. That was all.

Alex turned once more for the stables, thrusting aside the black mood threatening to envelop him—the sort of black mood that used to drive him to excess in his desperate bids to escape. Well, he was that man no more. He was happy. He would do everything he could to stop his demons from sullying his new life. And he would continue to protect Jane from the memory of Pikeford's attack. She did not need reminding of what had happened, not when she was recovering so well and seemed so happy.

Happy with *him*, as he was happy with her—a feeling he cherished and one he would fight to preserve.

Alex's resolution to make sense of his dreams didn't go as planned and he soon reverted to trying to block out his nightmares in the face of increasingly distressing visions and new, disturbing suspicions that taunted him. But those visions proved almost impossible to stop now they had started—it was as though he had opened Pandora's box and, try as he might, he couldn't shut the lid again. The only good part was that the more often the daytime visions occurred the less frequent his nightmares became.

They always began with the memory of Pikeford's attack…but then they would slide into something different.

Something dark and dangerous.

Something his instinct told him he must suppress at all costs.

He dared not reveal even a hint of what his memories—

if they were indeed memories—implied. Because it was no longer simply about protecting Jane from any reminders of Pikeford's attack. Because now, bubbling deep in his past— swirling in a murky cesspool of fear, disgust and horror, and creeping ever nearer—was something so huge...so dark...so dreadful...that Alex fought with every fibre of his being to stop that clouded vision from sharpening and becoming clear.

Because...once it did...once he *knew*...he feared there would be no going back.

Chapter Ten

'I must go into High Wycombe this morning,' Alex said one day as they breakfasted together. 'Would you care to accompany me, Janey?'

'I should like that. Thank you.'

Jane kept the frown from her forehead. Where had the friendly, easy banter disappeared to? She didn't understand it, but she sensed a growing distance between them. She was certain it wasn't her imagination that Alex appeared to be holding her at arm's length. Not physically—he still made love to her most nights with tender skill—but Alex himself, the man, was steadily becoming more unreachable.

He hated her asking if anything was troubling him, but it was hard to stay silent when every instinct she possessed told her *something* was wrong. Was he tiring of married life already? Had she simply fooled herself that the bond between them had been strengthening since their marriage? Had she imagined their growing closeness and intimacy? Was it wishful thinking on her part—the feeble hope her childhood dreams could really come true?

She tried to ignore her doubts as she went upstairs to change into her new yellow carriage gown, admiring herself in the pier glass: the colour really did bring out the colour and shine of her hair. She donned her dark blue spencer and bonnet, picked up her gloves and her cloak, and hurried downstairs. Alex was waiting at the foot of the stairs and Jane saw some strong emotion flash across his face.

'What is it?' Her stomach tightened with the familiar anxiety that had plagued her in the presence of her stepmother. 'Have I kept you waiting?'

His gaze swept her from head to toe, a muscle bunching in his jaw.

'Do you not like my gown?' Jane persisted when he did not answer her. She saw the effort it took him to smile at her.

'It suits you very well, Janey,' he said. 'I shall be the envy of every man in High Wycombe.'

That empty compliment did nothing to reassure Jane as Alex helped her with her cloak. Her thoughts whirled as she tried to understand what had upset him, but she couldn't work it out and to question him further would likely only result in an uncomfortable journey for them both. She wanted to enjoy this outing, so she let the subject drop, suppressing her sigh at her avoidance, yet again, of a contentious subject. She had always known Alex was a complex man—she mustn't expect him to suddenly turn into an easy man to understand. But she would keep trying.

High Wycombe, one of the principal towns of Buckinghamshire, was a leisurely hour's drive from Foxbourne. The sun was shining, but a breeze kept the weather fresh and Jane enjoyed the journey through the beautiful Buckinghamshire countryside, with its rolling Chiltern Hills and wooded valleys, the trees a stunning autumnal mix of russet, orange and gold as their leaves turned colour before they dropped.

In town, Alex dealt with his business and then escorted Jane along the High Street, a broad thoroughfare where the market was in full swing. Jane, still planning ahead for their Christmas visit to Devonshire, bought a pretty ivory hair comb for Susie and set of brightly painted wooden toy soldiers each for Thomas, Julius and Sebastian. She hadn't yet decided what to make for baby George, but she had enough colourful fabric at home to make ragdolls plus matching hair ribbons for Christabel, Florence, Sophie and Daisy and she'd found some beautiful ruby-red satin in a trunk at Foxbourne with which she planned to make a waistcoat for Alex.

Alex treated Jane to a beautiful shawl of flowered silk, edged with local lace, and, after she admired a pair of the Windsor chairs for which High Wycombe was famous, he bought those, too, arranging for their delivery to Foxbourne where Jane planned to put them either side of the fireplace in the morning parlour. After a pleasant few hours, they returned to the Red Lion, where they had left the horses, and enjoyed a glass of wine and a sandwich before setting off on the journey home.

'Well, Janey? Did you like High Wycombe? It cannot offer the variety of goods you can buy in London, but it does boast a decent collection of shops.'

'I loved it, Alex! Thank you.'

'You don't have to thank me, Janey. We're a married couple. You are welcome to accompany me whenever I go into town.'

'Many married couples spend little time together, Alex. You need not feel obliged to invite me along every time you go into town.' She captured his gaze. 'Earlier, when

I came downstairs, I thought you regretted asking me to accompany you.'

His brow furrowed. Then it cleared and laughter danced in his amber eyes as he grabbed her hand, pulled off her glove and pressed hot lips to her bare skin.

'Of course I didn't regret it, my sweet Janey. I was taken aback—I have never seen you wear yellow before, but I was not merely flattering you when I said it suits you very well. You look lovely and you could not have chosen better for such a pleasant day.'

He tipped up her chin, then, and kissed her. She returned his kiss, but pulled away when he began to deepen it.

'Alex!' She laughed, batting his hand away. 'It is broad daylight! What if someone should see us?'

'What if they should? Why should I not kiss my own wife whenever I choose?'

His teasing soothed her and her worries seemed far away.

'You should keep your eyes on the road,' she said, mock severely. 'What if we should have an accident?'

'My horses are too fly to collide with anything or to run us into a ditch.' But Alex did turn his attention back to his driving, taking the reins in one hand as he slipped his arm around Jane and pulled her in close. She relaxed against him, laying her head on his shoulder, contentment flowing through her as the steady beat of the horses' hooves lulled her.

Alex had worked hard to hide the increasing strain he was under, but it was obvious Jane had noticed something was wrong. She knew him too well—she had always been an observant soul and he had always been hopeless at concealing his moods—his entire family could attest to that—no matter how adept he was at concealing the cause of those moods.

But how could he admit Pikeford's attack was leading to increasingly frequent visions that appeared to be linked to his mother's death, even though he had no conscious memory of finding her body? He knew Jane—she would blame herself for being the cause, even though it was not her fault.

It was taking its toll on him. He couldn't even decide if they were real memories, or whether his imagination was resurrecting those awful visions out of his nightmares. And, if the latter, did it mean he was losing his mind? The very thought terrified him—in his youth he had once visited Bethlem Hospital with a group of friends, before it moved to its current location at St George's Fields in Southwark. He shuddered at the memory.

What if I am going mad?

He swallowed down that fear and resolutely directed his attention to the road ahead. Jane's head grew heavy on his shoulder, her face shielded by the brim of her bonnet, peacefully slumbering as the curricle rumbled over the stony track. That yellow gown *had* taken him by surprise. For a split second, when he first saw her, he had felt nothing but terror and he'd failed miserably to hide his reaction. It was odd. Yellow had never affected him before—he could only think that flash of fear and dread was linked to the yellow gown in his visions.

They drove over a humpback bridge and Alex urged the horses into a trot as they approached the long, slow pull up the lane towards home. Jane stirred.

'Are we nearly home?' Her voice sounded thick. Sleepy.

'Not far now, Janey. Close your eyes again, if you like.'

Jane pushed herself upright and straightened her bonnet. 'I was *not* asleep.'

Alex caught her eye and grinned. An answering smile slowly stretched her lips, but she stuck her nose in the air before turning to watch teams of men and plough horses working in an adjacent field until it was masked from view by a copse.

A scream suddenly rent the air and a vivid image hit Alex with the force of a physical blow, followed by a feeling of such powerlessness, such hopelessness, such panic…a pair of boots…her yellow gown and matching slippers…the colour of daffodils…the scent of roses…the rough wood against his cheek…

His gorge rose to crowd his throat as his mind spun remorselessly in a black, choking vortex of terror and chills racked his body. The sound of ripping cloth… *What…no… please*—a woman's voice…pleading. The vision continued—those boots and the slippers, moving…to and fro…as though in a dance. Two figures, sinking towards the floor…a cry, choked off…his heart beating so hard it might burst…the grunts…

A new image began to form.

'Alex?' It seemed to come from far away, and he focused on that voice…safety…reassurance…hope… He clambered out of the past, back to the present, away from that hazy image of his father's face.

People ran when they heard my screams. They told me. And Father came, too… That's all that means. Isn't it?

'Alex?' Jane's hand was on his, her voice urgent. 'What is it? What's wrong?'

He forced open eyes that had screwed shut. 'The…' His voice croaked. He cleared his throat. Tried again. 'That scream…'

'Scream? You mean the children? They're just playing.'

Jane pointed back along the lane, towards the copse, now fifty yards behind them. Alex, his vision clearing,

saw the children—no doubt belonging to the ploughmen—
darting in and out of the trees.

It was all normal. Thoroughly normal.

The horses had halted and Jane now held the reins. Alex
rubbed his forehead. He had no memory of her taking over.

'The horses took fright,' she said. 'I had to stop them.'

He stared at her, trying to make sense of it all.

'What happened, Alex?' She made no attempt to start
the horses. 'One minute we were bowling along quite happily, then you jerked the reins hard and went quite rigid
and pale. It was like…you weren't there. I-It was spooky.
It frightened *me*, never mind the horses.'

'I don't know what happened.' He felt as he did when
he emerged from a nightmare, as though his brain were
stuffed with wool. 'I really don't know.'

She offered the reins and he shook his head. 'You drive.'

They drove home in silence, Alex conscious of the many
concerned glances Jane sent his way. By the time they arrived, his clenched jaw ached. He'd spent his entire life
suffering not only the sympathy and pity of his family, but
also their misguided efforts to snap him out of his moods.
He was damned if he wanted to undergo the same treatment from his wife—he could only pray she would soon
forget about it and he would suffer no further lapses in
front of her. All he wanted now was to get away…to be
alone so he could think about what had happened.

Jane didn't mention the incident again, lulling him into
believing she would let it pass. He should have known better. She waited until after their evening meal, until they
had settled in the drawing room by the fire crackling in
the huge stone fireplace for, even though the days were
warm, the nights were drawing in. Jane settled on the sofa,
reached for her sewing box and removed her lucet, with

which she was making silk cords for the reticules she'd made. Alex quashed his guilt that he still hadn't told her they wouldn't be going to the Abbey at Christmas. She wouldn't be pleased after she had lavished so much care and attention on gifts for the family, but they could at least be sent on. He promised himself he would tell her soon.

'Shall I continue to read to you, while you work?'

Alex picked up *Waverley*. They were already halfway through the story of the Jacobite rebellion of 1745 and he enjoyed the cosy companionship and even the domesticity of reading aloud while Jane sewed. His younger self would have stared to see how he had changed.

'I would rather you didn't.' Jane didn't look at him, her head bent over her work. 'Not tonight, if you don't mind. I would rather talk.'

Hell and damnation!

He wasn't always the most perceptive of men, but he couldn't miss her resolve. Jane lifted her head and his teeth clenched.

'Very well. How long will it be until the kittens are fully weaned, do you suppose?'

Jane's eyes remained steady on his. 'Not long now, but it is not that I wish to talk about.'

Alex huffed a laugh. 'You sound far too serious for this time of night, Janey.' He sat next to her and trailed one finger down her cheek to her neck, and around her neckline. 'Let's go to bed early, sweetheart.' He nipped her earlobe, then sucked at it.

He thought his distraction had worked. Jane moved her head to capture his lips and kissed him, moving her full lips over his, firing his blood. But she took his face between her palms and eased her mouth from his long before he was ready to end their kiss.

'Alex…you do know how much I care for you, don't you?'

He pulled back, frowning. 'Of course I know, Janey. As I care for you.'

'Do you? Really?' She shook her head. 'How can you care for someone if you do not trust them?'

He straightened, staring at her. 'I *do* trust you!'

'I thought you did. But now…' She paused, chewing her lip, and his heart squeezed, knowing he was the cause of her worry. 'You're hiding something, Alex. What happened to you this afternoon? Are you ill? Ought you to see a physician?'

'I'm not ill and I don't need a physician.'

'But…what happened? You mentioned the scream…did it remind you of what happened with Pikeford?'

He'd thought to protect her by not mentioning that bastard, but it seemed she'd reached that conclusion anyway.

'I think of him sometimes, you know.'

Alex stiffened. 'Who?'

'Pikeford. About that day.'

'You've never said.'

'I didn't want to worry you. But that makes me as bad as you—hiding the truth to protect you.'

'When do you think about him? When we make love?' He loathed the very thought.

'No!' She caressed his hand. 'You have helped me so much, Alex. I never think of him at those times. But it *has* affected me—I went for a walk in the woods and I couldn't go on. I couldn't rid myself of the conviction someone was following me.'

'Janey! I had no idea.'

Guilt and shame swirled through him. What kind of man didn't notice his wife's distress?

'And I've had flashes of memory of what happened. For a few seconds it is as though it is actually happening again.

I can't breathe and I can't move, and the fear…it wells up and, even though I know it's not real, it still *feels* real.'

She swallowed audibly and he squeezed her hand, even as his heart thudded against his ribs. That sounded exactly how he reacted to those accursed visions.

'I wish you had told me sooner, Janey. You must have known I would want to help.'

She stared at him, her eyes serious. 'As I want to help you.'

He could see her willing him to confide in her. But he couldn't. He straightened, holding her hands as he gazed into her eyes.

'You must tell me if it happens to you again, Janey. I will help you to get over it, I promise you.'

She didn't try to hide her frustration.

'But… Alex…what about today? I hate any reminder of Pikeford, but that scream didn't affect me. Why would it have that effect on you?'

An image exploded into his head—his mother…the shadowy figure of a man…a struggle. He couldn't tell her! Hell, he didn't know for sure what he was 'seeing' in those visions. Were any of them true? Had he actually witnessed—?

He swiped that question aside and leapt to his feet, fear he was going mad scorching through him.

'Alex?' Jane stood, grabbing his hand, stopping him from leaving. 'What is it? *Please* tell me.'

'It's nothing. You're imagining it. I have the headache so I shall sleep in my own room tonight.'

She didn't release him. 'No. Please do not. Come to bed with me… I promise I shan't plague you with any more questions.' She pressed her lips to his hand. 'But I do wish you would trust me enough to *talk* to me.'

Dear God! How he wished he *could* confide in her. But

how could he when he didn't even know if they were real memories or a fiction conjured up by years of nightmares? And what if he was losing his grasp of what was real and what was inside his head? What then? What would the future hold?

He quashed his fears and forced a smile.

'There is nothing to tell, Honeybee. Nothing at all. Come to bed.'

Chapter Eleven

Jane was relieved when Alex's funny turn, as she came to think of it, didn't recur, but something was clearly bothering him although he tried to hide it. It couldn't be money… the ledgers confirmed their finances were healthy. She was almost certain it wasn't her… Alex would never manage to hide it if he truly regretted their marriage. She'd be left in no doubt if she was at fault.

She told herself it was her imagination…she was being over-sensitive…but as the days got shorter and the nights closed in those doubts simply would not go away and, rather than reassure her, Alex's lovemaking slowly but surely started to echo everything that was going wrong in their marriage. One morning as they lay together in a post-coital glow, Jane could no longer deny her frustration. Physically, she was fully satisfied. Alex was everything she could wish for. But emotionally… She frowned as she pondered the source of her disquiet. She couldn't deny the suspicion that, emotionally—in bed as well as out of it—he was holding back. Those barriers behind which he had always protected himself—the ones she believed were crumbling—were firmly back in place.

The mattress dipped as Alex rolled over to face her. He

traced between her brows with his forefinger. 'Why the frown, Janey?'

But how could she explain when she barely understood it herself? All she could do was to keep proving he could trust her and hope he would eventually confide in her. His lovemaking was so controlled, reminding her of a rider who put his horse at a hedge, but spent the approach ensuring every aid was perfection. She longed for Alex to release his control and 'throw his heart over'.

She lied. 'I was thinking your nightmares have improved.'

'That's good, though. Isn't it?'

It was his turn to frown now, staring unseeingly across the room as Jane laid her hand against his whisker-rough cheek.

'Have you had any more episodes such as that day we went to High Wycombe?'

She'd not broached the subject since and she hadn't seen anything, but that didn't mean they hadn't happened and she knew Alex would never voluntarily admit it to her.

'Why should the subject of my nightmares cause you to think about that?' His amber eyes turned wary. 'The two are unconnected.'

She cuddled into him, her cheek to his chest. 'I wasn't sure they *were* unconnected.'

She remained convinced he was hiding his troubles to protect her. If only he would talk to her about his mother. About the day he found her body. It couldn't be good for him to keep those memories inside.

'I think that child's scream reminded you of Pikeford's attack and, because it happened in the same place as your mother—'

He tipped up her face and kissed her, his lips moving over hers with practised skill, and her thoughts scattered as she responded to the coaxing caress of his tongue. The kiss ended and Alex rolled from the bed in one smooth movement.

'Come on, lazybones. There's work to be done.'

He tugged the covers from her body and picked her up, kissing her again before allowing her body to slide down his until her feet touched the floor. The cool caress of the morning air shook her thoughts back to their conversation… and his blatant attempt to distract her.

'Wait!'

His eyes narrowed. 'Don't think about that day, Janey. Pikeford isn't worthy of a single second of your time.'

'I know. But…your nightmares…they got worse after—'

'And now they are improving. I'm always the same when I go back to the Abbey…the nightmares were not linked to Pikeford's attack and there's no reason whatsoever why a random scream should resurrect anything.'

Was he trying to convince himself, or her?

'I hope that does not mean we can never go to the Abbey, especially as I've already accepted your stepmother's invitation to spend Christmas there.'

She'd hoped to diffuse the tension shimmering between them, but Alex refused to meet her eyes as he shrugged into his banyan.

'I remember you saying so.'

Jane frowned. That seemed somewhat non-committal, but she was reluctant to pursue the subject. There were enough difficulties already in their relationship without cultivating more.

After a few days of heavy rain when they couldn't continue Pearl's education, they took advantage of a dry morning to work together on schooling her.

'She's ready for you to ride out,' Alex said as they

strolled back to the house together. 'What do you say to taking her out early tomorrow? We can ride around the fields and get her used to all the sights and sounds.'

'I say that sounds perfect.' Jane couldn't wait for Pearl's education to be complete. 'And you haven't forgotten I am to visit Mrs Phillips again today, have you?'

Mrs Phillips was several years Jane's senior, but they had much in common, and Jane had promised her support for the vicar's various charitable endeavours on behalf of the poor of the district.

'I hadn't forgotten. Would you like me to drive you to the village or are you comfortable driving yourself?'

'I can drive myself.' Although still wary of walking alone in the countryside she had no fear of driving. She looked forward to the freedom of riding out alone, too, once Pearl was ready. 'There's no need to waste your time and I know you won't miss the neighbourly gossip.' The very idea of Alex sitting making polite small talk with any of their neighbours, let alone a vicar's wife, was laughable. 'I've asked Lilley to have the pony and trap ready at two.'

Jane had spent a pleasant hour visiting Mrs Phillips, hearing all about the usual Christmas activities in Malton—decorating the Church on Christmas Eve and the morning church service after which the poor of the village were invited to an open kitchen at the vicarage. As she and Alex would be away during Christmastide, Jane promised to arrange for food to be sent to the vicarage to help feed the poor, many of whom, Mrs Phillips said, would afterwards go wassailing around the district, hoping to be given gifts of money, food or drink.

When it was time to leave, Mrs Phillips handed Jane a bunch of silvery-pink roses.

'I hope you will accept these? This rose flowers right

up to the first frost and I thought you might enjoy a few fresh flowers.'

'Thank you.' Jane smiled with pleasure, raising the blooms to her nose. 'The fragrance is glorious.' She frowned. 'Do you know…although the gardens at Fox-bourne are extensive, I cannot recall seeing any roses.'

'That's odd. The late Lady Rockbeare definitely grew them. Maybe they had to be dug out?'

'I shall ask the gardeners. Goodbye, Mrs Phillips, and thank you.'

Jane tapped the pony with the reins to drive home, but she had barely left the village behind when she heard someone call her name. Pikeford shot into her brain. Suppressing her quiver of fear, she glanced over her shoulder to see Tommy, the postmaster's son, on his pony. She breathed easier and halted the trap.

'Good afternoon, milady. I have a letter for the Manor.' Tommy grinned at her disarmingly as he withdrew a let-ter from his shoulder bag. 'You'll save me some time if you don't mind taking it. My other deliveries are out to-wards Cucklow.'

Jane opened her reticule. 'Of course I don't mind, Tommy. How much is the postage?'

'Sixpence, milady.' Jane passed him the coins. 'It's from St Albans.' He wheeled his pony around and trotted away.

That must surely mean it was from Zach—Alex had written to ask for his help with an exceptionally fast and handsome stallion who had been badly treated and har-boured a deep mistrust of humans, biting and kicking any-one who entered his stall. Alex had saved him from certain destruction, hoping to use him for breeding if he could sat-isfy himself Nelson's viciousness was the result of the ill treatment and not a trait he might pass on to his offspring. The stallion, however, was proving a challenge.

* * *

Back at the stable yard, Lilley informed Jane that Alex was indoors so, one arm full of roses and the letter in her other hand, Jane walked up to the house.

Home. She already felt a deep sense of peace being here and marvelled at her unexpected good fortune. Her heart full of joy, she went straight to Alex's business room. He was at the window behind his large mahogany desk, his back to the room, arms folded across his chest.

'I thought to find you hard at work, but here you are daydreaming.'

Jane crossed the room and rounded the desk, laying the roses and the letter on its gleaming surface.

Alex started as she spoke and faced her. She clasped his upper arms and aimed a kiss at his cheek, but he moved his head so their lips met. He cradled her face as he explored her mouth in a kiss that melted her insides.

Would she ever get used to this? The man of her dreams, now her husband. Hers. Heat pooled low in her belly and, with an effort, she pulled away. He quirked a brow, his tiger eyes aglow.

'Is that it? You've been gone hours and all I get is one measly...'

His face blanked. Jane frowned. His eyes looked... empty, somehow. Unseeing. His lips were tight and his chest rose and fell in a rapid rhythm.

'Alex? What is it?'

He screwed his eyes shut and then opened them again, to look at her. Then his gaze shifted to one side, and beyond Jane—to the roses on the desk.

'Get them out of here,' he growled.

'I... Why? What is—?'

'Do it!'

'But…Mrs Phillips gave them to me. They have the most beautiful scent.'

Jane reached for the bunch and held them up to Alex. He dashed them from her hand and spun to face the window again.

'I said get them out of here. No roses. Ever. Do you understand?'

'But…' Her brain scrambled to understand. 'Why?'

She moved so she could see his profile—jaw muscle bunched tight, lips colourless.

'Alex? I don't understand.'

Her voice wobbled and tears stung. She swallowed to keep them at bay.

'Get rid of them.'

The easy option was to mindlessly obey, but why should he get away with barking orders at her when she'd done nothing wrong? She'd had enough of her stepmother browbeating her…she wouldn't accept that kind of treatment from Alex.

'What is wrong with roses?'

His chest continued to heave and his hands clenched into fists at his sides. 'The smell makes me sick. Take them. Go.'

Jane, still puzzled, sensed she would get no more from him while the roses were in the room. Silently she gathered the scattered blooms and left, vowing this would not be the end of the matter.

'Mrs Kent?' The housekeeper was in the kitchen, sharing a cup of tea with the new cook, Mrs Godfrey. 'Would you care to have these roses for your quarters? It seems His Lordship does not care for their scent.'

'Oh, my!' Mrs Kent shot to her feet and almost snatched the flowers from Jane. 'I am sorry, milady. Mayhap I should have warned you, but I thought you would know, having known His Lordship such a long time. It's a strict rule. No roses in the house. Nor in the garden. He made poor Scully dig them all out. Near broke his heart, it did, destroying Lady Rockbeare's pride and joy that way.'

That might underline the fact Alex hated roses, but it explained nothing. Maybe Alex would tell her the real reason once he had calmed down. Jane smiled at Mrs Kent, handing her the flowers.

'It would be a pity to waste them now they have been cut. And His Lordship will never know you have them unless you tell him.'

Needing comfort, Jane headed to see the kittens, who were now eating and drinking for themselves, although they were still with their mother. In the outhouse, Dora—who could come and go through an open window—was absent. Jane sat on a cushion and distracted herself from what had happened with Alex by rolling a pine cone for the kittens to chase. When they tired of the game they piled on to Jane's lap and fell asleep. The smallest, prettiest and fluffiest—grey and white, like Dora—was her favourite and she decided she would keep Mist, as she called her, as a pet.

'I thought I would find you in here.'

Her stomach tensed at Alex's voice. She did not look up.

He crouched next to her, touching her hand. 'I'm sorry. I should have warned you.'

Not much of an apology.

'Why do you dislike roses so much?'

He shrugged. 'I just do.'

It was the old Alex talking—abrupt and dismissive. The *mind your own business* Alex she had known since childhood. The *I don't need anyone's help* Alex. Had it been too much to hope he had changed? Perhaps it was inevitable their relationship would be two steps forward, one step back to begin with. She suspected that, in some way, his aversion was bound up with the past and the secrets that simmered deep inside him. And all she could do was to keep proving to him he could trust her and hope, in time, he would confide in her.

'Anyway, I have good news.' Alex waved the letter under her nose. 'It's from Zach. He's coming to help me and Aunt Cecily and Florence are coming with him. They arrive tomorrow.'

The carriage drew up outside the front door the following afternoon. Alex was down at the stables, but had promised to come up to the house as soon as their visitors arrived and, true to his word, Jane could see him striding in their direction as she went outside to greet the Graystokes. Myrtle had come, too, hopping around on her three legs, her whole body wriggling in delight.

Aunt Cecily enveloped Jane in an apple-blossom-scented embrace. 'I hope you don't mind us all coming? When Alex wrote to Zach about Nelson we thought it the perfect opportunity.'

Jane hugged her back. 'Of course we don't mind. We're delighted to see you all.'

As Alex kissed his aunt and shook hands with Zach, Jane scooped up Florence and kissed her cheek. Two pudgy arms wound around her neck and dusky curls tickled Jane's nose as Alex watched them, his expression wistful. Would he make a good father? She hoped so, but it was obvious he hadn't had much practice with children, unlike Dominic, who was a natural with their young half-sister and brother, and with their cousins. Never mind. She loved Alex and would help him become the man and father she sensed he wanted to be.

Her arms quickly ached with holding Florence's solid

little body but, before she could put the child down, Zach was there, taking his daughter gently.

'You gradually get used to the increasing weight as your child grows, I find. But it is surprisingly fatiguing when you are not accustomed to it.'

Jane smiled up at him, feeling a little shy. She had only met Zach for the first time in the summer and she found him a little unnerving, with his dark soulful eyes and the glinting diamond he wore in his ear.

'It is a pleasure to meet you again, Jane.'

'And you, Uncle…um… Mr Graystoke.'

'Zach will do, my dear.'

She smiled again. 'Come inside. I will show you to your bedchamber—there will be a tea tray in the drawing room in half an hour.'

Chapter Twelve

It was fun having guests to stay and Jane was in her element, playing hostess in her own establishment—a role she had feared she might never fulfil. Her hopes had dwindled as the Seasons passed, but now—when she had finally lost all hope—her dreams had come true and she was married to the love of her life. Who was proving every bit as challenging as she had thought he would.

But while they had guests, Jane pushed any concerns about Alex to the back of her mind—neither of them referred again to his reaction to those roses and their nights together were still full of passion as he coaxed responses from her body as a talented musician might coax exquisite tunes from his instrument.

Alex, for his part, proved he could play the perfect host. He and Zach spent much of their time at the stable yard, working with Nelson—even when it rained—while Jane, Aunt Cecily and, usually, Florence, went for walks whenever the weather allowed, chatting about all manner of subjects, including the planned Christmas family gathering at the Abbey. The only subject they did not touch upon…the subject Jane longed to broach but did not quite dare…was Alex and his past. Until the day before the Graystokes' departure.

Florence was napping, so Jane and Aunt Cecily walked alone.

No sooner was the Manor out of sight than Aunt Cecily said, 'Alex seems very settled at the moment but…' She sighed and slid a sideways glance at Jane. 'I cannot help but worry about him. He is…complex.'

'He is.'

As Jane pondered how to elaborate, Aunt Cecily continued, 'I hope I have not offended you by my frank speaking. You must say if you would feel it would be disloyal to discuss Alex with me.'

Jane almost laughed. 'No. I do not consider it disloyal to want to help my husband. I know he loves you like a mother.'

It was easier to start with something simple. If anything about her frustrating husband could be deemed simple.

'Do you know why he dislikes roses?'

'*Roses?* I didn't know he disliked them. Why…' Aunt Cecily paused. 'Now I come to think of it…he specified no roses at your wedding. I was so busy I didn't question it at the time. And…your garden. There are no roses. And yet I particularly remember Leo mentioned a rose garden when he described the place to me at the time he was thinking of buying it.'

'Apparently Alex ordered the gardener to dig them all up. I only found out by chance—he became quite…well, *agitated*…when the vicar's wife gave me a bunch of roses for the house. I wondered if it might be linked to his discovering his mother's body?'

'Oh!' Aunt Cecily halted. 'That could be it. Margaret… the perfume she always wore was rose-scented and smells *do* prompt memories, do they not? At least, they do for me. Mayhap roses remind him of that day?'

More than ever Jane believed Pikeford's attack *had* revived Alex's memory of that dreadful day.

'Poor little boy,' Aunt Cecily continued. 'He didn't speak for nigh on a year afterwards. I was so afraid he would never talk again…and he clung to me so…he wouldn't even trust his own father. I suppose he was afraid he might lose me, too, like he lost his mother.'

'Did he ever tell you about discovering his mother's body? After he regained his speech?'

'No. I tried to talk to him about it, but he became so agitated Leo decided we should leave it in the past. He thought it would be better for all three children to look forward, not back, so we rarely spoke of Margaret unless one of the children mentioned her. And that was seldom.'

Jane could believe that. As long as she had known Alex, he'd avoided the subject of his mother.

'How sad he avoids all memories of his mother because of that one day. Surely he must have happy memories of her, too?'

'I think Margaret's death supersedes everything in Alex's mind. Besides, she was not the best of mothers to those children. Although…' Aunt Cecily linked her arm through Jane's and they resumed walking '…she *was* attempting to change. Leo stopped her frequent jaunts up to London and, not long before she died, she told me she wanted to become a better mother.'

They let the subject drop, but it left Jane with plenty to mull over. Alex's dislike of roses was something she could accept, but she would love to help him overcome his aversion to his father and to the Abbey. His wistful expression sometimes when he saw Dominic or Olivia with their father was all the encouragement she needed to believe that there, at least, she could help. Perhaps Christmas at the Abbey could be a turning point.

They emerged on to a lane, turning in the opposite direction to the village.

'Halsdon Manor is up here,' Jane said. 'There's been great excitement in Malton because it will soon be occupied, for the first time in over five years. Alex tells me it is owned by your cousin, Mr Lascelles.'

'Oh, heavens. Now *there* is a name from the past. Has he returned to England?'

'Nobody knows for sure, but they say it's been let, so that must mean a tenant.'

'Just as well,' Aunt Cecily muttered.

'Why do you say that?'

'Has Alex not told you the story?'

'He told me Mr Lascelles is your illegitimate cousin and he resents your brother being the duke, but nothing more.'

'Probably because he doesn't know much more, other than what happened five years ago. I doubt he remembers him from his childhood because Anthony has lived overseas for most of his adult life, apart from a couple of brief returns. But he came back and bought Halsdon Manor five years ago and Leo and Vernon came here to try to mend the breach between Leo and Anthony. But I believe that resentment runs too deep for them to ever get along. That trip proved worthwhile, however, because Leo met Rosalind, and he also discovered Foxbourne Manor was for sale and, now, here you are.'

'In that case, I am grateful they at least attempted to heal that breach. This Mr Lascelles sounds unpleasant, to transfer his father's sins on to the Duke.'

'I always tried to give him the benefit of the doubt because I understand his frustration that his life might have been very different. But he *is* a troublemaker. When Leo and Rosalind were courting he took a shine to her and when she rejected him, he abducted Susie in an attempt to force Rosalind to marry him.'

'Abducted Susie? How evil! She must have been terrified.'

'She was only eight when Rosalind took her in—although she seemed younger, a poor little scrap of a thing—and I don't think she understood much of what happened. Luckily, Leo found out and averted disaster, with Alex's help, and Leo persuaded Anthony he would fare better out of the country for a while.'

As he did with Sir Denzil. It clearly doesn't pay to make an enemy of such a powerful duke.

They reached the entrance of Halsdon Manor and paused to gaze at the house, at the head of a straight drive.

'I confess to some relief he won't be returning himself.'

'You probably need not worry even if he did, Jane. Anthony never bore any resentment towards the rest of us, only Leo. But you'd still be wise to be cautious, should you ever meet. He has a great deal of charm, but he *is* clever and manipulative.'

They continued back to Foxbourne, their path taking them past the paddock where Alex and Zach were working with Nelson. Zach strolled over to join them when they paused by the fence to watch.

'Did you have a pleasant walk, my dove?' He stroked his wife's cheek with his forefinger, his dark eyes on her face.

A touch of envy stirred inside Jane. She was content with Alex, but would he ever look at her in that way, with his heart in his eyes? She loved him so much, but would he ever lower his guard enough to love her in return?

'Very pleasant, my darling. I love to walk with Florence, but it was nice to have the chance to talk in peace, was it not, Jane?'

'It was.' Jane's gaze strayed to where Alex—holding out an apple—approached the stallion, who was watching him, head high, the huge muscles in his haunches bunched. 'Is Alex safe in there, Zach?'

'Nelson no longer attacks, now he is not in a confined space. He *wants* to trust us, but he suspects a trick.'

Nelson wheeled around and trotted away from Alex who, rather than continuing to coax the stallion, turned his own back and walked to the opposite end of the paddock. Nelson stood stock-still, ears pricked, before lowering his neck and shaking his head. He took a tentative step towards Alex, followed by another. When he drew near, Alex walked away again, following the fence around. Nelson shadowed him.

'Ah…' Zach breathed. 'He won't be coaxed, but he'll follow of his own accord. He wants to trust Alex, but on his own terms.'

Nelson continued to follow Alex, slowly nearing him until his nose was mere inches from his shoulder. Alex halted and before very long Nelson was crunching an apple contentedly, juice dripping from his lips, as Alex stroked him, murmuring praise.

Having Aunt Cecily, Zach and Florence to stay proved the perfect distraction to stop Alex fretting over his overreaction when Jane brought those roses into his business room. He'd avoided roses over the years, most likely because they prompted memories of Mother, but he'd learned to control that response. Roses, after all, were almost impossible to avoid completely—all manner of social occasions included flowers, and roses were widely used—but his vow to be reasonable and to control his dark moods had shattered the second that smell summoned such a vivid flash of memory. Nausea roiled his stomach whenever that memory edged into his thoughts over the next few days, but although he consciously thrust it aside, afraid of examining it too closely, he could not dismiss it entirely.

This time, as with the child's scream, there had been

no image of Pikeford's attack to warn him, just the instant immersion into…what? The past? A fragment of his old nightmares? He still wasn't sure, but the fear of that vision being true was now equal to the fear he was losing his mind. All he knew was the scent of roses had triggered the same scene—the yellow gown and slippers, and that pair of gleaming boots, the quietly furious voices, the two figures sinking to the floor. But that image had shimmered, fading, and then a new image began to form—something horrifying; something that stole his breath and made his heart thump in his chest and cold sweat gather on his brow. The cries…the grunts…a slender neck…large hands around it…

And he'd panicked, dashing the roses aside, petrified of allowing that picture to fully form, some primal instinct screaming at him that it would be disastrous for not only his own peace of mind, but also the future happiness of his entire family.

Why was this happening to him? Why now? Since Pikeford's attack it seemed a leak had sprung in the barrier between his conscious mind and the deep well of memories of the day his mother died.

These visions were driving him close to despair so he welcomed the distraction of having guests to stay and he strived to behave as normally as possible. The intensity of working with Zach on Nelson helped push his worries to the back of his mind and he genuinely loved having his aunt to stay. Little Florence made him yearn for children of his own—he found himself watching Jane, both with and without Florence, and imagining her with their children. *That* image never failed to bring a smile to his lips and hope into his heart.

I have so much to be thankful for. I couldn't wish for a better wife and I have Foxbourne.

He silently recited the refrain every day, but it never seemed enough to protect against the past that lurked, waiting to leap out and destroy his life if ever he allowed his guard to drop.

He thought he'd done an excellent job of covering his fears and tension, but he might have known Aunt Cecily and, in particular, Zach would not easily be fooled. On the last night of their visit, as Alex and Zach lingered over their after-dinner port, Zach came straight to the point.

'You are troubled, Alex. Both Cecily and I sense it. Have the nightmares continued?'

He supposed it was inevitable. The entire family must know his nightmares had returned at the Abbey—it was impossible to keep such a secret when servants gossiped about their masters so freely. But…he eyed Zach. Could he tell him part of the truth? It would be a relief to let some of his worries out. The other man's calm, non-judgemental attitude positively invited confidences.

'It's not only nightmares.' He strode to the window, gazing out on the night. 'They started again at the Abbey, as you know, but the attack on Jane somehow became muddled into them and they became…worse.'

He walked back to his chair and sat. Myrtle scuttled over to him and laid her head on his knee, staring up at him with worried eyes. Alex fondled her ear. 'I do sleep better now I am with Jane, but…'

He hesitated. How much could he reveal? And would Zach think he was losing his mind? He took a chance.

'It is almost as though, now my nightmares are more bearable at night, they are hovering at the edge of my mind during the day. And something…a sound, a sight, a smell…will suddenly trigger…' He paused, frowning. 'I'm not sure they're even memories; they could just be fragments of nightmares. I don't know what is real and what is imagined any more. And, at times, I fear I am going mad.'

But the greater fear now lurked out there. The fear he had actually witnessed his own mother's murder. And that was a fear he could reveal to no one. Not until he was certain, for how on earth could he voice that other suspicion that prowled around the shadowed edges of his memory? The suspicion fed by those images of his father that followed the visions. He could swear Zach to secrecy, but he and Aunt Cecily were so very close it would be unfair, especially when it could simply be the befuddled recall of a terrified child.

He swallowed past the knot in his throat. Dragged in a breath.

'They conjure up such *feelings*. Feelings that have the power…have the power…' He swallowed again. 'I am afraid of what I will learn if I allow those memories to surface fully, Zach.'

His father's face materialised once again in his mind's eye.

And not just for me. For the entire family.

'If the memories are close and if your mind is ready to remember the past, then perhaps you might be wise to allow them to form fully so you can examine them from a man's perspective,' Zach said. 'At least then you would know exactly what memories still haunt you after all these years. Otherwise, how can you ever move on from the past? Is it not worth facing up to your fears for the sake of your marriage? For Jane?'

'It's not as easy as that. It's all right for you. You've never had—'

'You are wrong.' Zach's dark gaze penetrated Alex. 'I have bad memories that threatened my sanity at times. But I allowed them into the light and they lost some of their power over me. And, with the help and love of your aunt, I confronted my past. Memories cannot destroy us unless we allow them to. They can cause pain and tears and regrets, but once we acknowledge them they are always less powerful than if they are suppressed. If we do not confront our fears, we give them the power to haunt our present and our future. Is that what you want? This dark cloud hanging over you, casting gloom over your life and over your marriage?

'Maybe it is time for you to remember, Alex. You are a man, no longer a seven-year-old child afraid of monsters under the bed. Whatever we speak of tonight will stay between us but, if you will take my advice, you will confide in Jane. She is honest and straightforward. And she loves you.'

'*Loves* me? I...'

He paused, his thoughts whirling. He'd never even considered love, but it made sense of how he occasionally caught Jane looking at him and how, ever since he had known her, she had tried to help him, even when he was being foul to her. He'd always thought love wasn't possible for a man like him, but...he recalled that whisper of hope on their wedding day and the feeling that had grown— the feeling he couldn't imagine his life without her in it. Could it be...?

But even if what he felt for her was love, how could he confide in her? *He* was the man of the house. It was for him to be strong—how could he humble himself by confessing to his wife that the terrors of a small boy still had the power to bring him to his knees? How could she love and respect such a weakling?

Besides, as soon as he admitted he might have witnessed his mother's murder, the questions would start. Who did he see? Who killed her? He couldn't face those questions. He didn't know the answer…he didn't *want* to know the answer. The reason behind those hazy images of his father's face was what scared him the most, threatening his entire family, and the same reason he couldn't burden Zach with the full extent of his fears also applied to Jane.

No. He must deal with this himself.

'Maybe she does,' he said, 'in which case I am a fortunate man. And you are right… If I stop trying to suppress what happened, maybe the truth will not be as dreadful as I fear.' He said the words, but he did not believe them. 'Your advice, as ever, is sound. Thank you.'

Dark, knowing eyes surveyed Alex and his stomach squirmed at the directness of that gaze. Zach always seemed to see what others kept concealed in their hearts and Alex knew he had not fooled him. But he also knew Zach would interfere no further. He had said his piece and he would leave it to Alex to decide whether or not to take his advice.

They finished their drinks in silence.

Chapter Thirteen

A few weeks later Alex again awoke bathed in sweat, his head brim-full of incomplete images and his heart hammering with utter terror.

'Alex?' Jane embraced him, drawing his head to her breast. 'You're safe. It's all right. I'm here. It wasn't real.'

But it *was* real—Mother *had* been murdered. He just didn't know if he'd witnessed it or if his imagination had embellished the truth over the years.

He thrust the memories down and slammed a lid on them.

'Shhh...'

Cool fingers caressed his forehead. His cheek. Combed through his hair. Almost against his will, his eyelids grew heavy and they drifted shut and his unquiet mind stilled as he sank towards blessed oblivion.

It was his first thought when he awoke. At some point in the night they had swapped over, and he lay on his back, Jane slumbering peacefully in his arms, her glorious bosoms pressed to his naked chest and one slim leg flung across his. He was already painfully hard. What better way to start the day and banish the nightmare? He tilted her face to his, waited until her lids flickered and she began to rouse, then kissed her. Gently. One thing he had learned about his wife was that she did not awaken all bright and breezy. She took time to surface. But he knew the perfect way to help her, and he stroked the length of her back, tracing each vertebra, watching her face the whole time.

Her eyes opened, dazed, heavy-lidded. Then widened. She wriggled free and sat up.

'You had a nightmare.'

'Hush. Never mind about that.'

But Jane stared down at him, utterly awake, her expression a mixture of concern and determination. He put his hand on her thigh and caressed her, moving steadily upwards. Jane placed her hand on his and held it still.

'Janey…sweetheart…' Quite apart from now wishing to distract her—as well as himself—from the subject of nightmares, Alex simply wanted to bury himself inside his wife. 'We'll talk later.'

Not likely! But she needn't know that.

But to his dismay, Jane shook her head. 'We *could* talk later, but you forget…I *know* you, Alexander Beauchamp. You will discover a million and one ways to avoid me until you think I have forgotten. However…' she wriggled her way down in the bed until she was also lying flat and wrapped her fingers around his length '…indulge me now and *I* shall indulge you afterwards. To your heart's content.'

She squeezed, and Alex couldn't hold in his moan. God, how he wanted her but he would allow no one, not even Jane, to manipulate him. There was nothing anyone could do to help—the suspicion still haunted him that he had indeed witnessed his mother's murder and, if that was true, he could no longer deny he must have seen her killer.

And only one man's face kept appearing in connection with that day.

His father. The Duke of Cheriton.

Even just *thinking* that made his stomach heave, forcing hot, sour bile into his throat.

It couldn't be true!

That inexplicable aversion towards his father had driven him to rebel throughout his youth but, deep down, he had always *wanted* to love him. Unconditionally. But now... that suspicion gnawed at him endlessly...

He cupped Jane's face, smoothing his thumb over her soft skin. He would feed her a white lie, and then he would bury all thought of nightmares and do what he did best... satisfy them both.

'I don't remember any details—just that I woke up, and you were there.' He rolled to face her, and laid his hand on her waist. 'I went back to sleep and I didn't have another one.' His hand slid up to her breast and cupped it. He leaned across to press his lips to her naked shoulder. 'Thank you, my darling.' He nuzzled her neck, then stopped as Jane's hand landed on his shoulder, preventing him from lowering his torso to hers. He raised his head. Met her eyes. Widened his. 'What?'

Her own eyes narrowed. 'Don't you play the innocent with me, Alexander.' Her face softened. 'Please. I only want to help. Please tell me about it.'

But there was nothing he *could* tell her. He knew how the nightmare began but the rest was still murky, and the thought of allowing those fragments of horror to fully form—as Zach had suggested—was enough to break him out into a sweat again. He simply wasn't ready. Wasn't brave enough.

'What *do* you remember? There must be something.'

He tried not to resent her pushing him, telling himself her intentions were good. Jane was his wife, and she naturally wanted to share his troubles but *he* was entitled to make the decision not to share them.

'I only remember the very start. It is always the same. I hide from our tutor, Mr Brockley, and then I am outside playing. Then I walk towards the summer house, and then I wake up.'

But he couldn't tell her that, in his dreams, his mother walked by his side. Not when everyone believed what really happened was her dead body had been waiting for him in the summer house.

He was afraid to know if that was the truth, let alone where, and how, his father fitted in.

His throat thickened but he forced a nonchalant tone.

'See? It's nothing. I know what happened, because I've been told. But I cannot remember, and I have no wish to, either. The nightmare is the dread of what's inside the summer house. I wake up before I get there, and it's over.'

She held his gaze before releasing his shoulder and moving her hand to his chest. He released his breath in relief as her eyes darkened and her lips parted, and he leaned in to kiss her, his prick springing back into life.

Later that day, Alex found Jane outside, discussing the kitchen garden with Scully.

'Would you care to ride with me, my dear? Nelson is ready to hack out and the men are all busy.' The stallion had come on marvellously since Alex found the key to unlocking his distrust. 'Pearl will set him the perfect example, she's so well behaved.'

Jane beamed. 'I should love to! Give me ten minutes to change my gown.'

They were soon on their way, Jane dressed in a deep red riding habit, her hat trimmed with netting. They rode through the estate and then out on to the local lanes, nattering away, but, thankfully, both avoiding the subject of nightmares. Nelson soon settled, after a few excited jinks at all the new sights and sounds. The weather was cold and dull but dry, and there was little wind—perfect weather to try out a green youngster, with no shadows across the ground to goggle at, and no sudden gusts to upset him.

They stayed out for half an hour and were on their way back, close to home, when they saw a solitary horseman—a stranger, but clearly a gentleman—riding towards them on a rangy black.

'I wonder if that is our new neighbour?' Jane said.

'It's about time, if it is.' Halsdon Manor had been ready since late October, but still no one knew the identity of the tenant and the house remained empty.

'I hope he is a married gentleman with a family. It will be pleasant to have new neighbours.'

They fell silent as the stranger neared. Alex frowned, studying him intently. There was something…

'Hell and damnation!'

'What is it?'

Alex couldn't tear his attention from the other rider, now near enough for there to be no mistake.

'Leave the talking to me,' Alex muttered to Jane. He raised his voice. 'Lascelles. I was unaware you were back in the country.'

Anthony Lascelles inclined his head. 'Alexander. I heard you now live at Foxbourne.' His teeth gleamed in his tanned face as he smiled. 'How do you do?' His dark gaze slid sideways to Jane. 'I also heard about your recent nuptials. My felicitations to you both.' He bowed again, and raised his hat to reveal close-cropped silver-grey hair—a contrast to the jet-black it had been a mere five years before. 'I am charmed to meet you, Lady Alexander.'

'It is Lady Jane,' Alex bit out, his mind whirling at the awkwardness of this meeting after what Lascelles had done. 'She's Stowford's daughter.'

'Ah. The girl next door. How sweet. And how are the family? I regret my failure to stay in touch while I was overseas but, in view of the misunderstanding before I… er…left so precipitously—'

'*Misunderstanding?*' At Alex's exclamation Nelson sidestepped into Pearl, causing her to bare her teeth at him. Alex smoothed the stallion's neck to settle him. 'There was no misunderstanding, Lascelles. You forget. I was there. And you didn't leave; we *put* you on that ship.'

'You did. And I am most grateful to you.'

'Grateful? Hah! You expect us to believe that?'

Lascelles arched one brow. 'It is the truth, however.'

'Alex…' Jane laid her hand on his arm. 'The horses are growing restless. Maybe now is not the time for this discussion?'

She was right. Both horses were young and green and if Alex was tense it would harm their progress.

'Your lady is correct,' said Lascelles.

Alex longed to snarl at him that it was none of his business but he held his temper.

'Might I…?' Lascelles hesitated, looking uncertain—an uncharacteristic expression for the man Alex remembered. Five years ago, Lascelles had been smooth and assured with, it seemed, the thickest of skins. He was the only man Alex had ever met who openly mocked and challenged his father. Not many dared.

'Well? What is it? I want to keep our horses moving.'

Between his thighs Nelson was quivering with nerves… not helped by Lascelles' horse, who snaked his head in Nelson's direction several times. Although his teeth clashed harmlessly in mid-air, Nelson was on edge.

Lascelles cleared his throat. 'I should appreciate the opportunity to clear the air with you, Alexander, as we are to be neighbours. Might I perhaps accompany you back to the Manor and explain. I am aware I owe you, and your parents, an apology.' He smiled ruefully at Jane. 'A man can change, can he not? Do I not deserve the opportunity to make amends?'

Alex knew exactly how Jane would respond to that—she always wanted to see the best in people.

'Alex?' Her brown eyes pleaded with him.

It went against his better judgement but it wouldn't hurt to hear the man out—they were to be neighbours after all, so they must learn to rub along together somehow. 'Very well. Come to the house. We can talk over a drink.'

Lascelles smiled, and reined his black aside to allow Alex and Jane to ride ahead of him.

'Thank you,' Jane whispered. 'Surely everyone deserves a chance to prove they've changed.'

Superficially, Anthony Lascelles could not have been more charming. Jane had ordered refreshments—a tea tray and Madeira—and they settled down to talk. He declined the Madeira in favour of a cup of tea. Jane poured the tea and passed him a cup.

'Thank you.'

'You are welcome, sir.'

'Oh, you must call me Anthony.'

He surveyed Jane and she suppressed an involuntary shiver. His eye were the nearest to black she had ever seen. They gave the impression of staring into an abyss.

So empty. I wonder what is really going on inside his head.

She scolded herself for that fanciful thought, feeling guilty that she was judging him after such short acquaintance, but she couldn't shake off the odd feeling that assailed her. He looked every inch the gentleman but there was something about him—now he was in her home—

that set the hairs on the back of her neck to rise. Surely, though, it was only Aunt Cecily's warning that was behind her instinctive distrust of the man? She vowed to quash her doubts and to give Anthony Lascelles the chance he had asked for—the opportunity to prove he was a changed man.

Lascelles sipped his tea before addressing Alex directly, giving Jane the opportunity to study him as they talked. Tall, without an ounce of superfluous flesh on him, he was a good-looking man for his age, which she judged to be near to fifty. He was unmistakeably a Beauchamp, with the same cast of features shared by all the Beauchamp men. Lascelles' face and hands were tanned and he looked healthy and vigorous, his silver-grey hair lending him a distinguished air. But there was also a suggestion of arrogance. Well concealed beneath the charm, but there none the less. That was hardly sufficient to condemn him though. Many gentlemen in their world emanated that same air of superiority although, in Lascelles' case, that conceit seemed at odds with his illegitimacy.

Still. His father *was* a duke. Maybe he should be forgiven a little arrogance.

Jane concentrated on the men's conversation.

'I mentioned an apology, and an explanation as to my past behaviour, Alexander. Allow me to offer the apology first—I am sorry for what happened. Events spiralled out of my control. Has that never happened to you?'

His tone implied he knew the answer to that question all too well, for five years ago Alex had been on the brink of losing everything, from what Jane's stepmother had gleefully announced on her return from the London Season. That had been the year before Jane's debut.

'On occasion.' Alex remained brusque.

'The trouble is…your father and I always enjoyed a

similar taste in ladies. I was smitten by Rosalind but the best man won.'

Alex merely grunted as he stared into his glass of Madeira, reverting to the prickly, monosyllabic man he became whenever he was with someone he did not trust. The same man, Jane realised, he became in his own father's presence. She was still hoping Christmas at the Abbey might provide an opportunity to begin healing that rift between the two of them.

'It is humiliating to confess—particularly within hearing of your charming bride—but I became somewhat obsessed by Rosalind and, when it seemed I was to lose her to your father, it became too much to bear. Looking back, I see that I temporarily lost my reason. I became determined to win her at any cost and behaved in ways I now bitterly regret.'

He paused as though hoping for some response from Alex. When none was forthcoming, he continued, 'I hope to offer my apologies to your father and stepmother at the earliest opportunity but, in the meantime, I should deem it a favour if you refrain from telling them of my return. I should much prefer to meet them on neutral territory, such as in London, rather than suddenly appear at Cheriton Abbey.'

Alex raised his head at that. 'You could write to them.'

One corner of Lascelles' mouth lifted in a half-smile. 'I have thought of that, but this is something I need to do in person.'

An awkward silence fell, which Jane felt obliged to fill. 'Where did you go, when you went overseas, Anthony?'

Alex barked a harsh laugh. 'He didn't leave of his own free will, Jane. He had no choice. We put him on a ship bound for China, and Father paid the captain very well to ensure his new crew member had no opportunity to abscond until they reached their destination.'

'Ah…' Lascelles drained his teacup and placed it with its saucer on a nearby side table. He smoothed one hand along his breeches-clad thigh. 'Dear Captain Cheng. We struck up quite a rapport, don't you know, and he—in return for a substantial further payment I was fortunate enough to be in a position to make—allowed me to disembark in Cape Town.'

Alex's eyes narrowed. 'I don't believe you. Where did you get that sort of money?'

Lascelles smiled. 'Alex… Alex…you cannot blame me for making my plight less desperate, surely? Granted, I was imprisoned upon that ship until it sailed, but the Captain understood very well I might have need of replacement clothing and so forth and, as luck would have it, I had planned to leave London that very day. My trunk—containing cash and banker's drafts to cover my expenses—was ready packed. One of the crew went to my house to collect my trunk, for which kindness I rewarded him substantially.'

Alex's mouth twitched and reluctant admiration lit his tawny eyes. He shook his head, and his mouth widened in a reluctant smile. 'Uncle Vernon said you always come up smelling of roses.'

Lascelles smiled back. 'It is a talent. A useful one.'

'Would you care for another cup of tea, Anthony?'

Jane rose to pour a fresh cup for herself.

'I think not, dear lady. I have said what I came to say and I can only hope we might start afresh, Alexander. Just because your father and I have never been on comfortable terms is no reason for us not to get along, I should hope.'

'You've always resented Father.'

'It is true I have always begrudged the circumstances of my birth as, I think, would most men in my position. My father and mother were together for many years and, if he had married her, I would be the duke and my life would be very different. I have never denied my resentment, but these past five years I have realised that to cling on to that bitterness hurts me more than anyone.' His gaze flicked down, and then back to Alex. 'I also blamed your father for your mother's untimely death.'

The colour drained from Alex's face but he made no sound.

'Your father and I might never have seen eye to eye, but Margaret and I were friends long before she wed your father. I didn't know if you were aware of that.'

'No. I know nothing about you, other than what happened five years ago. I don't recall you visiting the Abbey.'

'I visited once or twice in the early days of their marriage but it was clear I was unwelcome and, because your father and I often argued, Margaret asked me to stay away. Shortly afterwards, I went to the Americas. Now,' Lascelles stood, 'I have outstayed my welcome, so I will bid you good day.' He bowed to Jane. 'It was a pleasure to make your acquaintance, Lady Jane. I hope we shall meet again soon.'

There was a slight questioning lilt to his final words and, before she realised what she was doing, Jane said, 'You must join us for dinner some time.'

Lascelles smiled. 'But what a generous invitation. When did you have in mind?'

Jane glanced at Alex, who shrugged. 'Um…well…what about next week?' she said. 'Tuesday?'

Lascelles' smile faded. 'Unfortunately I have a prior engagement.'

Jane's relief was short-lived as he added, 'I am, however, free on Thursday.' His teeth gleamed in a smile.

Jane forced herself to return it. 'We shall look forward to it.'

'I'll walk you down to the stables,' Alex said.

When he returned, Jane expected him to be annoyed she had invited Lascelles to dine, but he merely laughed when she apologised.

'You were right,' he said. 'We're neighbours and I don't want to be on bad terms with him, so it will do no harm. Besides, it will be interesting to talk to someone who knew my mother—none of the family ever talk about her and *my* memories are…'

He trailed into silence, his expression darkening. Jane put her arms around him.

'I'm sure it will help to replace your memories with happier images of your mother, even if they are secondhand.'

She pressed against him, a thrill running through her at the feeling of his lean hard body against hers. His arms wrapped around her waist and he pulled her closer still to graze his lips over hers. Lascelles was soon forgotten as passion overtook them.

Chapter Fourteen

They returned to the subject of their new neighbour over dinner.

'I have been thinking,' said Alex.

'About?'

'Lascelles. I might call upon him tomorrow. I should like to talk to him about my mother and I think he will talk more freely if it's only the two of us.'

Disquiet threaded through Jane.

'I am in two minds about him, Alex. I find him… Oh, I don't know…disconcerting, I suppose.' The word wasn't quite strong enough, but it would do until she knew him better. 'However, I couldn't help but sympathise when he spoke of his father. It would surely be enough to make any man bitter. But…do be careful.' The warning left her lips before she could help it.

Alex stared for a moment, then laughed. '*Careful?* What do you think he might do? Abduct me like he abducted Susie and tried to abduct Rosalind?'

Jane's cheeks burned. He was right. Alex was no child, he was a grown man, but…Lascelles…there was something…

'Your aunt is the least judgemental person I've ever

met, and she warned me to be cautious if we should ever meet. And your father—'

'My father has nothing to say about who I associate with.' Alex scowled as he spooned gooseberry pie into his mouth.

Jane bit her lip against the urge to probe Alex's touchy relationship with his father. He was already irritated with her.

'I am just...uneasy about Lascelles, Alex.'

And now she was irritated with herself. What had happened to her resolve to speak her mind in this marriage?

'And I do not like him asking us to keep his return from your family. Are we meant to keep it secret when we go to the Abbey for Christmas? That will be difficult...and, when your father finds out—'

'Don't start worrying about something that may never happen.'

Jane stared at Alex's sharp tone. What had she said? 'Alex... I—'

'I'm sorry. That was uncalled for.' Alex laid down his knife and fork and reached for Jane's hand. 'You goose. Lascelles is just a man. He's no threat to me, but he *does* give me the chance to learn more about my mother.' He folded his fingers around hers and gently squeezed. 'Dear Honeybee. I can see you're still fretting but please believe me—I know what Lascelles is capable of, and I promise I shall stay on my guard.

'I want you to be happy, Janey—not constantly worrying over me. If you keep this up you'll have me wondering how on earth I've managed all these years without you to watch my back.' His grin took the sting out of the rebuke, but she recognised it as such nevertheless.

She squeezed in return. 'I am happy, Alex. More than you know.'

And it was true. Mostly. But the shadows were there, nipping at their heels. Shadows that hid Alex's past. A past he was no nearer to sharing with her, as far as she could see, and a past that seemed to be steadily widening the rift between them. Against that, the problem of Lascelles seemed trivial.

Alex stood, and tugged her to her feet. 'And I am happy, too, sweetheart. Now, come. I have a wish to listen to music.'

That night, Alex lay on his back staring up through the darkness, mulling over the day's events. Who would have thought Lascelles would return? Father would be furious. That fact alone made his mind up—he would tell none of the family, because it would bring Father straight to Foxbourne to confront Lascelles.

And Alex did not want him here. He had enough to contend with, with these confounded dreams, or memories, or whatever they were. They continued to plague him. More and more frequently. More and more vividly, bringing him nearer and nearer the brink of a place he didn't want to be. Instinct told him Father's presence would make them worse, not better, and then how would he find the strength to hold back the vision that threatened destruction for his family?

He was afraid his suspicions would show in his face.

He simply couldn't face his father at the moment. He recalled Jane's worry about hiding Lascelles' return but that was the least of Alex's concerns. He'd never intended to go to the Abbey for Christmas but now he had even more reason to shun the place and his family. But he must break the news to Jane soon. He really couldn't keep shirking that difficult conversation.

Lascelles, though…he might prove a Godsend. What

if talking to him about Mother could help Alex sort fact from fiction? If he learned more about her life might that help overshadow the day of her death? He had no wish to revisit that day, merely to forget it all together. Was that really too much to ask? He had overcome his nightmares before. Why was he finding it so hard to do so again?

He had so much to look forward to and he'd do anything to stop these terrible suspicions—and the shocking speculation they spawned—ruining the happy future within his grasp.

With this thought, he turned to snuggle close to Jane. Finally, he slept.

The following day he rode Frost to Halsdon Manor, studying the brick-built house as he trotted up the drive, its three-bay central section crowned by a pediment and flanked by symmetrical wings. A flight of stone steps led to the central front door which, as he neared, opened. Lascelles himself emerged.

'Alexander! What a pleasant surprise. Is this a fleeting visit, or will you come inside?'

Alex dismounted. 'I'll come in if I may?'

'But of course, dear boy. Burnley?' A footman appeared behind him. 'Take Lord Alexander's horse to the stables and tell Watkins to do what's necessary.'

Inside the house, Lascelles preceded Alex into the entrance hall where a maid took his hat and gloves.

'Tea?' asked Lascelles. 'Or something stronger? I would value your opinion on a claret I recently discovered, if you care to try it?'

'Claret sounds ideal.'

'Carter! Bring a bottle and two glasses to the salon.'

The maid curtsied. 'Yes, sir.'

Alex followed Lascelles into a salon, lavishly decorated in red and gold.

'The décor is sadly outmoded, I am afraid. I have plans to refurbish the place, however.' Lascelles gestured to a chair. 'Please, do take a seat. I am delighted you have called… I find it so much easier when there are no females around to restrict the conversation, don't you?'

'Indeed.' Alex had come here to establish a rapport with Lascelles so it suited him to agree. He knew many men felt the same, hence the popularity of the gentlemen's clubs in Town.

They discussed general topics—politics, their estates, agriculture—until the claret had been poured and the door closed behind the maidservant. As soon as they were alone, Lascelles raised his glass.

'To neighbourliness, and to new beginnings.'

They touched glasses and then sampled the claret.

'This is excellent,' Alex said, diverted by the quality of the wine. 'You must tell me where you got it.'

'A backstreet vintner in Bordeaux. I returned to England with a couple of cases, and he has agreed to supply more. I shall send a case over to Foxbourne.'

'No! That is far too generous. I cannot possibly accept.'

Lascelles smiled, and leaned back in his chair. 'Oh, but I insist. We *are* family, after all, as well as neighbours. It is the least I can do, for one of dear Margaret's sons, and I dare to hope we, too, might become friends in time. Gifts between friends come with no hidden agenda, is that not the case?' He leaned forward, grasping Alex's knee. 'Allow me to do this, m'boy—it would give me pleasure and I hope before long you will see I have truly changed.' His mouth pursed, and a tiny frown stitched the skin between his brows. 'I do know I have to prove myself to you, Alexander, before I earn your trust. I hope you will give me that chance. Your father might never be able to forgive me, but…' He paused. Shook his head. 'No. I should not ask… I cannot expect you to act contrary to what your father would want. It is unfair of me to even suggest it.'

'My father does not rule *my* life, Anthony.'

Lascelles cocked his head to one side. 'Do I detect a touch of antagonism, m'boy? I do recall there was a— shall we say, a certain tension between you and your father when we met before in London. Have matters between you not improved?'

Alex shrugged. 'My father rarely impacts upon my life. I am my own man.'

'Of course you are, dear boy. It is just…the Duke…he can be quite *forceful*. I have never yet seen any man—or woman—get the better of him.'

'He does not rule my life,' Alex repeated. 'I make my own friends and my own decisions.'

'I am pleased to hear it.' Lascelles sipped his claret, and then raised his glass once more. 'To new friends.'

'New friends.' Alex raised his own glass.

I'll not forget what you did to Rosalind, though.

'Now then.' Lascelles put down his glass and steepled his fingers, propping his chin on them, reminding Alex of Father, who he'd seen in a similar stance more times than he cared to remember.

'I confess to some curiosity, Alexander. Is this merely a courtesy call?' Lascelles cocked his head. 'Or do you have something in particular you would like to discuss?'

He'd wanted to lead into the subject of his mother gradually…almost as an afterthought. This was too obvious. Caution whispered through him: *Don't let him know how much it means to you.* There would be time to talk of Mother, even if he must leave it for another day.

'It is merely a courtesy call, Anthony. And a way to satisfy my curiosity—I've lived at Foxbourne five years now, and this is my first visit to Halsdon.'

'Then you must allow me to show you around.' Anthony rose to his feet. 'At least, around the ground floor. I cannot believe you have any desire to view the bedchambers or servants' quarters.'

'Not likely!'

The first room they entered was a billiards room.

'Do you have a billiards room at Foxbourne?'

'No.' Alex swept the room with envious eyes. 'There's no space. But even if there were, I'd have no one to play with.' The thought of knocking balls around a table on his own held no appeal.

Lascelles raised a brow. 'Jane might learn the game. Your mama was quite an accomplished player, you know.'

'Was she?' This is what he had come for. Knowledge of his mother, of the person she had been. 'You played with her?'

'Oh, yes. Several times, at various house parties at which we were both guests. She was as good as any man, and often won games.' He laughed softly, his eyes far away. 'She could be quite ruthless once she gained an advantage, both in billiards and at the card table. And…' He paused, his dark eyes on Alex. 'And she was a popular young lady.'

Alex frowned. Lascelles had been going to say something different, he was sure. He was aware his mother had had a reputation for taking lovers…of course Lascelles would not speak of that. And Alex didn't want to hear it, either.

'When did you meet?'

'Let me see…it was her debut year. We were both eighteen—you must know she was three years older than your father?'

Alex nodded.

'We were friends from the outset. But, of course, a bastard like me wasn't deemed suitable company for a gently born and bred young lady. But, despite her parents' objections, we remained friends. She confided in me.'

'About…?'

Lascelles smiled. 'Alex… Alex…dear boy. A confidence is a confidence, even if the confessor is no longer with us. But, a marriage made in haste, my boy… I am sure you can fill in the gaps.' His features hardened. 'Your grandfather was sick…fretting over the succession of the dukedom. But if my father had married my mother and made me his heir…' He clamped his mouth shut. 'My apologies. That is naught but ancient history.' His expression softened. 'You remind me of her. You have her colouring. Those eyes…such a tragic waste.' He sighed, and clasped Alex's shoulder. 'You must feel free to come over any time you choose, my boy. *Any* time. We can play billiards, or cards. Or…just talk, if you wish. A man—especially one who has just married—needs male company, I find. Dear Margaret's son will always find a welcome here.'

'Thank you. I might take you up on that.'

'Do. In fact…do you recall that, when your good lady invited me to dine on Tuesday next, I had to decline?'

Alex nodded.

'I am hosting a small gathering—just a few friends to enjoy a day or two hunting and shooting. You must come by one evening for a few games. Billiards and cards… Oh! Have no fear, low-stakes games only. I cannot allow my guests to beggar themselves under my roof! There are more than enough gaming hells in Town should they wish to follow *that* road to penury. Gentlemen only, I'm afraid, so I am unable to extend my invitation to include Lady Jane…but I am sure she will understand if you wish to join us one evening. My guests arrive tomorrow, so shall we say Saturday? Or…' his head dipped to one side again, a ghost of a smile playing across his lips '…might dear Jane disapprove? I should *hate* to be the cause of disharmony between newlyweds.'

'Jane will not object. She doesn't keep me on a leash, you know.'

Lascelles inclined his head, that knowing smile still lurking, setting Alex's hackles to rise. 'Of *course* she does not, dear boy. Acquit me, I beg you…it was never my intention to imply such a thing.'

Chapter Fifteen

'*Tonight?*'

It was Saturday, and Jane and Alex had just returned from a hack on Pearl and Nelson. They had even seen a shooting party on Halsdon land, and Alex had told her Lascelles was entertaining a party of gentlemen at the Manor, but even then he hadn't thought to mention he'd been invited to join them for dinner that evening.

'Yes. You don't mind, do you?'

'But...' Jane frowned. 'When was this arranged? I wasn't aware you had seen Anthony since you went over there on Thursday.'

'I haven't.'

'But you didn't think to tell me he had invited you to dine tonight?'

'I didn't think I needed permission to accept an invitation on my own behalf. I'm sorry you're not included, but it's a male-only gathering.' He grinned at her. 'Not your idea of an enjoyable evening at all, I'll wager.'

He didn't even seem to realise how unreasonable he was being. She tightly folded her arms, as if to keep her anger inside.

'You should have told me. I could have warned Mrs

Godfrey. She'll have prepared a meal for two…if I'd known I would be dining alone, I'd have been happy with only one course.'

Alex scowled. 'Why should the cook care? It's just a meal.'

'And how do you think it makes *me* look, that I didn't even know my husband intended to dine out tonight?'

Alex's jaw set and Jane turned away, hurt he hadn't told her—like he hadn't told her anything about his visit to Lascelles, despite her asking. It was as though he were excluding her, reminding her of the old Alex…going his own way without being beholden to anyone. It made her feel…incidental. Shut out. First his nightmares. Now this.

'Come on, Janey.' He pulled her round into a hug, and kissed her cheek. 'Don't be cross. I'm still learning this husband thing… I dare say I'm too used to coming and going as I please. I'll do better. I promise.'

He held her at arms' length and his rueful smile melted her anger.

'I'm not so much cross as hurt you didn't tell me.'

'I know. I understand. I'll do better. And, to prove it, I should tell you Anthony has invited me over to play billiards any time I like.' He arched one brow. 'Do you mind?'

'No. Of course not.' How could she say anything different now? She consoled herself with the thought he was unlikely to go regularly. 'Although—'

She bit her lip, locking her words inside. He'd already objected when she'd warned him to be careful. Sometimes it was hard not to recall his troubled boyhood and the scrapes he had dived into headlong…hard to relinquish the role of the sensible one who tried to prevent the worst of his excesses. But that was many years ago—their lives had led in different directions: his to school, university and the life of a man about Town whereas she had remained at home, only seeing him when she went to Town for the Season since he stopped visiting the Abbey.

'Although?' His lips continued to smile, but there was glint of annoyance in his tiger-gold eyes.

'Although I will miss you.'

'That's my girl!' He swung her around and, as he set her down again, he kissed her. 'At least you'll have Mist for company.'

Mist had joyfully adapted to her new life as Jane's pet, clearly relishing the life of luxury, while Dora and the rest of the litter had returned to life in the stables. But a kitten was no substitute for her husband. Jane strove to conceal her dismay.

'Do you know who his guests are?' Olivia had told her of the time certain gentlemen had attempted to ruin Alex in order to wreak revenge on his father. What if any of those shady types were among Lascelles' friends? Or what if— and her stomach tumbled at the thought—Lascelles himself harboured thoughts of revenge through Alex?

'Yes and they're all eminently respectable. Anyway. I've enough time to help Lilley work with that team of chestnuts before I need to change my clothes, so I'll see you later, my adorable wife.'

He kissed her nose but his attention was already on the four ready-harnessed horses being led from the stalls.

The walk back to the house was surprisingly lonely and Jane spent the time scolding herself. On their wedding day she had vowed never to be a needy wife, nor to complain if Alex continued his own pursuits, but in the early weeks of their marriage she had grown accustomed to them spending time together. Maybe she had become complacent, believing that was how their life here at Foxbourne would always be, but Alex had led a full life before their marriage and she shouldn't expect him to change his entire life to accommodate her. He had work to do. Although Jane was useful at certain times, it would be odd indeed if she expected to be included in every aspect of Alex's work.

Besides, not only would Alex soon resent being tied too closely to anyone, even his wife, she also had responsibilities. She had the house to run; the staff to manage; she had those Christmas gifts to finish making, and she had also taken over the regular updating of the ledgers.

But those barriers between her and Alex—the feeling of being shut out of parts of his life—troubled her. That was the Alex of old, keeping everyone at bay. Hiding his innermost feelings. The initial happy contentment of their marriage seemed to be slipping further and further out of reach. She suppressed a sigh as she let herself in through the front door. How she wished her husband was easier to understand.

She went straight to Alex's business room. She would work on the ledgers for a while before she changed her riding habit for a gown and her solitary dinner.

That is where Alex found her half an hour later. He breezed through the door, bringing with him the smell of fresh air and horses.

'There you are!' He rounded the desk, took the pen from her and tugged her to her feet. 'No one knew where you were…they all thought you were still outside with me.'

He tilted her chin up as he wrapped one arm around her waist and pulled her close.

'I was worried. I went upstairs and saw you hadn't been up there to change.' His tawny gaze darkened as it fastened on her mouth, and her heart thumped in response. 'I thought you might still be cross with me for not telling you sooner about tonight.'

'Of course I am not.' Love for him filled her heart even

as she warned herself this would not be the only time he would disappoint her. He was a complex man. She already knew that when she married him. If she'd wanted a paragon...an easy life...then Lord Alexander Beauchamp would have been the very last name on her list.

She smiled tenderly. 'I don't deny it was a surprise but I'm not annoyed with you.' The need to speak the words battered at her. 'I love you, Alex. I want you to be happy.'

He blinked, and a slow smile stretched his lips. 'Darling Honeybee.' He possessed her mouth in a slow, dreamy, lingering kiss.

Desire flamed inside, sizzling through her as his lips feathered to her ear and he nibbled her lobe, burning away her disappointment that he hadn't said those three words in return.

'I think it's time you got out of those clothes, Janey.'

He unbuttoned her jacket and pulled her shirt free, deftly scooping her breast from her corset. She gasped, her nipple tightening as Alex bent his head. Hot lips sucked the tight bud into his mouth. His tongue swirled and pure need sparked along her veins. He reached for her skirts, and hoisted them high before slipping one finger between her thighs. She moaned, her core throbbing, already wet for him. She reached between them, unbuttoned the fall of his breeches, freed his straining erection and stroked along his hot, hard length before gently circling the tip.

'Temptress.' The low growl vibrated in her ear.

His hands still full of her skirts, he cupped her bottom and hoisted her up, perching her on the very edge of the desk as he parted her knees and moved between her thighs. He nuzzled her neck and then bit her lobe as he entered her with one swift thrust. She clutched at his shoulders, her head back, her legs wrapped around him as he stilled, his hands supporting her back. She lifted her head to look at him, and found him watching her with a wondering look in those tiger eyes of his.

'Who knew?' he whispered. 'Who could possibly know the fiery wanton lurking inside quiet Janey?'

He started to move. 'Thank you, my Honeybee, for making my life so sweet.'

Later, Jane watched Alex leave for Halsdon Manor with a heavy heart. For all his lovemaking, and all his sweet words, she still couldn't quite shake the feeling that some kind of Rubicon had been crossed. Mayhap it was inevitable—they must settle into a humdrum daily existence. But it felt…*she* felt…as though shadows were starting to close in. She huffed a laugh at such a fanciful thought, and yet she couldn't convince herself it was all in her imagination. There was a growing barrier between them, as though Alex had withdrawn from her—mentally if not physically. And, for her, that diminished the pleasure of their lovemaking.

He shared his body but not his thoughts.

He accepted her comfort at night when he suffered nightmares, but rejected her attempts to help him by bringing those nightmares into the open.

He was a stubborn man. He would tell himself he was protecting her. He would tell himself he was the man of the house and mustn't show weakness. He would tell himself there was nothing she could do to help him come to terms with what had happened the day his mother was murdered.

Jane, however, remained convinced he was wrong. To talk about his memories was, she was certain, the key to stopping them haunting him and, more importantly, the way to stop him retreating behind those impenetrable barriers he had erected against the world, including her.

She must keep trying. She might be defeated for now; she was not defeated for good.

After her lonely dinner, Jane went to the drawing room. She played with Mist, who was turning into an adorable bundle of mischief. When she wasn't running up the curtains, sharp claws scrabbling, she was climbing on the furniture, leaving paw prints on the polished surfaces, much to Mrs Kent's chagrin. Then she worked on the Christmas gift she'd made for Alex—a beautiful ruby-red satin waistcoat which she was embroidering with cream and pale green silk thread.

She meant to wait up for Alex but it grew late and she could barely keep her eyes open. Eventually, she gave in and went to bed where, ironically, sleep eluded her for what seemed like hours. Finally she must have slept because she was roused by Alex stumbling against the bed.

'What time is it?' she asked groggily.

'Late. Gone four. Shhh—go back to sleep.'

A short while later she was vaguely conscious of him lying close behind her, one arm draped over to cup her breast, and then she slept again.

She was woken by Peg opening the curtains to allow light to flood the room. Alex was no longer spooned against her back and, when Jane rolled over, his side of the bed was cold and empty.

'Where is His Lordship?'

'In his own bedchamber; he felt sick in the night.' Peg's pursed lips made her disapproval clear. 'Drabble says he moved so's not to disturb you.' She lifted a tray from the dressing table. 'I brought your chocolate and rolls, milady.'

Jane sat up, tugging the pillow up behind her to lean against. 'Thank you, Peg. Is he awake yet?'

Peg placed the tray on Jane's legs and snorted. 'Not he! I don't doubt he'll still be abed at noon, complaining of his head a-banging. Well, he won't get no sympathy from me, that's for sure.'

'Now, Peg. Do not forget who pays your wages. If Lord Alex hears you talking like that, you'll be out on your ear.'

Peg laughed. 'I've known Lord Alex as long as you have, milady. He'd not dare.' Then she nodded. 'Not but what you're right. Me 'n' Drabble might have a grumble now and then, but you know we wouldn't see no harm come to him. And nor would we say such things in front of them others below stairs.'

'I'm relieved to hear it.'

As soon as Jane finished her breakfast, she tiptoed into Alex's bedchamber. He was lying on his side, curled into a ball, the covers up around his ears. Jane sat gently on the bed and smoothed his hair from his forehead. He looked so angelic she wanted to just hold him in her arms and protect him always.

She smiled as she imagined his horror if he knew what she was thinking. He would be utterly insulted. In his mind—and that of most men—*they* were the ones who did the protecting. She continued to stroke as her thoughts roamed. Perhaps a better word would be nurture. To nurture those they loved came naturally to a woman. Her thoughts drifted on to babies—how she longed to be a mother and to have babies to love and care for.

Alex stirred, mumbling, a frown creasing his forehead. He cranked open one eyelid, then closed it again with a groan.

'Head hurts…'

'Has Drabble brought you anything for it?'

'What…? Who…? Ugh…no. Nothing. Thirsty…'

Jane brushed her lips across his brow. 'There's water here. Let me help you drink, then I'll bring you something later to relieve your head.'

She slipped her arm under his shoulders, helped him up, held the glass to his lips, then laid him gently back. His eyes slitted open.

'You're too good to me, Janey.'

Jane huffed a laugh. 'Yes. I know I am.' She feathered a kiss to his brow. 'Sleep now. I'll bring up the remedy before I go to church.'

Outside the bedchamber door she paused, anxiety that Alex might be lured back into the excesses of his youth churning her stomach. Although surely it was too soon to begin fretting over Lascelles' influence, even if she couldn't trust him—Alex had too much to lose now, with Foxbourne and his beloved horses.

Logically, that made sense. But whenever had Alex and logic walked hand in hand?

She dressed, and then headed downstairs to mix up a remedy to soothe his head, vowing to talk to him about Lascelles as soon as he recovered.

After church, Jane mingled with the villagers.

'Good morning, My Lady.' Mrs Phillips stopped to chat, one of her daughters by her side. 'No Lord Alexander this morning?'

'I'm afraid not. He is unwell.'

'Nothing serious, I hope?'

'No. We think he ate something that disagreed with him.' As the white lie slipped from her lips, she caught sight of Anthony Lascelles, his dark gaze on her. She hadn't noticed him in the church but *he* clearly wasn't suffering the after-effects of last night as Alex was. 'If you will excuse me, Mrs Phillips, I need to speak to Mr Lascelles, but would you care to call at Foxbourne on Wednesday? I am eager to lend more practical help to your charity work for the poor.'

They had discussed the vicar's charity work before, but

had arranged nothing definite, with Jane still settling into her new role. Now, though, she realised if she was to cope with Alex leading his own life some of the time, then she must seek some fulfilment from other sources. It could only help if she cultivated interests of her own.

'Thank you, Lady Jane. I shall be there.'

Jane crossed to where Lascelles was talking to one of the local farmers.

'Good morning.' She encompassed both of them in her smile of greeting.

Lascelles bowed. 'Good morning to you, Lady Jane. Or…might we dispense with the formalities, as we are family?'

'Of course.' She could hardly object—he'd already asked her to call him Anthony.

The farmer mumbled a greeting. 'I'll see what I can do, sir,' he then said to Lascelles. 'You leave it with me. Good day to you both.'

He nodded before ambling away, watched by Lascelles. 'One of my tenants. I need a new estate manager, and he knows of a chap over Cucklow way in need of a new position.'

'I hope he proves suitable.'

Lascelles smiled. 'As do I. I have no wish to spend too much of my time here…its very closeness to London proves far too great an enticement to a lonely bachelor such as myself.' His words eased some of Jane's concern. 'Oh, not that local society is not welcoming, of course. I cast no aspersions. But it consists of families in the main, and I know from experience there is only so much we will have in common.'

'Maybe it is time to seek a wife?' The words came out before she could stop them. 'Oh! I apologise. I did not mean to be impertinent.'

Lascelles smiled. 'There is no necessity to apologise, my dear. You may be right. Perhaps it *is* time I took my chance and experienced domestic bliss. After all, if Alexander can take the plunge... What *were* the circumstances of your betrothal, if you do not mind me asking? I understand Alexander visited the Abbey in the summer but, having been friends for several years, it does seem to have happened without much...now, how can I put it? Without much forethought. A hurried affair, I gathered.'

Shock momentarily stole her breath. Her skin crawled at the thought of Alex discussing anything so intimate with anyone.

'Alex told you about our wedding?'

'No, no. Not in so many words but...reading between the lines, as it were...and me a student of human nature...' He fell silent, his gaze wandering over the people gathered outside the church before turning his attention back to Jane. 'How *is* dear Alexander this morning? I noted his absence. Is his head very sore? I did try to dissuade him from indulging quite so freely but...well, my dear. You know our Alex. He is not easily brought back to heel once he's been allowed off the leash, is he?'

'He has only the slightest of headaches.' Anger clawed Jane at the insinuation she kept Alex tied to her. 'He had urgent business, so he could not attend church.'

'I *see*.' A smile hovered on Lascelles' lips. 'I wonder... when you return home could you remind him Sir Henry will call tomorrow at noon to examine that bay mare he has for sale?' Jane knew the mare he referred to. It was one she had helped to school. 'I am sure it won't have slipped Alex's mind but...just in case, you understand.'

His falsely sympathetic tone and the glimmer of laughter in his eyes set Jane's teeth on edge.

'I shall remind him, sir.'

'Anthony,' he prompted gently.

Jane swallowed her irritation. 'Anthony.'

Their talk had reinforced her feeling there was something distrustful about Anthony Lascelles and she couldn't wait to escape him.

'I must be going. They're waiting for me.' She indicated the members of the Foxbourne staff who had also attended the church service and were now waiting in a huddle by the two vehicles that had conveyed them into Malton. 'Good day to you, Anthony.'

'I shall see you on Thursday, if our paths do not cross tomorrow, dear Jane.' He raised his hat, and his hair shone silver as it caught the sunlight. 'Farewell.' He strolled away, swinging his cane.

Jane watched him go, her feelings in turmoil. Was this instinctive distrust she felt for him unreasonable? It felt as though there was a subtle innuendo in almost everything he said…a hidden message beneath the actual meaning of his words. Or was her imagination playing tricks on her? One thing was for sure, she would be unable to avoid him. She must hope he would tire of country life very quickly, and return to London.

And, in the meantime—should she risk Alex's anger by again voicing her doubts about Lascelles? She walked over to the servants and they were soon on their way home, Jane's head full of ways to warn her stubborn husband against Lascelles without inadvertently driving him closer to the man.

Chapter Sixteen

'Don't worry, Janey. I shan't make a habit of it… I have no wish to repeat the way I feel today.' Alex's head still throbbed like the Devil, albeit less ferociously than earlier. 'All I want is for today to be over, knowing I will feel better in the morning. I fear I cannot hold my liquor as I used to.'

Alex had finally hauled himself from his bed and shaved and dressed. He'd found Jane in the drawing room stuffing strips of fabric into what looked like a purple velvet bag with legs.

'I am relieved to hear that. I do not like to see you in such pain.'

'What *is* that?'

She held it up. 'It's a ragdoll rabbit for baby George. I've made ragdolls for the girls and then thought of making this for George. It's soft so there are no hard edges to hurt him.'

Alex's stomach twisted. He *still* hadn't told Jane they weren't going to the Abbey for Christmas but he couldn't face that conversation now. He would tell her soon, he vowed. 'Very nice.'

He sat beside Jane, and plucked the toy rabbit from her hands. He might appreciate her industriousness in making gifts for the family but, right at this moment, he wanted her undivided attention. He'd barely seen her all day, and he'd missed her.

As he played with an errant lock of hair that had escaped its pin Jane said, 'Anthony came to church this morning.'

Alex grinned. 'Is that a subtle way of asking why I've been fit for nothing for the entire day and yet he was unaffected?'

Jane remained straight-faced as she denied it, but the mischievous glint in her eyes told him he'd guessed right.

'I am out of practice, clearly, although Anthony took his responsibilities as host seriously and limited his intake of spirits. What did he say about last night?'

'Nothing much.'

Alex sensed she wanted to say more.

'He asked about the circumstances that led to our marriage. He implied there was something dubious about it.' She sent him a sidelong glance. 'You didn't let slip anything about…about…' She hauled in a shaky breath. 'About Pikeford, did you?'

'Janey!' Alex wrapped his arms around her and hugged her. 'Do you really think me so crass? I told him nothing, but that didn't stop him asking plenty of questions.' He frowned as a thought occurred. 'I suspect he was using questions about our betrothal and wedding to find out more about the family and the Abbey. That's another thing Uncle Vernon told me about Anthony… He is obsessed not only with Father but also with the Abbey itself. No doubt because he feels it should belong to him! And I can't deny I would likely feel the same in his position. Anyway, enough about him—unless you truly find him riveting as a topic of conversation, in which case…do I need to be jealous?'

'You? Jealous? How absurd.'

The words might mock but, if anything, Jane looked delighted at that idea, and Alex recalled her telling him she loved him. He shifted his shoulders, uncomfortable with the topic; uncomfortable with delving into feelings. That wasn't what this marriage was about, was it? It was a marriage between good friends, borne out of necessity. He'd saved Jane from Pikeford and that witch of a stepmother, and she was already proving herself so invaluable he couldn't quite imagine his life without her now. But jealousy, and love, did not come into it.

'Absurd indeed,' he said lightly, ignoring the stab of guilt as Jane's teasing smile slipped.

'About Anthony, though…' She hesitated, her cheeks colouring.

'Yes?'

Her chest rose as she hauled in a breath. 'I can't *help* worrying about him, Alex… He bears your father an ages-old grudge and Aunt Cecily warned me he is clever and manipulative and to be cautious. I would be happier if we kept our distance from him as far as possible.'

What was it with his family? He removed his arm from Jane's shoulders, resentment bubbling through him. They never thought him capable of managing his own affairs. Could they never see him as a grown man? An adult? Would they always see him as a boy who needed guidance and protection? And now Aunt Cecily had infected his wife with the same doubts about his judgement.

'I think I'm old enough to make my own mind up about Anthony, don't you?'

Jane shook her head, and held his gaze, frustration brimming in her brown eyes. 'I am entitled to my opinion, Alexander. Or are you suggesting I should always bite my tongue?'

He stared at her frowning face. 'When have I *ever* prevented you from saying what you think?'

But you are now, aren't you? Simply by not listening to her, you are dismissing her opinion as worthless.

'I apologise,' he said quickly, before she could respond. 'Of course you are entitled to your opinion, Janey. Go on. I am listening.'

'Thank you.'

She smiled, but it was hesitant and he hated that she felt inhibited. But he didn't hate it enough to allow her to dictate who he might socialise with.

'I am worried, Alex.' She covered his hand with hers. 'There is something about Anthony that makes me uneasy.'

'Why? What has he said?'

'It is not what he says but the *way* he says it...as though everything he says has a hidden meaning.'

It was his turn to frown. 'So you will condemn the man because your overactive imagination has conjured up underlying implications to his every word? That does not sound like you, Jane. You always see the best in people. Let's face it, you must do, to still be friends with me after all these years.' It was true. She was the kindest, most forgiving person he knew. 'Do you know what I think?'

Her eyes widened. 'No. What do you think?'

'I think Pikeford's attack has made you ready to suspect monsters where there are none. You said yourself Anthony has said nothing to cause offence, so why do you insist on taking it? You are being overly sensitive.'

'That is unfair, Alex.' She snatched her hand away, as though his skin was red-hot. 'Don't turn this into an attack on me. I am your wife. I'm trying to help you.'

Of course she was trying to help. It was what she did... helped to heal the sick and wounded. Rescued starving kittens. He gritted his teeth. Was that how she viewed him? As a man who needed rescuing? He leapt to his feet and paced away, then back again.

'I know you only want to help but all I am doing is following *your* advice. You begged me to talk about my mother. Well, be happy. Because I am. To Anthony. He knew her—I'll learn far more from him than going round in circles talking to you about someone you never knew, or about a day…an incident…even *I* cannot remember.'

He hardened his heart as hurt flashed across her face.

'Alex…please…be reasonable… Yes, I think it will help you to talk about your mother, but I am unconvinced a man you barely know—and a man with a dubious past as far as your family is concerned—is the right confidant.'

His jaw locked, and it took effort to release it to say, 'It is not my intention to confide in Anthony, merely to pick his brains to see if it helps restore my memory.'

She searched his gaze. 'Very well. I shall say no more.' She was uncharacteristically abrupt. 'You know your own mind best.' Then she sighed. 'Tell me, how is your headache now? Did the remedy help?'

He was grateful for the change of subject. 'Better. And, yes, it did. Thank you. And, Janey…?' He reached for her hand and raised it to his lips. Her brows lifted. 'I *shall* take care with Anthony, I promise. You are not to worry.'

'Thank you. Oh! I almost forgot… Anthony asked me to remind you about Sir Henry coming to view that bay mare tomorrow. And will you want me to be there, to ride her for him?'

'I didn't need reminding. I wasn't that badly foxed.' Jane levelled one of her looks at him, prompting a chuckle. 'I can't fool you for one minute, can I, Janey? Very well. I confess it had slipped my mind until you mentioned it. And yes. If you don't mind, I should like your help to show her manners and paces.'

'Of course. I shall be happy to help.'

Alex picked up their current book, *Sense and Sensi-*

bility. 'Shall I read to you while you finish stuffing that rabbit?'

He said it with an air of doing her a favour but, in truth, he was as eager as Jane to discover the fate of both Elinor and Marianne Dashwood.

'If you feel well enough and it will not prove too much of a trial for you, that would be lovely.' A smile quivered on her lips. 'Thank you.'

The talk over dinner at the Halsdon Manor gathering had consisted mainly of politics and business, and the presence of Sir Henry Jacobsen, a Member of Parliament, together with several other respectable gentlemen, had helped lull Alex's suspicions about Anthony Lascelles. The one objectionable guest was Colin Theobald—a fellow Alex had known, and avoided, for many years. Alex had never liked him, plus he was infamous for his harsh treatment of his horses—an unforgiveable sin in Alex's book. He'd managed to avoid Theobald on Saturday evening and was dismayed to see him accompanying Anthony and Sir Henry when they came to view the bay mare for Lady Jacobsen.

'I trust you've no objection to me tagging along, Beauchamp?' Theobald's head swivelled from side to side as he took in everything, his eyes sharp with curiosity. 'I'm in the market for a team of four...thought I'd see if you've anything suitable.'

Alex had many objections but he kept them to himself. 'Of course I have no objection. Unfortunately, though, I have nothing currently available.'

He was damned if he would willingly sell any of his animals to Theobald. One look at the horse he rode in on— the dullness of its eyes and the barely healed scars on its flanks—made that decision easy, business be damned.

Jane chose that moment to arrive at the stable yard.

'My wife, Lady Jane,' said Alex. 'She will ride the mare to demonstrate her paces. My dear, this is Sir Henry Jacobsen and Mr Theobald.'

It felt good, to introduce her as his wife. To have someone at his side…a feeling he'd seldom experienced in his life. Her smile warmed his heart and pride suffused him as she greeted all three visitors with the exact degree of courtesy and briskness required for what was, after all, a business gathering.

Lilley led out the bay mare, and Alex cupped his hands to help Jane mount. The mare behaved impeccably as Jane put her through her paces, and Sir Henry looked impressed.

'She cuts a neat figure on horseback,' Theobald commented as Jane executed a perfect figure of eight on the mare.

'She's a talented horsewoman,' Alex replied. 'One of the best I've seen.'

'That is praise indeed, coming from a member of your family,' Anthony said. 'I've never yet met a Beauchamp who is not a skilled rider.'

'That is true.' Theobald smirked. 'And your mother too…she was an *exceptionally* skilled rider, is that not the case, Tony? I remember—'

'She put the rest to shame on the hunting field, for certain.' A muscle ticked in Anthony's jaw, and Alex caught the scowl he directed at the other man. 'And she could handle a horse as well as anyone.'

'Oh, indeed,' said the other man smoothly.

Alex tamped down his anger…he knew damned well what Theobald implied and, although he knew of his mother's reputation for taking lovers, he didn't appreciate having the subject thrust under his nose by some uninvited, insensitive sneaksby. He was grateful for Anthony's intervention… He

wanted to conclude a deal with Sir Henry, not frighten a cus-
tomer away by thumping Theobald on the nose. Anthony had
interrupted Theobald at the perfect moment for Alex to pretend he'd missed Theobald's insinuation. He shot Anthony a
grateful look and received a wink in return.

Jane halted the mare, and Sir Henry crossed the paddock
to examine her. Alex took two paces, then slammed to a
halt as a vision—sudden and shocking in its intensity—
flooded his mind, freezing all coherent thought.

The perfume…roses…voices, arguing. That yellow
skirt flowing around a pair of elegant ankles. The polished boots, back and forth, in step with a pair of yellow
slippers. A woman's pleas. A slap, and the rip of cloth.
Two figures sinking to the floor.

Alex clamped his hands to his ears, desperate to block
those sounds, but they were coming from inside his head.

I will never let you go. You won't abandon me again.

A man's voice. Harsh. Vicious.

A cry…Mother…large hands around her neck…the desperate rasp of choking.

He saw again the blackness when he screwed his eyes
shut. Felt the rough wooden planks chafe his skin. Smelled
again her scent of roses, then felt the burn of his lungs as
he held his breath. Then a heartfelt groan, and the scrape
of boots against the floor, followed by a terrifying silence,
broken only by his own tortured breaths.

He relived the shudder that racked him when he finally
opened his eyes to the froth of her crumpled yellow gown.
Yellow that filled his vision. A naked leg. One hand out-
flung, fingers slightly curled. Still. Oval nails, smooth
and perfect.

Alex's head throbbed as he fought to banish the images,
sounds and smells of the past. Then gorge erupted, forcing
its way up his throat as that horrific scene was replaced by

an image of his father's face. His stomach cramped as he desperately scrabbled his way out of the nightmare vision and back to reality, battling the urge to drop to the ground and curl into a ball, one thread of his mind still linking him to the present and screaming at him to keep it hidden.

An arm landed across his shoulders. 'What is it? You've turned ghostly, m'boy. Are you quite well?'

Anthony's voice. Low. Concerned. Alex couldn't muster a reply, his head pounding with questions.

Why the hell has this happened now?

There was no scream or scuffle. No scent of roses. Nothing. Except a random mention of his mother.

How could any sane mind conjure up such a vision? Am I going mad?

'Alex?'

He forced his attention to Anthony.

'I'm all right.'

He looked across the paddock to where Theobald had followed Sir Henry over to Jane and the mare. Thankfully neither man seemed to have noticed what happened, although Jane glanced over several times even as she responded to Sir Henry's questions. He would face an interrogation later, that was for sure. How much longer could he fob her off? He couldn't tell her about this. It would be utterly unfair, for he could no longer avoid thinking the unthinkable— what if he hadn't just discovered his mother's body all those years ago, as everyone had told him?

What if he had *been* there? Seen and heard what happened?

He felt sweat bead his forehead and upper lip. What if he had seen her killer? His lungs heaved, dragging in breaths that simply did not satisfy his need, as though he had been running full tilt. His vision swam. His legs felt like jelly.

Anthony gripped his arm, guiding him to a nearby fence he could lean against for support.

'Take a minute,' he murmured before calling to the others: 'We'll be with you in a moment.' He lowered his voice again. 'I'll tell them we're discussing business and, if that does not fool them, I shall blame it on your unaccustomed excess of alcohol the other night. Make a jest about you being a sober and upright citizen these days. So very insensitive of Colin to bring up the subject of your dear mama in that way. Such a blow to a young child, to lose a parent to such a heinous crime. I presume your father did tell you what happened to her?'

'I found her.' The words came out before Alex could swallow them. 'I found her body.'

'*You* found her? But…what were you doing there? I… From what I've been told, she was in the summer house. Were you not in lessons?'

'I was meant to be. I hid from our tutor so I could play in the copse. I… I don't remember what happened. They say I found her body. The gardeners heard me screaming.'

'Oh, you poor, poor boy.' Anthony squeezed Alex's shoulder. 'But it was fortunate you did not run into the scoundrel who killed her.'

'Yes. I was lucky.'

He avoided eye contact with the other man as he lied. How could he ever admit his visions of that day? He wished…oh, how he wished it would all go away. He dragged in a deep breath and levered himself away from the fence, the muscles in his legs still shaky. 'I'm sorry. Please forget this—it's in the past. I don't want to think about it. I'm more interested in learning about my mother when she was alive, if you will talk to me about her?'

'Of course I will, my boy. I shall be delighted.'

'When did you last see her? I know you have lived abroad much of your life.'

'That is true. I left England soon after your parents' marriage and returned...now, let me see...it was the year before your mother died. I intended to settle in England but I grew restless and left just a week before dear Margaret's death. I was back in America when I received the shocking news. I have never been so distressed, but I was grateful I'd had the opportunity to renew our acquaintance.'

They headed towards the others, Anthony's hand on Alex's shoulder. 'Your mother was a very special lady; one I fear your father never fully appreciated. But, then, he was so young when they wed... I daresay he would treat her differently now. With greater understanding.'

They left the subject while Alex concluded the sale of the mare to Sir Henry, and then their visitors left, leaving him and Jane standing outside the stable yard, watching the three men ride away.

'What happened?'

No preamble. Trust Jane... No skirting around the subject, but straight in. He wasn't surprised...she'd never been afraid, in her quiet way, to challenge him and hold him to account. But neither did she used to pity him, and he could read that emotion more and more in her eyes. In her voice. In her expression.

In her words.

And he loathed it.

'Nothing. It was the alcohol from the other night.'

'Still?' Jane's voice rang with scepticism. 'Alex...*do* you need a physician? Please...I am worried. These turns you've been having...what if it's nothing to do with visiting the Abbey and your old nightmares but something more serious? Something medical?'

'It's not medical. Stop worrying. I am perfectly well. If

you must know, Theobald made some derogatory remark about my mother, and I had to take a few minutes to stop myself from punching him on the nose.'

He looked at the worry in her kind eyes. Resentment twisted through him even though he knew that was unfair and he despised himself for it. The early part of their marriage, when they had grown closer and closer, seemed a far-off memory and the dangers in marriage to someone as perceptive as Jane were ever more apparent. He knew she was trying to help but he couldn't allow her to stray into those areas of his life where *nobody* was allowed. The distance between them was widening, the barriers between them solidifying, in his attempts to hide the slowly emerging truth of his past because he knew, instinctively, that once those memories fully surfaced the pain they would cause…the heartbreak…would destroy the family he loved more than life itself, even if he couldn't always show that love.

He touched her cheek. 'Janey. If I thought I needed a physician, I would tell you. I promise.' He tried a grin but her expression told him she wasn't fooled. 'You know what I can be like. Unpredictable. You've said it yourself. Can we not count it a success that I *didn't* thump Theobald? You know in the past I wouldn't have hesitated.'

His attempt to reassure her hadn't worked, judging by the worry and, again, pity he could read in her expression. How long would it be before that was all she saw when she looked at him? A mass of troubles…the sum of his past rather than the successful horse breeder and trainer he had worked so hard to become? He had struggled all his adult life to leave the past behind him but his family still watched him, on tenterhooks in case he slipped back into old habits. Must he now expect the same from his wife?

Well, he was damned if he'd let that happen.

'You should thank Anthony for stopping me doing something I might regret, Jane. I for one am most grateful to him.'

Jane's mouth set in a tight line, but he'd spoken the truth. What might have happened had Anthony not been there? At the very least he would've made an utter fool of himself. At the worst… He didn't like to think of the worst.

He was starting to believe Zach was right—if he tried hard to recall that day, would knowing the full truth—the identity of the killer—help? God knows it couldn't be worse than this speculation.

And if his suspicions were true then he would have to learn to deal with it.

On his own. As always.

Chapter Seventeen

After experiencing Anthony's talents as a host on Saturday, Alex was unsurprised he proved an entertaining dinner guest on Thursday. Jane, he could see, warmed to Anthony during the meal and laughed out loud several times as he regaled them with interesting tales of his time living overseas.

'I shall leave you to your port.'

Jane stood to leave the room when they finished eating. Both Alex and Anthony rose to their feet and Alex waited for Anthony to suggest they drank their port in the drawing room rather than leave Jane on her own. He said nothing, however, and Alex felt obliged to follow his guest's lead.

'We will join you shortly, my dear,' he said as Jane left the dining room.

Once the port was poured, Anthony leaned back in his chair and sighed contentedly. 'You keep a fine table, my boy. My compliments to your cook.'

'I'll pass them on.' Alex sipped his port. 'I suggest we finish these quickly and join Jane.'

He found himself the focus of those dark eyes and a knowing smile. 'Yes. I gathered from our conversation after church that your good lady rather expects you to dance attendance on her.'

Alex frowned but, before he could frame a suitable retort, Anthony continued, 'Oh, not that I blame either of you—it is natural for young lovers to wish to spend every minute together, after all.' His head tilted, and he adopted a sympathetic air. 'But it is…disappointing…when the wife of a dear friend… Now, how may I put this? When she seeks to curtail that friend's enjoyment in the company of other gentlemen in the fear he has not outgrown his youthful indiscretions.'

'My *youthful indiscretions*?' Alex found it hard to believe Jane had discussed any such thing with Anthony.

'Dear Jane… It is understandable that she will worry about your welfare, Alexander. I am convinced she will learn to trust you.'

It was true. She constantly worried about him, much to his annoyance. He wondered exactly what she had said to Anthony—he would not lower himself to ask but neither would he rush to finish his drink and join her. Dance attendance on her indeed.

Instead he persuaded Anthony to talk of his mother, and his memories of her youth. Finally, Alex drained his glass and stood up, but then sat again abruptly as he recalled something Anthony said that had been bothering him.

'The first day we met, you said you blamed my father for my mother's death. What did you mean?'

Anthony frowned. 'It is hardly a proper subject to discuss with you, Alex. Leo is your father, and deserves your respect.'

'Allow me to decide who deserves my respect, Anthony. It was a simple question. Did you have a reason for saying that, or was it your dislike for my father that prompted it?'

He held his breath as he awaited the answer although

quite what he expected he didn't know. After a long pause, Lascelles shrugged.

'I was fond of dear Margaret…as a friend, of course. I daresay I am somewhat prejudiced against your father but, over the years, I have often wondered how some vagrant happened upon the summer house, where I understand she was killed.'

Alex suppressed his shudder at the mention of the summer house.

'It was, after all, in the middle of the estate and not so very far from the Abbey itself. How, I wonder, did the killer find his way there? And why? Think of the risk… If he'd wanted to ravage some poor, unsuspecting female he could surely have found a less risky target?'

Alex's mouth dried and his heart pounded. He felt sweat dampen his brow, and he wiped it with his handkerchief.

'There…' Anthony rounded the table to put his hand on Alex's shoulder. 'I've upset you, speaking of such painful matters. Come. Let us join your charming wife.'

'You go ahead, Anthony. I shall follow soon.'

He couldn't face Jane just yet. She would see in a moment he was upset, and she would, of course, blame Anthony. But this was Alex's fault. He *had* asked, after all.

Jane had dreaded Anthony Lascelles coming to dinner, but he'd proved excellent company and she felt quite in charity with him as she waited for the men to join her, although she was disappointed they left her alone for such a long time. Finally the door opened but only Anthony entered. He strolled across to where she sat on the sofa, Mist curled on her knee, and bowed.

'I do beg your pardon, my dear Jane. I suggested we brought our port in here to keep you company, but dear Alex…well, it is natural for a man to crave the release of other male company from time to time, I am sure you agree?'

Jane fought to conceal her hurt. 'Of course.'

'I hope you will forgive us—I should hate for you to be reluctant to extend invitations to me in future in the fear I will always monopolise your husband.'

He tipped his head sideways, with an ingratiating smile that did not reach his eyes. Jane nodded, suppressing her involuntary shiver. No matter how entertaining his raconteur skills, he still made her uneasy.

'There is nothing to forgive, Anthony. I've been quite content with my book and with Mist for company.' She laid her hand on the kitten's soft fur, and was rewarded with a rumbling purr.

'What a sweet kitten.'

'Where *is* Alex?'

'He will join us soon, my dear. He… Ah, here he is now. Alex, dear boy, your good lady has forgiven our lapse in manners in not joining her sooner, and I dare to hope I shall still be welcome in your lovely home in future. I shall look forward to further reminiscences but, for now, I shall say my farewells.'

'Will you not stay and take tea before you leave, Anthony?'

Jane voiced the invitation from obligation, not from the desire to extend the time in Anthony's company. Alex clearly noticed her reticence, darting a glance of disapproval at her, but Anthony appeared oblivious.

'I thank you, dear lady, but I shall decline. I make no doubt you young newlyweds are finding an old man like me distinctly *de trop*.' He bowed and, as he straightened, his dark gaze pinned Jane. 'I shall leave you both to your pleasures…' He paused long enough for Jane to question his true meaning, then—with a flash of teeth—he smiled and added, '…for I am certain you are eager to discover what happens next in your novel.'

Jane stretched her lips in a smile. 'Then I bid you goodnight, Anthony.'

Alex clapped Lascelles on the shoulder, shaking his hand. 'Thank you for answering all my questions—you've been very patient.' He shot another reproachful glance at Jane. '*And* most helpful. I'll show you out myself.'

He said nothing, however, when he returned.

'Shall we go up?'

Jane frowned. 'Will you not tell me what you've been talking about? Did you learn much about your mother?'

'Yes, a great deal but I shan't bore you with it. After all, you didn't know her.'

Jane tried hard not to care. Alex had always been this way—always kept the different parts of his life separate. She didn't doubt he cared for her but she was still excluded from parts of his life…parts of him…and she had no idea how to reach the core of the man trapped behind that barrier.

She swallowed back her disappointment. 'I am tired,' she said. 'I think I will go up now.'

Alex didn't quite meet her eyes. 'Now I think about it, though, I'm not ready to retire just yet.' He helped Jane to her feet and kissed the tip of her nose. 'Sleep well.'

Jane lay awake, staring blindly into the darkness, worrying. Alex was still downstairs and, if she was honest, it was something of a relief. Lately, when they made love, although she was always physically satiated, she ended up feeling flat. Emotionally hungry. Dissatisfied.

And his moods seemed to be worsening. Was it simply pride that kept him from confessing what he was so afraid of? Because he *was* afraid. She saw the fear haunting his eyes, especially since Monday when, whatever he might tell her, she was convinced he'd had another of his funny turns. And that fear, she was certain, was new. He had always been haunted. But he had not been afraid. Rather, he had always been fearless. She frowned. At least, he had always *appeared* fearless. On the surface.

If only he would trust her. He must know she wouldn't think any the less of him, or love him any less, no matter what. But he stubbornly refused to even admit anything was wrong and, try as she might, she couldn't find a way to break through the barrier he had thrown up between them.

Finally, weary of her ever-circling thoughts that appeared to get her nowhere, she rolled over and slept.

My husband is the most frustrating man I know!

The refrain ran through Jane's thoughts a minimum of twice a day in the days and weeks that followed. Alex continued to act all strong and manly, denying there was anything wrong and, despite knowing that pestering him to talk only made him irritable, Jane could not help herself. She was worried sick about him. If only he would trust her…she was certain they could resolve whatever it was that shadowed his eyes and was robbing him of his appetite.

A voice inside Alex's head warned he was in danger of becoming obsessed with finding out everything he could about his mother. Most days, either Anthony visited Foxbourne, or Alex rode over to Halsdon and if, for whatever reason, they did not meet for a few days a panicky feeling would take root in his gut, growing there until the next time he saw their neighbour.

He shoved aside Jane's concerns—this was his problem, and he would find a solution. He couldn't risk giving her even the slightest hint of what was going on inside his head until it was clear in his own mind, and it was a long way from being clear. Talking to Anthony helped, however, and those distressing visions became less frequent—he even coped with the smell of the rose-scented perfume worn by a lady seated in front of him in church one Sunday without making an utter fool of himself. It helped to breathe through his mouth and to concentrate his thoughts on the sermon… It was surely the first time he had *ever* paid so much attention to a vicar's discourse.

Things were improving. Except for that deep dread that assailed him whenever a mental image of his father formed in his mind's eye. But was his father's face linked to his memories of that day because it was he who had carried seven-year-old Alex back to the Abbey or was there a more sinister reason? What if those dreadful suspicions were true? What if his father had killed his mother? That thought alone was enough to make him feel physically sick.

Alex and Lilley were debating which of their young stock to sell to ensure a sufficient stock of winter fodder one day when Anthony rode up to them.

'Would you care to come up to the house?' Alex asked. 'There's a real nip in the air this morning. I dare say you would appreciate a glass of something to counter it.'

Anthony's gaze slid away from Alex, as though embarrassed. 'I should not like to presume. I…' He shook his head. 'No. I am being over-sensitive. Yes. Thank you, Alexander. I accept with pleasure.'

Alex frowned. 'What do you mean…presume? There is nothing presumptuous about accepting an invitation from a man to join him for a glass of wine.'

'No, of course there is not. Ignore me, I beg of you.'

'No. Tell me what you meant. Has…has Jane made you feel unwelcome?'

'Not at all! Please do not think… I am certain she did not mean…after all, I *have* been a frequent visitor. It would be no wonder if a bride resented a friend who distracted her husband. Not that a word of criticism has left her lips, I assure you. She has been all that is civil.'

Civil? Alex had been on the receiving end of Jane's civility when she disapproved of something but it was her duty as lady of the house to make *all* visitors feel welcome, without regard to personal feelings. His inner voice urged him not to fly in and throw accusations at Jane—she'd warned him she didn't care for Anthony, and it was true he visited Foxbourne frequently.

The last thing they needed was even more conflict between them—it was bad enough with her constantly on at him to talk about his mother, and what had happened. She seemed unable to accept it was part of his life separate from their marriage and their life at Foxbourne. Plus, at the back of his mind, was the nagging realisation that he still hadn't told her they wouldn't be going to the Abbey for Christmas. It never seemed to be the right time but he was horribly aware he couldn't put it off much longer.

'Well, you may take it from me that you are welcome to visit any time you choose, Anthony. After all, I visit Halsdon as often as you come here.'

'Thank you, my boy. You have no idea how much that means to me, coming from Margaret's boy. If I had ever been blessed with a son, I would wish for him to be just like you.'

Once indoors, Alex led the way to his business room.

'I do suggest, though, that you might visit me at Halsdon more often instead,' Anthony continued as Alex stood aside for the older man to precede him into the room. 'At least there we can be sure we are not disturbing— Oh! I do beg your pardon, Jane. I am sure neither of us had any notion you might be in here.'

Alex entered to see Jane standing on the far side of the desk, his quill knife in her hand.

'You may rest assured you are in no way disturbing me, Anthony,' she said. 'I have merely come to borrow Alex's knife as I have mislaid my own and I am writing to my father.'

She smiled, but it did not reach her eyes. She rounded the desk and headed for the door, saying, 'Please excuse me. I must go and attend to my correspondence.'

Alex poured them both a glass of Madeira.

After they had settled, Anthony said, 'I am reluctant to broach the subject, but I hope Rosalind is content with your father? I know I forfeited any right to concern after my despicable actions five years ago, but I still care enough to wish her happy in her marriage.'

Alex always tried to avoid the subject of his father but Anthony was persistent in introducing him into conversation.

'Yes. They are happy together.'

'I am glad. She is more fortunate than poor Margaret. Her life with your father was far from happy.'

He'd told Alex that many times, as he'd recounted his memories of Alex's mother. He sipped his wine. 'Speaking of your father...'

Alex tensed. He might have grown closer to Anthony but he was conscious the man had never put aside his hatred and jealousy of Alex's father.

'What about him?' he asked when Anthony seemed reluctant to continue.

Anthony shrugged. 'Oh. It is of no importance. Not really. But I cannot help but wonder why your own relationship with him has not improved? Five years ago, you were still a headstrong young man, for ever in trouble…as I remember, that is. Forgive me if I have misinterpreted the events of that year.'

Alex scowled. 'No. Your memory is correct. But I do not see your point.'

Anthony waved his arm, indicating the room. 'I am curious why—five years later, with you a responsible estate owner, running a business, and, from my observations, no longer in thrall to your previous wild existence—you are still at odds with the Duke?'

When Alex failed to respond, Anthony continued, 'Have I touched upon a nerve? My dear Alexander, please forgive me. It is family business. I understand.' He leaned forward, patting Alex's knee. 'But if you ever need someone to listen, you know where I am. I know you have family loyalty at heart—and you're aware your father and I can never be friends—but if anyone can understand, it is I.

'It is hard to be the outsider; the only one, seemingly, out of step. Your father is universally admired. And the rest of your…of *our*…family love him unconditionally.' He shook his head. 'I sometimes wonder why I cannot do likewise.' He raised his glass. 'You and I, m'boy, are kindred spirits. We should take strength from that. Cheers.'

He smiled, and drank, and Alex automatically responded to his toast although the very notion he and Anthony Lascelles were alike bothered him. Intensely. Anthony had always resented and loathed Father. That was his conscious decision, driven by resentment and jealousy. It wasn't the same with Alex. He'd always longed to love his father unconditionally, as Dominic did, but that natural filial love had always eluded him.

And he didn't know why; unless these accursed visions were trying to expose the reason. The familiar dread coiled in his gut. He no longer doubted he had witnessed his mother's murder. But…could his father *really* be her killer?

'What is it?' Anthony's voice seemed far away. 'Alexander? You are pale, my boy. Are you unwell?'

'No. I'm all right. It's nothing.' Alex drained his glass and rose to his feet. 'Thank you for calling in, Anthony, but I really must return to the stables…there are decisions to be made.'

Lascelles was soon mounted, ready to leave. He touched the brim of his hat in farewell.

'Don't be a stranger, Alexander. Call upon me whenever you wish…you will always find a warm welcome.'

Later, Alex found Jane in the drawing room, embroidering initials on the handkerchiefs she'd made for Christmas.

'Anthony feels unwelcome here.'

'Does he?' She captured Alex's gaze. 'I am sorry, Alex, but I have said nothing to make him feel that way. I'm aware of my duties as hostess, and I say all the right words. I cannot help it if my inner feelings reveal an aversion to Lascelles, the same as *he* seems unable to prevent his inner…*offensiveness*…from peeking through at times.' Her lips tightened before she added, 'There is something not right about the man.'

'You shouldn't allow Aunt Cecily's prejudice to infect you. You are positively searching for reasons to object to him.'

Jane leapt to her feet, her eyes shooting sparks. 'I am not! You are being unfair, Alex. I am polite to him because he is your guest, but you cannot force me to like him. *I* cannot understand why *you* don't recognise his deviousness.'

'He knew my mother! I—'

'But that doesn't stop him being devious!' He winced as she raised her voice. What had happened to quiet, inoffensive Jane? 'Why do you *always* find time for him yet hardly have any time to talk to me?'

Anger roared through him, partly fuelled by knowing she was correct. He sought out Anthony to talk about his mother, and yet his mother was the very reason he avoided talking to Jane. The irony wasn't lost on him. He paced the room, desperately tamping down that rage. How ridiculous, to allow a neighbour to cause such a row.

'You know I need to find out about Mother.' He stopped pacing and took Jane's hands. 'Let's not quarrel, Janey. I hate it when you're cross with me.'

Jane's face softened. 'I hate it, too. But please don't expect me to mindlessly obey you when it goes counter to what I believe. I *will* continue to speak my mind—but I only ever do it out of love for you.'

Shame now held him in its grip. She was far too good for him. His hands slid up her arms to her shoulders.

'I do know it. But I won't stop seeing Anthony. I cannot. Please accept that.'

'I do.' Her soft hand caressed his cheek. 'But I wish you would trust *me* enough to talk to me, Alex. You are remembering something from the past, but what can be so dreadful that you are unable to tell me?'

He stiffened. He didn't want this discussion. Not again.

'Whatever it is you're afraid of, I can help. Please. Just tell—'

Alex jerked away from her. 'There's nothing. I *have* told you. Time after time. Why won't *you* trust *me* when I say there's nothing wrong?'

He spun on his heel and slammed out of the room.

Chapter Eighteen

Jane picked up her discarded sewing, her throat a painful mass of unshed tears. Her hands shook and, after pricking her finger twice, she gave up trying to control her emotions. She crossed to the window, staring blindly out, as she relived every moment and every word of their argument. Her arms wrapped around her waist, her hands fisting in the fabric of her gown. Should she have apologised, and promised to be less mistrustful of Lascelles? Should she give in, and accept Alex's refusal to talk about whatever was troubling him? She *could* be the easy, supportive wife who never questioned her husband's judgement and decisions but she believed, with her whole heart, that was the wrong path.

Despite Alex's fury. Despite his refusal to confide in her. Despite her distress at his reaction…she still believed she was right to keep encouraging him to trust her.

Or nagging him, as he would no doubt see it.

She hauled in a deep breath, and lifted her chin. She *knew* Alex. She'd seen these tactics time after time, from way back when she first knew him. It was how he kept the world at arm's length—his brother, his sister, his aunt and uncle. His father. He kept them all away, never allowing them to probe too deeply. It was his defence…the way he pretended nothing mattered…nothing could touch him… hurt him. But he *was* hurting, deep inside. She knew it.

And that fear still haunted him. She had glimpsed it too many times, shadowing his tiger eyes before his expression would blank, his jaw tight. It had started with his stay at the Abbey, and Pikeford's attack, and it linked to that day he had discovered his mother's body. The entire family counted it as a blessing he couldn't remember, believing ignorance protected him. Jane wasn't so sure.

Now…was he remembering the details of that day after all? Could he now picture his mother's brutalised body as he had found her? Jane shuddered, the memory of Pikeford close. He'd hit her. He was drunk…she'd been unable to reason with him… How far would he have gone had Alex not intervened? Another shudder racked her body, her skin crawling with gooseflesh and, of a sudden, all she wanted was to turn to Alex, to feel his arms around her, his strength and his comfort.

Her heart ached that he would not turn to her in his distress, but chose to turn to Lascelles. With a muttered exclamation she swiped the tears wetting her cheeks. Crying wouldn't help. She didn't know what would help. Or… yes, she did.

Alex.

She couldn't bear to leave his anger to fester…she hated it when they quarrelled. For her own sake, she would apologise for now but it wouldn't stop her trying again. She'd lived too long with her stepmother—having to edit every word before she spoke—to be prepared to tiptoe around within her own marriage.

She spun on her heel and half ran to the door, which opened as she reached it.

Alex. Contrition on his face.

Jane stepped back. 'I was coming to find you. To say I'm sorry.'

'No. It's me who is sorry.' He hugged her close. 'I'm a brute. I know you are trying to help me, but...' He shrugged. 'I am too used to fending for myself.' He tipped up her chin, searched her eyes. 'Forgive me, Honeybee?'

She bit her lip. 'I forgive you, Alex. But...I still want you to trust me. I really do believe it will help you to talk about whatever is haunting you. Unless, of course, you have already confided in Anthony?'

She couldn't help herself, even though she was aware she was playing with fire by revisiting the very reason they had argued. A myriad of emotions played across Alex's face. Jane braced herself for him to lose his temper again, but he sighed, and Jane released her own breath, knowing he would not fly up into the boughs again. This time.

'Jane...sweetheart...there's nothing to tell. Your imagination is conjuring up ghosts where there are only figures draped in sheets. They are of no concern. Now...come for a ride with me? I want to inspect the two-year-olds in the north paddock. Lilley and I have been discussing which of them to sell and which to keep. I'd value your opinion.'

Jane knew a distraction when she saw one. Alex was a master at deflecting attention from subjects he refused to discuss. She suppressed another sigh as she accepted her husband's latest olive branch.

It was the first day of December, and Jane had just finished writing to Olivia when Kent came into the parlour.

'Mr Lascelles is here, milady—he brought a letter with him. He met Tommy on his way to the village. I told him His Lordship is away from home, and he asked for you.'

Jane stood, her insides clenching. The prospect of being

alone with Lascelles unnerved her, with Alex absent from the house.

'Thank you, Kent. Have you offered him refreshments?'

'Yes, milady. He declined. He said he will not linger but didn't wish to leave without paying his respects. He is waiting in the library.'

'Thank you.'

Jane smoothed her clammy palms down her skirt before she preceded Kent into the hall. The letter lay on the console table and she recognised Liberty's neat hand. Her heart lifted. Liberty's letters were always entertaining— almost as good as chatting face-to-face. They'd become firm friends since their first meeting, before Dominic and Liberty's marriage.

But before she could read it, there was Lascelles to face. She longed to ask for a maid to come and sit with them but was embarrassed to reveal her mistrust in Lascelles.

As she passed Kent into the library, however, he murmured, 'I shall be in the hallway should our visitor change his mind about refreshments, milady. You only have to call.'

Relief coursed through Jane. 'Thank you, Kent.'

She stepped into the room. Lascelles was perusing the titles in a bookcase. A movement on the top of the bookcase caught Jane's eye and, before she could shout a warning, a grey bundle of fluff launched itself, landing on Lascelles' shoulder. Lascelles swore viciously and grabbed Mist, turning back to the room as he did so. Jane froze, her stunned brain scrambling to make sense of what she was seeing, as Lascelles held the wriggling kitten tightly in his hands. His face distorted into a snarl as his grip tightened...squeezing...

At Mist's squeal of pain Jane broke free of her paralysis and charged at Lascelles.

'Let her go!' She shook his arm in her fury. 'You evil brute! *Let her go*, I said!'

'Gladly!'

Lascelles cast Mist across the room. She rolled several times, leapt to her feet and shot out through the door, fur on end, tail fluffed out to twice its normal size. Lascelles smoothed the sleeve of his coat, and stared down at Jane, eyes narrowed. They were so close the woody, sweet and spicy scent of his bay rum cologne filled her nostrils, and her ears detected his erratic breathing. He might look un-ruffled, but she suspected he was a mass of tension beneath the surface. That gave her courage, to realise he might be as rattled as her.

'I *ought* to apologise but I will not. Cats are vicious animals, totally unsuitable as house pets. They belong outside, with the rest of the vermin. That animal *attacked* me.'

Jane fought the instinct to retreat. 'I see no blood.' She forced the words through gritted teeth. 'Get out of my house and *never* come back. Do you hear me?'

Fury flashed in his eyes. '*Your* house? I think your hus-band might have something to say about *that*, my dear. He will not take kindly to you banishing me. Not when *I* have the information he craves.'

'He will not take kindly to you torturing an innocent animal.'

Lascelles sneered. 'Your word against mine, my dear. You are clearly distraught and your imagination is play-ing tricks.'

'Milady? Is everything all right?'

Jane didn't even glance at Kent, determined to hold Las-celles' gaze. 'Mr Lascelles is leaving, Kent. Please show him out.'

Lascelles' gaze hardened. He reached out, lifting her

chin with one finger. Jane refused to flinch. She wouldn't give him the satisfaction.

'Take care, Lady Jane.' His voice was a menacing whisper. He held her gaze for what seemed like an aeon before pivoting on his heel and striding from the room.

Jane squared her shoulders, determined not to succumb to her quivering nerves.

'Thank you, Kent. Please tell the rest of the staff Mr Lascelles is on no account to be allowed into the house unless His Lordship is at home.'

'Yes, milady.'

'Did you see where Mist went?'

'Upstairs, milady. I hope she wasn't hurt.'

'So do I, Kent.'

Jane found Mist trembling under her bed. She coaxed her out and sat on the bed to examine her, petting her and reassuring her. She appeared unharmed physically and, murmuring softly to calm her, Jane carried her downstairs to the parlour, collecting Liberty's letter on the way.

She settled Mist on her lap, smoothing her fur. It was an age before the kitten ceased trembling. Eventually, though, she slept, and Jane also dozed off, having already read Liberty's letter three times, squinting as she deciphered the crossed lines, but reluctant to disturb the sleeping kitten to fetch a book to read to pass the time.

Alex paused inside the parlour door, watching Jane before she was aware of his presence. Her eyes were closed, her lashes a dark crescent against the gentle bloom of her cheeks. Her lips were parted, her chest gently rising and falling with every breath. Her hair had escaped some of the pins, and tendrils stroked her neck, leaving her perfect shell-like ear peeping through. One hand rested on

Mist, curled on Jane's lap, her green eyes on Alex as one ear twitched. In the other was a letter.

Peace warmed his heart. No matter what horrors his visions stirred from the past, Jane was his life now and he vowed to try even harder to make her happy—their disagreement the other day had shaken him more than he believed possible and he had no wish to repeat it. But Jane hadn't mentioned nightmares or the past since, and she hated quarrelling as much as he did, so hopefully they could avoid the subject in future and all would be well.

As he walked towards her Mist suddenly leapt up and shot past him, out the door.

'Ouch!' Jane woke with a start, rubbing her leg. Her eyes widened when she saw Alex. 'I didn't know you were home. Why did Mist run off? Is Lascelles here?'

'Anthony? Why should he be here?' He crouched down next to Jane's chair. 'There's blood on your gown. Did Mist scratch you?'

'She dug her claws in as she jumped off.' Jane tutted as she examined the spot of blood. 'I shall have to change this, and sponge the blood out before it dries.'

'I'll come with you.' He nuzzled her neck, breathing in her jasmine scent, licking the hollow beneath her ear and nibbled her lobe. It was too long since they'd made love, the growing distance between them by day having its effect by night, too.

But Jane pulled away. 'Alex… Lascelles called. I caught him torturing Mist. *That's* why she ran away when you came in.'

'Torturing?' Anger brewed. 'What happened?'

'He was squeezing her. Hard enough to make her squeal. He claimed she attacked him, but she only jumped down onto his shoulder. He…he frightens me, Alex. I've told him not to come here again.'

Alex stood up, torn. He couldn't abide any kind of cruelty to animals, but…he *needed* Anthony. He was the only person who could help him know his mother and ultimately make sense of the past. 'You barred him from Foxbourne?'

'I did.' Her chin lifted. 'I hope you will support my decision. I will not be threatened in my own home.'

'He threatened you?' The anger boiled now. No man threatened his wife.

She nodded. 'Maybe not in so many words, but the threat was there.'

'What did he say?'

'He said, "Take care, Lady Jane".'

Alex frowned, and his anger eased. 'That doesn't sound threatening, Jane. Are you sure you aren't imagining it?'

She'd always been the same with Anthony, reading hidden menace in the most mundane conversation. What had happened to *Everyone deserves a chance to prove they've changed*?

'I am sure.' Jane's mouth settled into a stubborn line. 'It was the *way* he said it. I don't want him in my home again. Please, Alex.'

He folded his arms. 'I'll ask him to stay away. I can always go to Halsdon instead.' Jane's brows snapped together. 'I still need to talk to him about Mother, Jane. You must understand that.'

'But you cannot talk to me about her?'

Alex sighed. 'I will. One day. Once I understand it all.'

'Understand *what*?'

Her cry of anguish wrenched his heart but he turned away.

'Alex? Liberty has written to us.'

He turned back, relieved by the change of subject. Jane held the letter out to him, but the sight of those crossed and recrossed lines made his head throb. 'Perhaps you might paraphrase it?' He was rewarded with a laugh, even though it was strained.

'Firstly, she has shared the happy news that they are expecting their first child. Is that not wonderful? And, secondly, we're invited to stay at Clystfield Court next week, before we all go on to the Abbey for Christmas. She fears otherwise the weather might prevent us travelling.'

His heart lurched. He'd *still* not told Jane they weren't going to the Abbey. He could think of nothing worse, especially now with his suspicions about his father's role in his mother's death.

'No.'

Jane stared. 'No? What do you—? *Pfft!* That's a ridiculous question. I know exactly what you mean by "No". What I need to ask is "Why"? It will only be an extra week away, and Olivia, Hugo and the twins will be there, too. It will be—'

'I mean, no we are not going to the Abbey for Christmas.'

'*What?* But…we accepted…we're expected. Your entire family will be there.'

'Which is precisely why we are not going.'

Jane stood up and grabbed his hands. 'I don't believe you don't want to see your family. You *love* them. Why, Alex?'

He shrugged, pulling his hands from hers.

'Is this what our future holds?' Her voice sharpened. 'What if we have children? Would you deny them the opportunity to know their aunts and uncles and cousins? Not to mention their grandparents.'

'I've made my decision.'

Jane stared at him like he was a stranger. His gaze slid from hers and his insides shrivelled until he felt like an empty, useless shell. But he couldn't face his father. He simply couldn't.

'What about what *I* want? Or does my opinion not count? What *is* it you won't tell me, Alex?'

He couldn't tell her. How could she ever face any of his family again if she knew what he suspected? She would never be able to hide the truth from her eyes.

'If it's the Abbey…if you're afraid your nightmares will return…'

'It's not the Abbey! I can cope with a few bad dreams.'

'Your father then. We could compromise—go to Clyst-field and then come home. You wouldn't even need to see your father…'

The rest of her words faded as an image of his father erupted in his head.

He was in profile, his lips drawn back in a snarl. *I will never let you go!* Alex surged to his feet, utterly shaken. He'd accepted he had witnessed his mother's murder. He had suspected his father may have been involved but he had hoped…no…*prayed* it was not so. Prayed that the mental images of his father were simply his child's memory confusing his father—who had indisputably been there in the aftermath—with the man who attacked his mother.

But this was an image that shook his very foundations… the first time he had pictured his father actually playing a part in his mother's death. Not his father as he was now, but as he was then: lean, dark, dangerous. The image of *his* hands around Mother's neck. His greatest dread was true. He'd always blamed himself for his prickly relationship with his father. But now…the fault was not his. And that knowledge shattered him. He couldn't even begin to wonder at the impact of this on the rest of the family.

Nausea roiled his stomach, turning his legs weak and his breathing shallow.

'Alex? What is it? What's wrong?' Jane clung to his arm.

He needed to be alone.

'We're not going to the Abbey. That's my final word on it.'

How could he possibly go, knowing what he did? The very thought made him long to curl up into a ball and sleep for ever now he had the answer to his aversion to his own father. His father the killer.

The nausea rose up his throat: acid, burning, threatening to erupt.

'Alex…please…tell me…'

He must be alone. He snatched his arm free.

'I have work to do.'

He strode from the room before Jane could reply, and ran outside, hoping the fresh air might help clear his head. And defuse his anger. And obliterate that sudden, horrific image of his father, the sound of those words, gritted out through clenched teeth. Words of fury. Alex's stomach knotted, screwing tight, as his breathing grew shallow. He headed for the garden, to the arbour that used to support rambling roses but was now cloaked with honeysuckle every summer, and sank on to the bench, leaning forward, his forearms propped along his thighs.

His throat was thick, aching, and his head throbbed anew as it sank into his hands. He strove to rid his mind of all thought, but the images kept coming. Relentlessly. The yellow dress, the angry voices, the boots and the slippers, the breathless pleading: *'No. No. Please.'*

All while he had cowered beneath the chaise longue, where his mother had loved to recline on warm days. He'd done *nothing* to save her.

His stomach heaved, propelling him out of the arbour to the nearest bush where he retched until his stomach was empty. Tears burned behind his eyes.

I cannot stand this.

The visions were now crystal-clear, and that deep, deep

dread that had plagued his childhood and that he had managed to keep suppressed all these years—firstly with the help of alcohol and drugs and wild escapades and, latterly, by concentrating fiercely and wholeheartedly on his beloved horses—could no longer be ignored.

His stomach heaved again, his muscles clenched in pain. They'd had it wrong. Everyone had it wrong. He'd believed them because it had suited him to believe them…so he wouldn't have to face the truth that he hadn't just found his mother's murdered body, nor even that he had watched her being killed, but that he had watched her being throttled by his own father.

He sank to his knees, oblivious to the sharp sting of the gravel through his breeches. His arms wrapped around his torso as he bent forward and then rocked, images from the past…from that day…tumbling through his thoughts, clearer and sharper and, seemingly, unstoppable. He hadn't been seen. At no point had his father spotted him, cowering beneath the chaise longue, the floor rough against his cheek.

All these years. The truth had been there. Inside him. Waiting.

Again, his stomach clenched, a nest of snakes writhing inside. The lid on that day had cracked, and he had fallen through into a past of horrors. He could never rid himself now of that memory, and he had no choice but to somehow live with it.

He had watched his own father kill his mother.

He swallowed desperately, forcing his gorge back down his throat as chills raced across his skin. He could never admit the truth to a living soul, for it would tear the Beauchamp family apart. He thought about Dominic and Olivia, not to mention Christabel and Sebastian. How could he brand their father a murderer? He could never do that to his brothers and sisters, let alone to Rosalind and the rest of the family.

But how could he allow his mother's death to go un-avenged?

'Alex?'

Her call was distant. He couldn't talk to her. Not now. He scrambled to his feet.

'Alex?'

Nearer now. Panic set in. She knew him too well. Would know something drastic had happened. And she wouldn't give up…she would keep pushing him for an answer. And what if that rage roiling his insides should erupt at Jane? He couldn't take that risk, and he hadn't the strength to put on his customary brave face. He wasn't ready to bury it inside and pretend nothing was eating a hole in him. Not yet. Maybe in time…

Because if Jane should learn the truth… *He* also knew *her* too well. She could never dissemble with his family, and God forbid she should ever come face-to-face with his father. No. She must never know. But he must get his own emotions under control before he could attempt to fool her into believing nothing was wrong.

He turned and sprinted for the stable yard, despising himself but helpless to do anything else. He needed time to clear his head, and to work out how he could continue to face Jane—not to mention the rest of the world—with this new knowledge.

Chapter Nineteen

Alex regained some semblance of calm during the ride to Halsdon Manor, painfully aware it didn't bode well for the future of his marriage that he could face Anthony but not his own wife. He should never have wed. He was incapable of making any woman happy for long…his demons were too strong for that. And now he knew why. Anthony was the one person who shared Alex's distrust of his father and, right now, that's exactly what he needed. The freedom to admit there was something wrong. If his disdain for Father showed, Anthony would accept it whereas anyone else of his acquaintance would—as they always had—immediately try to persuade him he was wrong, and to use guilt to lever him into a filial love he had never felt.

And now never could.

He swallowed back a sob.

It would be better if I were dead. They'd all be better off without me.

The thought appeared from nowhere, shocking him. Jane's face materialised in his mind's eye, her brown eyes warm and trusting. She deserved so much better than him but he could see no way of being the husband she wanted him to be. Not now.

Servants were hurrying hither and thither when Alex arrived at Halsdon Manor.

'I leave for London this afternoon,' Anthony said, as he and Alex settled in the pair of wing back chairs in his salon.

'London?' The news hit Alex like a blow to the gut. 'I didn't know you were planning to leave this soon. How long will you be gone?'

Anthony shrugged. 'I had no intention of leaving yet, but I believe it will be for the best after this morning's unfortunate misunderstanding.'

'But…'

What about me? Who can I talk to if you're in London?

Sheer pride kept those words inside but now he felt even more compelled to discover as much as possible about his parents' marriage. To work out how a man like his father could be driven to murder. He was drowning, and Anthony was his lifeline…the only thing keeping his head above water.

Anthony speared him with a knowing look. 'We will talk again on my return, my boy. Never fear.'

Alex swallowed down his desperation. 'And when will that be?'

'I know not. Weeks? Months? It depends how long it takes your lady to forgive me, even though she utterly misread the situation.'

Belatedly, Alex recalled what Jane told him about Anthony and Mist. Shame piled upon shame. What kind of man didn't leap to the defence of his wife? If Anthony hadn't mentioned the incident, Alex would have completely forgotten, so bound up was he in his own troubles.

'How did she misread seeing you torture her kitten?'

'*Torture?* An exaggeration, my dear chap, I assure you. That is the trouble with females, is it not? They are prone to leap to conclusions, allowing their emotions to colour the facts before their eyes.'

Anthony put down his glass, leaned back in his chair, and steepled his fingers, propping his chin on them. The pose brought Father to mind—how many times had he seen both his father and Dominic adopt a similar pose? Nausea again churned his stomach. Would he feel like this every time his father was brought to mind?

Again, that scandalous idea crept into his thoughts. He thrust it aside, concentrating on what Anthony was saying.

'I bitterly regret what happened, my dear chap, but you must believe I had no intention of hurting the little creature. It startled me, leaping upon me from above as I browsed the bookshelves. Those claws are needle-sharp, and they dug straight into my scalp. I didn't know what attacked me—I swiped it away by reflex, and that was what Jane saw. She would not listen to reason, and so I beat my retreat.'

Alex recalled the spot of blood on Jane's gown…proof indeed of the sharpness of Mist's claws.

Anthony leaned forward. 'Surely you can see how that might be misinterpreted? Ladies' sensibilities are so easily upset, are they not?'

Alex did see how a misunderstanding might arise, but Jane was no fool and she was no delicate flower, prone to fits of the vapours. But, whatever the truth, the result was that Anthony was leaving for London and Alex *did* blame Jane for that.

'Indeed,' he said. 'But there is no need to leave on Jane's account, Anthony. I shall talk to her…explain it was a mis-understanding.'

'She has banned me from your house, dear boy.' Anthony's brows rose, and his eyes widened. 'I had so hoped to put to rest all those past disagreements with your branch of the family. I fear there is little hope now. Your lady wife will no doubt confide in the other Beauchamp ladies and, once your father gets to hear of it…' He sighed. 'He is an implacable enemy, Alexander. You will not have seen that side of him, but *I* have. Too often. What your poor, dear mother endured…but… There. I have said too much. Your family loyalty must of course be with your father.'

Tears burned behind Alex's eyes. He held his breath, desperately clamping down on all the emotion threatening to erupt.

'My dear boy! What have I said?'

Anthony's sympathetic tone was his undoing and, once the words began, he could no more stop the flow than he could stop the sun rising every morning.

Alex rode home two hours later, his spirits lighter after letting out all his pain and confusion. And Anthony was the perfect person to talk to—his loyalties never tested because there had never been any love lost between him and Alex's father. He had sworn on his life never to reveal what Alex told him, not to anyone, and Alex had no choice but to believe him for, by the time his brain had caught up with the torrent of his confession, the worst had been said and it was far too late to unsay it.

But nothing he said had persuaded Anthony to change his plans. He was leaving for London that afternoon.

Alex left his horse at the stables and headed for the house under a sky turned pewter by massing storm clouds. His pace faltered, despite the icy raindrops that spattered him. What to say to Jane? What explanation could he offer? His immediate crisis had passed…he was better able to control his feelings now he'd had his chance to vent…but he knew his wife. She would not let this go. She would want to know… He could hear her in his head.

What happened? Why did you run off? Where have you been?

Tension seized him again. He couldn't tell her. How would she ever face his family again? In time, *he* could face them although he would *never* willingly meet his father again. Ever. But Jane would never be able to keep her expression free of such dreadful knowledge.

He met Jane in the hall, at the foot of the stairs, her eyes puffy and pink. She stiffened when she saw him.

'You've come home, then?'

'As you see.'

'Alex…' She put her hand on his sleeve. 'I've been worried. Are you all right?'

'Yes, thank you.' His voice sounded raw to his ears. 'I'm sorry I stormed off.'

'No. *I* am sorry for plaguing you to talk to me. But…you *can* trust me, you know. I wouldn't think you less of a man for talking of your feelings as a child, if that makes sense?'

Her brown eyes were open and honest, warm and caring. She still harboured the hope he would share more of himself…his past…with her, as he'd known she would.

He stretched his lips in a smile. 'I know I can trust you, but there is nothing to tell. I spoke to Anthony, by the way, and you need worry no further. He leaves for London this afternoon.'

Jane stared at Alex. He'd gone to Lascelles? Run from her as though she were the devil incarnate, and gone straight to that evil…? She sucked in a deep breath, desperate to calm herself. The last thing she wanted was another argument but…could she really keep biting her tongue? Was this how she wanted to live her life? She'd had no choice while she was growing up. She did have a choice now.

'You said you had work to attend to.'

Alex scowled. 'I did it for you, Janey. You wanted me to tell him never to darken our doorstep again. That is what I did.'

She scanned his pale face; the shadows beneath his eyes; the deep grooves from nose to mouth. He appeared to have aged ten years since yesterday.

'Alex…please…'

He snatched his arm away. 'I've told you. There is nothing more so please stop nagging me. I cannot tell you what doesn't exist.'

Her hands clenched into fists. Infuriating man!

'Very well. I am going to consult with Mrs Godfrey about dinner.'

She pivoted on her heel and stalked down the hall to the kitchen, not trusting herself to say another word.

Early the next morning, Jane lay awake next to a still-sleeping Alex. He'd been restless, crying out several times in the night, but had not woken. Jane had soothed him each time, longing to shake him awake and demand to know what was troubling him, but she'd resisted, telling herself he needed his sleep. Telling herself she'd talk to him in the morning. But now that morning was here she realised that to badger him again would simply result in the same reaction. And an idea had come to her in the night.

She would agree to not spending Christmas at Cheriton Abbey but—in the hope Alex might confide in Dominic— she would try to persuade Alex to go to Clystfield Court. Today if possible, for hail had clattered against the window in the night and it was noticeably colder. If it should snow, they would be going nowhere.

If that failed, she had no idea what to do next, but she

was close to the end of her tether. Was it really asking too much to be allowed to help him?

She waited until they were at breakfast before broaching the subject.

'Alex. Please may we discuss going to Clystfield Court?'

His expression darkened as he put down his knife and fork. 'We discussed it yesterday. You know my decision.'

'I understand you don't wish to go to the Abbey, but could we not visit Dominic and Liberty? It will only mean two weeks away, including the travelling...surely we—'

Alex leapt to his feet, thumping the table with his fist, making the crockery rattle. 'No! Stop harassing me. I won't go. Let that be the end of it.'

'But *I* wish to go, Alex.'

'Then go, if it's so important to you. Go with my blessing. I'll even order the carriage for you.'

She stared at him, horrified at his implacable expression. He had called her bluff, knowing she would not go without him. But she couldn't give in. Not yet.

'Mayhap I shall.' Jane drank her coffee, holding his gaze.

Alex shrugged, and picked up his cutlery. Jane's cup rattled as she placed it in its saucer and she silently cursed her trembling hand. She wanted to sink her head in her hands so she could order her thoughts, but she refused to reveal her devastation. Her mouth was as dry as a desert, but she picked up her toast and bit into it, chewing as best she could while Alex continued to eat his bacon and eggs. An awkward silence ensued, until they were interrupted by Kent, bearing a note. Alex opened it, and Jane, perplexed, watched utter relief suffuse his expression.

'Who is it from?'

Alex looked up. 'Anthony.'

'What does he say?'

'He didn't leave yesterday after all.'

And Alex's relief not only made sense but it tore at her heart. What was going on? Why was Lascelles so essential to Alex?

Alex thrust back his chair. 'I have business to attend to, and then I'm going out. I shall see you later.'

No words of endearment, no teasing smile, just a stern-faced near-stranger who banged the door behind him. When he went out, would it be to see Lascelles?

Tears bubbled close to the surface.

If only I hadn't nagged him about Clystfield. If he does visit Lascelles, I have no one to blame but myself!

But it was not long before she realised she was doing what she always did—blaming herself when it was Alex who was being unreasonable, laying down the law without explanation. After a short while, she gathered herself together and rose from the table, determined not to allow the matter to rest there. Alfred, their new footman, was in the hall, waiting to clear the breakfast dishes.

'Did you see where His Lordship went, Alfred?'

'No, milady. But he did speak to Mrs Kent…' he pointed to where the housekeeper was talking to Sally on the stairs '…so she might know.'

The housekeeper looked around at her name.

'Mrs Kent, do you happen to know where His Lordship is, please?'

'He's gone out, my lady. I presumed to the stables. He asked me to put a letter in his business room, and then told me he's dining out tonight and not to expect him back till late.'

Jane's heart plummeted. He'd gone already? And he intended to dine out, without even informing her?

'Thank you.'

She marched to the business room. The letter must have

been the one from Lascelles, and she wanted to know exactly what that scoundrel had written.

She found the letter straight away and read it with an increasing sense of disbelief.

> *I am persuaded you need me more than ever, dear*
> *Alexander. You convinced me it is my duty as your*
> *friend to remain, at least until I can be of no further*
> *comfort in your hour of need.*
>
> *Come to Halsdon whenever you wish. Stay here as*
> *long as you need to. Come tonight to dine! We shall*
> *put the world to rights over a bottle of that claret*
> *you enjoy so much.*
> *Your loyal friend and confidant,*
> *Anthony Lascelles*

Confidant!

Fury raged through her as she stalked from the business room, swung her cloak around her shoulders and strode down to the stables, driven by the urge to follow Alex and challenge him. Except…she knew his stubbornness. Knew the more she reasoned with him, or badgered him…*whatever* tactic she might try to bring him to his senses…he would resist her.

And wasn't that exactly why he had gone to Lascelles now? Her nagging had driven him from her. Her anger seeped away and her shoulders slumped. What was she to do? Going along with whatever Alex decreed might satisfy him, but what if that made *her* unhappy? Yet standing up for herself merely widened the rift between them. If only he would listen—she was worn out with trying to get through to him.

She spent time petting Pearl, feeding her with slices of carrot she found in the feed store, at a loss to know what else to do with herself. Frost was gone, so Alex had definitely left Foxbourne. If he'd already gone to Halsdon, he would be all day and evening with that evil so-and-so, even though she'd told him what he'd done to Mist.

She wandered outside, one slice of carrot left, which she'd saved for Nelson who no longer attacked the men now he was turned out in a small paddock with an open-sided shelter rather than confined in a stall.

Jane tried everything to coax the horse to her, but he merely stared at her from the far fence. She let herself in the gate and approached him slowly, the carrot on her outstretched palm, but paused about ten feet from the horse, sensing he was about to run off.

'You are as difficult and prickly as your master,' she muttered, before walking back to the gate in defeat.

As she reached for the latch, she felt something stir her hair. She stilled, holding her breath. Then whiskers tickled her cheek, and a quiet snort confirmed Nelson had followed her. Remembering how Alex had handled the stallion, she didn't look at him.

'Good boy...you want to be friends, don't you, but you can't quite trust me yet.'

She put the carrot on her palm and held it in front of her. Nelson stretched his head over her shoulder, and whiffled at the carrot, before taking it gently between his lips. The crunch in her ear was loud, and pleasure filled her as she stroked his velvety nose. She let herself out of the gate before she faced Nelson. He moved away, but she didn't mind. He'd trusted her, and she felt a huge sense of achievement.

She shivered. The wind had picked up, sneaking around corners in eddies, and fingering its way through gaps in buildings and clothing alike, so she started back to the house, following the line of the fence. Nelson, still in the paddock, kept pace with her. Of a sudden, Jane halted, a blinding truth whirling through her brain.

All this time trying to persuade Alex to trust her and all she had succeeded in doing was to drive him away, straight to Lascelles. *That* was why he had gone this morning. Not because he desperately wanted to see Lascelles, but because he felt cornered. By *her*.

She shivered again, huddling in her cloak, wondering what to do. Kent had been muttering about winter setting in early and, if he was right, the weather would soon deny them any choice in the matter of travelling down to Devon.

It seemed unlikely they would go. Not now. Unless...

Jane headed back to the stables, where earlier she had heard the murmur of the grooms' voices from the tack room. Silence fell when she entered, and the three occupants stopped polishing tack and stood.

'Lilley, might I have a word, please?'

He followed Jane outside.

'Did His Lordship order the carriage to be prepared?'

'No, milady.'

She'd known his words were bravado. He never thought for one minute she would go without him.

Well, we shall see what you make of this, Lord Alexander Beauchamp.

Jane sighed theatrically, for Lilley's benefit. 'I *knew* he would forget! Have it ready at noon, if you please. I am going down to Lord Avon's estate. His Lordship will follow on later.'

Doubt chased disapproval across Lilley's craggy features. 'You're travelling alone, milady? I'm not—'

'It is all arranged, Lilley. Peg and Alfred will accompany me, so you need not fear for either propriety or for my safety.'

'Very good, milady.'

Jane headed back to the house, new purpose in her step. She didn't want to be apart from Alex, especially when he was so very troubled, but maybe the shock of her leaving would bring him to his senses. It was a gamble, but *he* had told her go. He had given her his blessing, so he couldn't accuse her of leaving him or disobeying him.

But would he follow her?

That was the gamble. But, even if he didn't, at least it would remind him she would not stay meekly at home, waiting for him to decide when—or if—he could trust his own wife.

Chapter Twenty

It was midnight when Alex returned to Foxbourne Manor. The wind had settled into a steady, biting blast from the east, and ragged clouds blew hurriedly across the moon, bathing the landscape alternately in a ghostly glow and a blanket of purple shadows. He really shouldn't have stayed at Halsdon all this time, but every time he had made a move to leave, Anthony had lured him into just one more drink…one more game of billiards…one more hand of cards.

One more story about his mother. His parents. The past.

He should have been stronger. More resolute. Jane would be… His stomach stirred uneasily as he recalled their last conversation. He had slammed out of the house. Again. And it had been easier to stay in the warm and put off facing his wife who would be, quite rightly, angry. And hurt.

He would make it up to her. Somehow.

He shivered as he slid from Frost's back and led him to his stall. Pat, one of the grooms, emerged from the tack room at the end of the row of stalls, yawning and rubbing his eyes, prodding Alex into an apology.

'Sorry to keep you up, Pat. I can see to Frost. You get off to bed.'

'No, milord. I'll do it. Mr Lilley left *me* in charge, so he did.'

'Well, you must catch up with your sleep in the morning.' Alex handed Frost's reins to Pat. 'If Lilley complains you're late tell him it was an order from me.'

Pat grinned. 'Thank you, milord, but I meant he left me in charge until he gets back. He thought you'd want him to drive milady to Devonshire himself, to protect her. Him and Nobby have both gone, sir, and taken the blunderbuss with them, too.'

Alex stilled. Then pivoted slowly to face the groom, his mind whirring as he worked out what conversation they were having. Surely…his brain dredged up that last conversation with Jane.

'But I *wish to go.'*

'Then go, if it's so important to you. Go with my blessing.'

And she'd done it! She'd taken him at his word and gone to Dominic's without a thought for him, and that he might need her. How could she *do* that to him?

'I am pleased he acted so responsibly.'

His voice remained level. Unconcerned. He wouldn't have the staff thinking he'd been unaware his wife was at this very minute *en route* to Devonshire, despite knowing he didn't wish to go. She would be staying in inns. Alone. That Lilley would take care to stop at only respectable establishments was immaterial. A lady should not travel without a male escort and Jane knew it. What the *hell* did she think she was playing at?

'I trust Her Ladyship got away on time?'

Pat was busy unsaddling Frost. 'Indeed, milord. They left about noon.'

'They?'

For one dreadful instant jealousy stabbed at Alex, even

though he knew damned well Jane would not go away
with another man.

'Her maid, sir, and that new footman.'

Peg and Alfred. At least she had sense enough to make
sure she had some sort of escort. But it wasn't him. Her
husband.

How could she leave me like this?

But you told her to go! With your blessing!

Alex shook his own words from his head. He didn't
want reasoned argument. His emotions tumbled and
churned as he abruptly bid Pat goodnight and strode up
to the house.

He stayed up half the night drinking, then slept in the
chair, where Drabble found him in the morning. Yesterday's events soon burst upon him but rather than feel sorry
for himself, as he had last night, he was angry. How dare
she defy him? He thrust aside that same voice which reminded him he had *told* her to go. She must have known
he'd said that in the heat of the moment. She must have
known he hadn't meant for her to go.

Follow her.

No! He would not go running after Jane the minute she
jerked on his leash. She'd no doubt done this believing he
would meekly follow but she would learn he was not so
easily manipulated.

His spirits dived further as he recalled the memory that
had triggered their argument. He'd not given a thought to
his father—he had been consumed with Jane leaving. But
the new facts of his life were unchanged, and he could no
more face any of his family today than he could yesterday.

He distracted himself all day with work. She wouldn't
be gone long. She would be back before Christmas, which

was only three weeks away. Although…he'd checked, and she'd taken all those Christmas gifts she'd made. But, no… she was making a point, that was all. And she wouldn't stay away for good—Pearl was still here, as was Mist. She would never leave them behind. Besides, Dominic wouldn't help her. They were brothers. Dominic had always had Alex's back, and he would do so this time.

His brave face lasted all that day, and the next. It lasted until he sat down to his solitary dinner on the second evening. He couldn't sustain his anger…all he could feel was pity. For himself. And that was pathetic. But there was guilt, too, that he had hurt Jane. She didn't deserve the way he had treated her…but she didn't understand what an impossible position he was in.

He stared down at his plate, and pushed the food around with his fork. What did he want?

Jane.

The answer came loud and clear as he realised, with a jolt, that he loved her. *Really* loved her. The man who thought he could never love anyone, loved his wife. To distraction. And the idea of following her, persuading her to come home, no longer seemed weak. It was a strong man who could admit when he was in the wrong. How many times had he heard his father say those words? He shuddered. And how long would it be before the thought of his father ceased to make him feel physically ill?

His appetite deserted him, and he rose from the table. He would go to bed early, and set off for Devonshire as soon as it was first light. As he left the dining room, Kent was on his way in, carrying a letter. Alex almost snatched it from him, hope blooming. But one glimpse at the writing on the outside revealed Anthony Lascelles' heavy black script.

'Mr Lascelles's man awaits a reply, milord.'

Alex broke the seal.

My dear Alexander,
I am concerned. I have not seen you for two days
now, and I seek confirmation that you have not sunk
in the doldrums after the shock of such a discovery.
You will note that I have not committed any facts to
this missive, in case the wrong eyes should see it!
I cannot bring myself to call in person after my
unfortunate misunderstanding with Jane but do, I
beg of you, write to assure me you are in good health
in both mind and body, or I shall have to overcome
my reluctance to further upset your good lady and
call at Foxbourne to set my mind at rest.
Your loyal cousin and friend,
Anthony Lascelles

Alex sighed. He should have foreseen this, but he had been so busy being busy, to prevent himself fretting over Jane, that he had not given Anthony a thought.

'Tell his man to wait for a reply.'

He sat at his desk. How much to reveal? Anthony knew about Dominic's invitation and that Alex's refusal had caused an argument with Jane. Anthony, he recalled, had tried to persuade Alex to go to Devonshire, to confront his father. At least Anthony would be pleased he was going, even if he had no intention of going anywhere near the Abbey and his father.

He dipped his pen into the inkwell and began to write.

'My lord?'

It was the following morning. Alex looked up from his plate of congealed eggs. The coming few days would be fraught. If only he could whisk Jane away from Clystfield without seeing or speaking to anyone else. If only… It was an impossible wish. He had the three days it would take him to travel to Clystfield to decide exactly what to say to Jane. And to his brother. And hadn't Jane said Olivia would be there, too? That would make his task even trickier. Olivia was never backward in challenging any member of the family if she scented trouble, and Alex had made a career out of being troubled.

'My lord?'

'Sorry, Kent. I was wool-gathering. What is it?'

'Mr Lascelles is here, milord.'

'*This* early?' Alex waved at his breakfast, and stood up. 'I've had enough, Kent. It can be cleared away. Thank you.'

Drabble was upstairs, packing for Alex's trip—he planned to leave within half an hour. Jane had the carriage, so Alex must drive his curricle to High Wycombe first, where he could hire a post-chaise. That would be an unwelcome delay—now he'd decided to follow Jane, he just wanted to get on with it.

And now, another delay.

'He awaits you in the hall, milord.'

Anthony—his greatcoat buttoned up, a muffler around his neck, gloves on, and his beaver hat in his hand—smiled when he saw Alex.

'Good morning, Alexander! It is perishing cold this morning, so I have provided hot bricks for the journey. My carriage is outside—if we set off now, we might make it as far as Andover by this evening. I know how eager you must be to settle your differences with dear Jane.'

'I… *We*?'

'Oh, do not think I shall interfere, dear boy, but I simply cannot bear the thought of you travelling such a distance alone. Not with such distressing thoughts to plague you. What kind of a friend would I be to abandon you to such a melancholy fate? I shall accompany you to Devonshire and then I shall return in my carriage while you and Jane will have your own carriage for transport home. She will never know I was there, you have my word.'

Alex ignored the warning in his head. He was exhausted. All he wanted was to see Jane. To talk to her. To bring her home. He had no energy to even think about anything else, let alone talk Anthony out of travelling with him—he was a difficult man to shake once he had set his sights on something. Besides...this would save him a good hour and a half now he didn't need to go to High Wycombe first, and Anthony was right. Left to his own devices, Alex would only brood all the way to Clystfield. At least Anthony would divert him from fretting endlessly over the whole sorry mess of his life.

Stuck in one another's company for three days on that interminable journey, however, Alex began to see Anthony Lascelles in a different light. He'd been tolerable—even entertaining—in small doses but his purpose in accompanying Alex soon became apparent. He was oblivious to Alex's reluctance to discuss his father as he dripped poisonous comments about him into the silence and tried everything to convince Alex to go to the Abbey and confront his father.

'Do you not feel it is your duty to expose your mother's killer?'

'How can you live with yourself if you allow him to get away with your mother's murder?'

'Why don't we travel on to the Abbey first? Once you have charged your father with the truth you will feel so much better, my boy...you will be able to rekindle your marriage with a clear conscience.'

Alex exploded at that. 'A clear conscience? What utter rot. I hid away while he strangled my mother and then denied the truth for eighteen years. How can my conscience ever be clear?'

'But my dear, dear Alexander…how can you possibly have prevented such a tragedy when you were only seven years old? And who's to say you didn't remember, in the beginning, and that your father convinced you of your mistake? He is an arch manipulator. What he wants is what he gets!'

A family trait, thought Alex as he eyed Anthony. *And one you share.*

And doubts slowly crept in about any similarities in character between his father and Anthony. The latter was… sly. He manoeuvred behind the scenes, manipulating people into doing his bidding. *Tricking* them.

Just as Jane warned you!

His father, though. He was a powerful duke…yes, he manipulated people and situations when he felt it justified, but he was never sly.

The closer they got to Devonshire, the more dread weighed on Alex until he was ready to scream. Or to punch someone. Preferably Anthony.

The only way he found peace was to feign sleep. After a few attempts at conversation, Anthony would lapse into silence, leaving Alex to silently plan what to say to Jane. If he wanted her to forgive him, and to believe he loved her, did he have any choice other than to tell her the truth regardless of the consequences?

Was his marriage worth that much to him?

He concluded it was.

The carriage pulled up at an inn a couple of miles from Dominic's estate at six o'clock on the third evening. Although desperate to see Jane, Alex felt grubby and ex-

hausted and in no fit state to convincingly persuade his
wife of his love for her.

*One more night. That's all. Then I will see her, and we
can put this behind us.*

Except they could never properly put it behind them,
not now he had decided his only option was to tell Jane
the brutal truth.

Another very good reason to delay speaking to her until
the morning. It would give him one more sleepless night
to plan what he would say. The only positive result of his
recent sleepless nights was that, gradually, he'd had no
need to feign sleep in the carriage. And Anthony seemed
to have finally accepted Alex would not confront his father, lapsing into a sullen silence on the final day of travel.
Alex couldn't wait for this evening to be over. He didn't
care if he never spoke to Anthony again, and he didn't
want to hear any more tales of his mother.

When Alex returned downstairs after washing, and
changing his clothes, it was clear from the slurring of his
words that Lascelles had been drinking in the taproom
the entire time.

They were served roast beef and game pie, which they
washed down with a full-bodied red wine, following which
they settled in a quiet parlour with a bottle of port. Alex
was determined to keep this final evening civil, conscious
that Anthony *had* provided the transport even though his
true purpose in accompanying Alex had nothing to do
with Alex's well-being and everything to do with causing
trouble for Alex's father.

'Drink up, m'boy.' Anthony filled Alex's glass, slop-
ping some on to the table. 'You look like a man in need of
fort…forti…fortification.'

Alex raised his glass. 'To the end of our journey.'

'What is your plan?' Anthony eyed Alex over the rim

of his glass, his black gaze slightly bleary. 'How shall you win back the fair Jane? What can you possibly say to help her understand the turmoil you were in?'

Alex shrugged. That was between him and Jane. 'I haven't planned it. I shall speak from the heart.'

He sipped his port. Anthony drained his glass, and re-filled it.

'You must tell her the truth,' he said.

Alex frowned. 'What truth?'

'About your father, of course.'

Alex said nothing.

'You will never find peace unless you do, my boy. Even if you fear to confront your father, you must at least re-veal the truth of your mother's death. Your brother Avon, too—he deserves to know. And your sister.'

How could he tell Dominic and Olivia? But, again, how could he not? Their mother was still their mother, no mat-ter how little she had cared for her children. But how could he burden them with the knowledge of their father's part in it? It was an impossible dilemma…never had he felt so conflicted as Lascelles droned on, topping up their glasses time after time.

'Poor Margaret. So vivacious…such a beautiful lady. What a tragic waste—she always looked so vital in yellow, my boy…pretty as a picture… She always had plenty of beaux swarming around her, you know, even after she wed your father.' His face blazed with sudden fury. 'She only married him for the title. All she cared for was the status… being the duchess. But later, when I knew her again…oh, then…' He sighed, his dark eyes distant. 'She tired quickly of the country life…she sobbed in my arms many times…' He sighed again. 'Such a beauty…skin like silk.'

'*What* did you say?' Alex leapt up, grabbing Lascelles' lapels and hauling him upright. Rage scorched through him, erupting like a volcano, shooting sparks, hot swathes of molten anger flowing from him. '*You* were her lover? You utter bastard! She was *my mother*.'

His fist landed square on Lascelles' nose. The older man staggered back, stumbling over his chair, landing hard on the floor. Alex followed, fists clenched, murder in his heart. All this time Lascelles had exuded sympathy…told Alex to treat him as a father…

Father! Sick anger churned his gut. He loomed over Lascelles, his lips drawn back in a snarl.

'When?'

That one question consumed him. Had Lascelles told the truth about going overseas after Mother and Father married, or could Lascelles be Alex's father? Is that why he'd always distrusted the Duke? Was it an inherited trait? The air whooshed from his lungs as he prayed it was not true. He hauled a moaning Lascelles up, thrusting his face close to the other man's.

'I asked you *when*, you bastard! When were you my mother's lover?'

Those dark eyes—still, somehow, mocking—narrowed.

'Never fear, m'boy. Your father made good and sure he sired every one of her children. But, once the girl was born, Margaret made certain she didn't have any more.' He frowned then. 'I was not her only lover—she swore she was true to me, but she lied. She might have had the title of duchess, but your mother was still a common slut!'

The roar began deep, deep inside Alex's chest and it echoed around the room as his fury erupted. He drew his fist back, but came to his senses when a prick to his throat announced Lascelles had a knife. Alex gritted his teeth, slowly releasing the other man's lapels.

'Sensible boy.'

Lascelles stepped back and then, before Alex realised

his intention, he upended the table, knocking Alex to the floor. When he scrambled to his feet, Lascelles had gone.

He was drained. His head hurt and his heart…his heart bled. And yet…the rumours about his mother—the rumours she had taken lovers—were not new. But having it confirmed like this—*now*—made the case against his father even blacker. Bleaker. Despair wrenched Alex's heart but it was the fact he'd misjudged everything that made him truly sick. He'd trusted his mother's former lover with the truth about his father rather than confide in his own wife. How had he been so stupid? He threw himself into an armchair and sank his head in his hands. But the truth still remained of that vision of his father with his hands around his mother's throat.

He gazed dully at the bracket clock on the mantel. Eight o'clock. He was only two miles from Clystfield. He needed to see Jane. He *needed* Jane. Tonight. He sprang out of the chair and thundered up the stairs. A quick glance into Lascelles' bedchamber confirmed he'd already gone. That was unimportant now. He could wait…and yet, what could Alex do about something that had happened so long ago? Beating Lascelles to a pulp wouldn't change the facts.

Downstairs, he rousted out an ostler and paid him handsomely to drive him to Clystfield in the inn's gig.

Chapter Twenty-One

She had only been at Clystfield Court two days but Jane was already weary of pretending Alex had been delayed by business; weary of deflecting probing questions about her absent husband; weary of smiling in the face of sympathetic glances cast in her direction. It was clear they suspected all was not well, and she longed to confide in them—after all, who knew Alex better than Dominic and Olivia? But she could not bring herself to tell them why she was there on her own because she didn't understand it fully herself.

Had it just been a moment of pique? An *'I'll show him'* moment? She was hurt he wouldn't confide in her, but was that *really* bad enough for her to leave without a word of explanation? She was supposed to love him, and yet her leaving would make whatever trauma he was suffering worse, not better. But as soon as she almost persuaded herself that her running off was unpardonable, the other side of the argument would rear its head—was the problem that plagued Alex genuinely so terrible he couldn't bring himself to talk to her about it? Or was this simply the same old stubborn, independent Alex who kept everyone who cared about him at arm's length?

The lengthy journey, and the two days at Clystfield with no word from Alex, had taken their toll on her and her reflection in the mirror confirmed the truth of Olivia's bald announcement that she looked worn to a frazzle. During the day it was easier to keep her thoughts from straying too often to her infuriating spouse, and from fretting about what he was hiding from her. She filled the hours with playing with Julius and Daisy who, although twins, were not identical, and sharing Liberty's excitement at being with child. There was always someone around to chat to, drowning out the arguments raging inside her head. But at night sleep proved elusive as she grappled in vain to find a solution to this impasse.

What if he did not follow her? Would she return, with her pride battered and bruised? Or would she...*could* she...stay strong? She wasn't oblivious to the fact that no one of her acquaintance—and certainly not Papa and her stepmother—would shelter a wife from her husband if he wanted her to return. Apart from, perhaps, the Duke. *He* might very well find a solution for her, but she knew that once he became involved, Alex would be lost to her.

Her throat thickened at that thought.

Alex was all she had ever wanted. But why did he have to be so complicated?

You knew what he was like before you wed him.

Yes, but I—

Would you rather be married to Pikeford?

No, but—

Be grateful for what you've got. So what if it isn't perfect. Life rarely is.

But it was *almost perfect! I just want to understand what went wrong!*

She was *utterly* weary.

That evening after dinner, Jane sat at the pianoforte while the others gathered around a card table but they had barely settled into their game of whist when a thunderous knocking at the front door interrupted them. Romeo, who had been dozing in front of the fire, shot to his feet, barking frenziedly. Jane's fingers stilled, her heart thudding, as Dominic strode from the room, Romeo dashing ahead of him.

'I do hope there is nothing amiss.' Liberty's hand rested protectively on her gently rounded belly.

Voices sounded in the hall—among them a voice that raised Jane's hopes as well as her hackles. Alex. And all her fragmented worries and arguments clarified, as if by magic.

Yes, she loved Alex, but he needn't think she would meekly return home simply because she was married to him. It was time for him to prove he had followed her for the right reasons, and not merely because she was his wife.

I must remain resolute if I want him to respect me and not take me for granted.

Liberty had recognised the voice, too, and she moved to stand behind Jane. She squeezed her shoulder.

'Know that we will stand by you, Jane.'

Jane reached up to pat Liberty's hand, grateful for her quiet support. They waited in silence as the low murmur of voices filtered into the room. Jane had heard Dominic pacifying Alex enough times over the years to imagine what was being said. She waited, her heart beating hard in her chest, her mouth dry. Then he came in, windblown and wild-eyed, and she couldn't stop herself.

'Alex!' She ran to him, taking the hands that reached for her. 'You look…' She stopped, realising the absurdity of anything she might say at this point.

You look distraught?

Of course, he would answer. *My wife left me.*

You look desperate?

The same answer.

You look angry.

The same.

His tiger eyes bore into hers as he moistened his lips. And she saw he was nervous, too, but she dredged up that resolve and hardened her heart. If she followed her usual instinct to soothe and to forgive, nothing would change. She wanted the early closeness of their marriage back but, more importantly, she needed to understand what had changed. And why.

But she knew Alex wouldn't easily share his innermost feelings or relinquish his secrets.

She slid her hands from his. 'You followed me. Why?'

'I missed you.'

She stayed silent, holding his gaze.

'I apologise for my behaviour.'

She turned aside, maintaining her blank expression as her heart sank. Same old Alex. An apology…words…it was too easy for them to be meaningless.

Olivia jumped up from the card table. 'I *knew* there was more to this than you told us, Jane.'

Hugo's arm shot out to restrain his wife. He rose, too, wrapping his arm around Olivia's waist and hugging her into his side.

'We'll leave you two to talk.'

'Hugo—'

'This is not our business, Trouble. Let us leave Alex and Jane to talk.'

Olivia bit her lip. 'Oh, very well. But if we don't see you again this evening, please note I expect you to be here in the morning, Alexander, so no slipping away at dead of night.'

'I'm going nowhere,' Alex said.

Fingers of desire stroked down Jane's spine at the resolve in his voice.

'Berty…' Dominic extended his hand to his wife.

Liberty went to him, but she hesitated as she passed Jane, her deep blue gaze questioning. Jane nodded, flicking her a reassuring smile, and Liberty and Dominic followed the other two from the room, closing the door behind them.

Alex immediately began to pace. Jane watched him a few moments before crossing to sit on the sofa, once more reining in that urge to go to him, to comfort him—such a natural part of her character, especially when it came to Alex. But she did help ease the way into the conversation they must have.

'Mayhap *I* should apologise to *you*?'

'What?'

He sat beside her, tried to gather her hands in his, but she pulled them away, swivelling to face him.

'You owe me no apology, Janey.' His brow furrowed as his tiger eyes searched her face. 'I don't blame you for coming here.'

'I didn't mean that. What I mean is… I am forced to wonder if, in trying to help you, I contributed to this…' she lifted her hands in a hopeless gesture '…this situation. You've been pushing me away, Alex. I could see the more I tried to persuade you to talk to me, the faster you retreated, and I know you felt unfairly harried. But I don't wish to be a wife who meekly accepts her husband's behaviour and can never challenge him. Especially when she is convinced he's in pain.

'I've had time to think in the days since I left. I am so afraid you will never allow anyone close enough to truly help you and I am *exhausted*. I cannot go on supporting you when you clearly do not trust me with what is troubling you.'

Alex leaned forward, propping his elbows on his knees, and thrust his fingers through his hair.

'I wanted to tell you the truth… I *want* to. But it's more complicated than you realise. What I know…it doesn't affect me alone.' He hauled in a tortured breath. 'But…you are right. We should have no secrets between us. I will tell you the truth.'

At last.

'Then tell me. *All* of it. Please, Alex. Help me understand what changed. I cannot bear the thought of going home with you, only for all this to start up all over again.'

'I will.' Alex scrubbed his hands over his face. 'I've been an utter fool, Janey. I thought I could cope with it myself. I was wrong.' He surged to his feet and again paced the room. 'How *stupid* can one man be?' The words spat out. 'I thought I was protecting you…protecting my family.'

'Tell me!'

Her nerves buzzed with the need to do something…to help…but how could she help when she still had no clue what he was talking about? This, surely, had to be about more than him finding his mother's body. Alex flung himself on to the sofa again.

'When the nightmares first returned at the Abbey, all I could recall was the beginning. They're always the same: I hide from our tutor, Mr Brockley, and then I am outside playing. And I find myself near the old summer house and I walk towards it. And then I would wake up.' He dragged in a deep breath. 'Then I realised that, in my dreams, my mother was walking by my side. And I thought it couldn't possibly be right because I knew what really happened was that her d-dead body was w-wait—' His voice thickened, and he stumbled over the words. He scrubbed his hands over his face again, clearing his throat. 'Was waiting for me in the summer house.'

He looked at her, his eyes clouded with pain. As a tear fell, she reached to brush it away.

'I thought my dreams weren't real. I thought they'd become confused with the image of Pikeford attacking you. I thought I knew what happened when my mother died, because everyone had told me. But…but…but…' He shook his head. 'I never wanted to remember what really happened that day, Janey. I convinced myself it was the dread of what was inside the summer house that shaped my nightmares.'

His attempt at a smile wobbled. He dashed one hand across his eyes, but he didn't even try to conceal his tears from her. Her heart opened, like a flower to the sun, and she moved closer, placing her hand on his thigh. Offering comfort.

'Then images began to flash into my mind. When I was awake.' He paused, swallowing audibly.

'She wore a yellow gown…smelled of roses… I remember his boots, moving in step with her slippers… He pushed her to the floor. I didn't understand what was happening at the time but I know now. He forced himself on her and, when she pleaded with him to stop, he put his hands around her neck…squeezing until she was still. I… I thought he would see me. He only had to turn his head, and I would see his face…his eyes…'

He shuddered, and buried his face in his hands as huge sobs ripped from him. Jane cradled him close, stroking his hair, until the storm of emotion passed, his words echoing through her mind. The yellow gown and the roses… Alex's extreme reactions began to make sense.

'You have kept that dreadful truth to yourself all these weeks? *Why*, Alex? Why could you not tell me? I could have helped—'

She fell silent as he turned haggard features in her direction, his red-rimmed eyes dull. She gasped as the full impact of his words hit her.

'But…Alex…that must mean…'

'I was there, Janey. I saw him kill her.'

She struggled to draw breath. 'Who?'

He buried his face in his hands yet again and Jane put her arms around him…it was like hugging a tree, he was so unyielding.

'Tell me. Let it out. It will feel better.'

He gulped—half laugh, half sob. 'That's what Zach said. He was wrong. I told Lascelles, but the relief was fleeting.'

A shard of pain stabbed Jane's heart. He'd told Anthony Lascelles the truth, but he'd been unable to trust her? She thrust down the hurt and the sense of betrayal to deal with later. At this moment, Alex was more important.

'Tell me. Come on, Alex. How bad—?'

'It was Father!'

Jane gasped. 'Your—? *No!* Alex…that *cannot* be true.'

'It is. My father killed my mother and I did nothing to stop him. And now…I don't know what to *do*, Janey. How can things ever be right, ever again?'

Sobs shuddered through him again. Jane held him, stroking his hair, struggling to assimilate what he'd told her. When he finally quieted, she said, 'I cannot believe you have kept this buried all this time.'

'What choice did I have? I wanted to protect you from having to face the others, and having to keep it secret. But now—somehow—you will have to manage.'

'Keep it *secret*? Alex! You cannot mean it. You must tell the others. Between you…between all of us…we will work out what to do.' She framed his face, searching his eyes. 'Are you absolutely certain it is a true memory, and not a nightmare come to haunt your waking hours?'

He shook his head. 'No. I wish I could believe that—it's what I told myself when I first saw him. But then…that day we argued about coming here… I saw him as clear as I see you now. They were *his* hands around her neck.'

Jane frowned. That was the day Lascelles had hurt Mist. She had told Alex about that, before their argument. Before he had run off. 'And you still went to Lascelles and talked to *him* rather than to me?'

'I regret that now, but I did it to protect you, and to protect my family. I wouldn't wish this knowledge on my worst enemy, let alone you. But…now you do know. And it is to stay between us, Jane.'

Jane leapt to her feet. 'No.'

Alex stared up at her. 'No?'

'We cannot keep this…this *abomination* to ourselves. If it *was* your father…he *killed* another person. He broke the law. We cannot keep that secret.

'Look what trouble you've caused already with your secrets and your conviction that you alone know what is best for everyone,' she added, unable to hide her bitterness. 'You have hurt me; you have shattered *my* trust in *you*, by choosing to confide in a man like Anthony Lascelles rather than in me, when I've *always* been your loyal friend, and—in choosing him over me—you have spoiled our marriage after we were so happy in the beginning…'

She paused, somewhat breathless after her tirade. She fought her burning need to try to resolve their personal differences here and now, guiltily aware this was the wrong time. First they must work out how to deal with this dreadful revelation about the Duke, and she must help Alex and the others find a solution.

'It will not do to keep this secret, Alex. You cannot make decisions of this magnitude on behalf of your entire family. At the very least you need to talk to Dominic.'

Alex slumped back, his brow furrowed. Jane waited. Finally, he pushed himself to his feet.

'Very well. If that is what it will take to make things right between us, we will talk to the others. I only hope you are right and this doesn't rip my entire family to shreds.' He grabbed Jane's hand and towed her to the door. 'Where is my brother?' he asked a passing maid.

The maid curtsied. 'I've just served the tea tray in the parlour, milord.'

Alex strode along the hall, Jane stumbling in his wake, until he slammed to a halt about six feet from the closed parlour door.

'I cannot,' he choked out. 'I don't know what to say... or how to say it.'

Jane placed her hand on his chest, feeling his heart thudding against her palm. 'You will find the words. And I will be there with you.'

He drew in a deep breath, squaring his shoulders, and she glimpsed the old Alex...the lad full of swagger no matter what trouble he was in. The Alex who never allowed doubt or fear to slow him down. The Alex who lived live to the full and to hell with the consequences. He'd changed as he had matured, but that same defiant, cocksure lad was still in there somewhere. It was then she knew he would cope with this, as he had coped with so much throughout his life.

Alex thrust the door open and stepped through it. Jane slipped past him to sit at the back of the room as the murmur of voices died away.

'I have something to tell you.'

Alex repeated his tale, punctuated by gasps of horror and vehement denial from his listeners, but Jane only half listened, her thoughts trapped in ever-circling questions about their future.

Alex had finally confided in her but only, in the end, because he'd been forced into it. She longed for the assurance that he saw her as more than just his wife. His possession. Even though, in law, that is what she was. She accepted she must return to Foxbourne—she had nowhere else to go, especially now with this news about the Duke—but she must stay strong and do so on her own terms.

A low cry jerked her from her thoughts. Olivia's head was bent into Hugo's chest, his arms around her trembling body. Liberty, eyes round with horror, appeared frozen in time. Dominic and Alex faced one another, nose to nose, fingers jabbing, Dominic's face dark with anger. They were so alike, especially in profile as they were now.

'You're wrong! Father would *never*…he's not that sort of man. When have you *ever* known him raise a hand to any of us? Never, that's when!'

Alex's chin jutted forth. 'I know what I saw. I couldn't make it up…the yellow dress, the wooden floor against my cheek. I *saw* it!'

Jane hated them arguing but she wasn't sorry she'd made Alex tell the others. He shouldn't carry this burden alone.

'But what reason could he have?' Dominic demanded. 'Why, Alex? Tell me. *Why* would he do it?'

'She had lovers. You've heard the rumours and innuendo, I know you have. Even Lascelles—'

'*Lascelles?* Anthony Lascelles? What the devil has he to do with this unholy mess?'

'He's back. Living at Halsdon Manor. He let it slip this evening—he was her lover! And he wasn't the only one!' Alex spun on his heel and marched across the room, murder in his eyes.

This evening? Jane's stomach lurched. Lascelles had come down to Devonshire with Alex? She'd thought…

hoped…Alex had come to save their marriage. Why would he bring Lascelles, knowing how she felt about the man?

'Who is Anthony Lascelles?' Liberty asked.

'He's my father's cousin and a slimy, evil scoundrel,' Olivia declared. 'I had no idea he was back in England. Does Papa know?'

'No.' Jane kept her attention on Alex, recognising the effort it was taking for him to pull himself together. 'He begged us not to tell any of the family… He said he wanted to meet your father in London, on neutral ground, in order to make his peace with him and your stepmother.'

'Hah! Make his peace. What a bouncer!' muttered Olivia, as Alex strode back to face Dominic again.

'*There* is your motive, Brother. Jealousy. Rage. He couldn't bear her playing him false. I *heard* him—"*I will never let you go!*"'

Jane started at Alex's words as they triggered a memory…she frowned, grasping for a thought that fluttered just beyond her reach. She put her hands over her ears to block out the raised voices, sifting through conversations about Alex's mother.

Someone… Aunt Cecily…what had she said? She surged to her feet. 'Alex!'

Five pairs of eyes locked on to her.

'Alex!' Her breath came in short bursts as her brain scrambled to make sense of an idea that swirled and swooped. 'Aunt Cecily…she told me your mother had agreed to settle at the Abbey. That she had changed, and wanted to put her children first. So why would your father say that? She wasn't threatening to leave him…she was going to *stay*.'

Dominic frowned. 'She is right. Aunt Cecily told me the same after Liberty and I got married. You are wrong, Alex. That was no motive.'

'You've never told me that before! How do I know you're not making it up?'

'Why would I make it up? And when have *any* of us ever really talked about Mother and what happened? It's been a taboo subject for years.'

They were nose to nose again. Two brothers. So alike—typical Beauchamp features, like their father and their uncle—and yet poles apart in temperament. Jane glanced at Liberty. Saw her concern mirrored in Liberty's expression—what if this caused a rift between Dominic and Alex that could never be healed? Jane's stomach squirmed. It would be her fault, for insisting Alex told the others.

No. It's the Duke's fault. Not mine. He's the one who killed their mother, not me.

And yet, she still could barely credit it. Alex's father, a cold-blooded killer? Now, if he had been like Lascelles, she might believe…

Her breath seized.

'Lascelles!'

Alex and Dominic stopped in mid-argument at Jane's yell, and turned as one to gape at her, as did the other three. She gabbled out her idea in fits and starts, afraid to take her time, petrified they would shoot it down before she could properly explain. When she eventually paused for breath she saw the hope on all five faces in the room.

Chapter Twenty-Two

Alex hardly dared to hope it could be true. He was the first to respond to Jane's blurted out idea.

'So…let me get this straight…you think I could have mistaken Anthony Lascelles for my own father? And that it was Lascelles who killed our mother?'

'Yes. All the Beauchamps have the same features. I noticed the resemblance when I first met Lascelles, even though his hair is grey.'

'It was black when I first met him,' Alex replied, frowning. 'Like Father's. But I still can't believe I would mistake a complete stranger for my own father.'

Lascelles? Could it be? By his own admission he'd been her lover.

While Alex pondered, Liberty spoke. 'Maybe it was easier to mistake a stranger for your father than someone you already knew? I thought you were Alex when we first met, Dominic, even though now I cannot imagine how I came to make such a mistake. Do you remember?'

A slow smile stretched Dominic's lips. 'Oh, yes. I remember being harangued on my father's doorstep by a hoyden with an umbrella.'

Liberty's answering smile at that memory—that private moment shared by her and Dominic—tweaked something deep inside Alex. A longing for the same. With Jane. They'd had it at the start of their marriage, until he'd ruined it. As he seemed to ruin everything he touched. Eventually.

'You and Alex have different hair and different colour eyes but all I saw were those aristocratic features, and that hint of arrogance—'

'Arrogance?'

Liberty laughed at Dominic's mock outrage but quickly sobered. 'I am making a serious point, Dominic.'

'And you were an adult, Liberty.' Olivia pulled away from Hugo. 'Alex was a small boy. A *terrified* small boy trapped in a scary and dangerous situation. Alex…is it possible?'

Dear God, I hope so.

'I don't know. His eyes are very different to Father's, but I never saw them. Mostly, all I saw was a pair of boots. And when…when…' He gulped. He was a grown man. He shouldn't be afraid to say what he saw, even though he hadn't understood it at the time. 'When he raped and strangled her, he was in profile.'

'Luckily for you,' Dominic said. 'If you'd seen the colour of his eyes…'

Alex didn't want to think about what might have happened had the killer spotted him cowering under the chaise longue. He paced the room, thrusting his hand through his hair from time to time. He always thought more clearly when he was active, and the surge of hope he now experienced swept through the foggy tangled mess that had filled his brain for too long. How he wanted this to be true. To be finally free of that baffling mistrust that had dogged his relationship with his father since boyhood.

'If Aunt Cecily is right and Mother did intend to spend

more time at the Abbey, and with us…' He paused. 'She didn't send me back to old Brockley that day. I hid from him, and then sneaked outside, into the copse. She saw me, on her way to the lake.' He glanced around the room. 'She walked by the lake every day when she was home, and she always stopped to rest in the summer house. I thought she would send me back to lessons but, instead, sh-she said I could go with her.'

'You lucky devil!' Dominic said. 'I asked to go with her that day, too, but she sent *me* back to old Brockley. But… I think Aunt Cecily is right. She did seem different—I expected her to snap at me for asking, but she patted my cheek and said maybe we could go out later. She seemed happy, and it's the only time I can remember her showing any spontaneous affection for me. That was the last time I saw her.' His voice hitched. 'Carry on, Alex.'

'We collected all manner of things as we walked—fir cones and pebbles and sticks and leaves—but when we reached the summer house she wanted to read and so I settled down to play behind the chaise longue.' The thought then struck him. 'She wasn't *expecting* any one.'

'So,' said Dominic, 'we know it wasn't an assignation.'

'Lascelles said he learned of Mother's death when he was in America, but we only have his word for that.'

'I wouldn't believe a single word he ever said,' declared Olivia. 'I remember Rosalind was *really* scared of him, even before he snatched Susie. He would lie about anything if it suited his purpose.'

'That's true.' Alex took another turn around the room. 'This is all my fault. I should never have allowed myself to be taken in by him—he was always dripping poison about Father and encouraging my distrust. That didn't surprise me with what I knew of his past but now…how can I know if *anything* he said about Mother was true?'

'Do you believe he was her lover, Alex?' Dominic asked. 'That's surely the most relevant question. If he *was* her lover—and she renounced him to spend more time at home with us, as Aunt Cecily claimed—then that could easily provoke a man such as he into a rage. He could have gone to the Abbey to confront her.'

'Yes. I'm certain that's true...he never meant to tell me. He let it slip when he'd been drinking. He said—'

He stopped. His pulse hammered. Anger and disbelief churned his guts as his jaw clenched tight. He'd had him. He'd had his hands on him, and he'd allowed the slippery bastard to escape.

'Alex?' Jane touched his hand. 'What is it?'

'"*She always looked so vital in yellow.*" His words. Last night. I should've killed him there and then.'

He stared round at the incomprehension of the others, sick rage at his own incompetence battering his heart and his mind.

'You don't see it! But I should have realised it there and then. I never told him any details. The only way Lascelles could know Mother wore a yellow gown is if he saw her that day.'

A messenger was sent to Cheriton Abbey—a two-hour ride to the west of Clystfield Court—to warn the Duke that Lascelles was in the vicinity, and to announce the arrival of his three children, their spouses and his twin grand-children the next day.

None of them slept much that night. They paced. They talked. They planned. They occasionally dozed. But all of them were waiting for dawn and the chance to take action.

Jane and Liberty both went to bed at one point but, within a couple of hours, both were back in the drawing room with the others, unable to settle. Jane watched Alex.

His entire focus was on the need to find out exactly what had happened that day in the summer house; the need to find Lascelles; the need to talk to his father.

She recognised his preoccupation; understood it; tried hard not to care that he had no energy left to worry about their marriage, and about her. The threat from Lascelles was immediate. Their relationship could wait. But a small, selfish part of her—a part that, when she thought about it, made her squirm slightly with shame—wanted his full attention and longed for him to make *her* his priority. When he did come to sit by her on the sofa—ousting a grumpy Romeo, who was nestled between her and Liberty—it was only to say, 'Why do you not go back to bed? You cannot do anything here.'

And despite knowing he said it out of concern for her, it also felt as though she were being excluded: as though she wasn't fully a member of the family; as though her support was incidental. Much as she had felt in the last weeks of their marriage, since Lascelles' arrival.

'I cannot sleep, so I may as well be here as anywhere.' She stood up and crossed to the window where there was the faintest lightening in the eastern sky. Soon the servants—who had been sent to bed—would be up and about and, after breakfast, the Beauchamps would set out for Cheriton Abbey.

Alex came up behind her, cupped her upper arms and caressed them through her shawl, encouraging her to lean back into his body. Jane stiffened, resisting him. She couldn't help it.

'Janey?'

The pain in his voice raked her, but she couldn't shake her hurt over his betrayal. The fact he had confided in Lascelles and not her. She faced him, searching his shadowed expression, seeking... She looked away. It mattered not what she wanted from him...it still was no time to make demands. He needed to resolve this business with his father and Lascelles and she needed...*yearned*...to feel more secure in his feelings for her.

When she'd accepted his proposal she'd thought *her* love was enough for them both. She hadn't foreseen how painful that one-sided state would prove to be.

'Why did you bring Lascelles to Devonshire with you, Alex?'

'He invited himself along. He turned up with his carriage that morning and...' He shrugged. 'I was anxious to get going. By accepting his offer it saved me going to High Wycombe to hire a chaise-and-four.' He pivoted away, and paced across the room and back again. 'As it happens, it was fortunate. I might never have discovered the truth had he not let slip about his affair with Mother.'

Jane lowered her voice, not wishing the others to hear their conversation. 'But you knew my feelings about him, particularly after his cruelty to Mist. And yet you still confided in him. You still travelled with him. Are my opinions... my feelings...so very unimportant to you?'

Alex stiffened. 'Of course they're not,' he hissed. 'I came to take you home. I—I *missed* you, Janey. So much.' He thrust his hand through his hair. 'Look. I can barely think straight. You *have* to forgive me, sweet Janey. The alternative...' His brows snapped together. 'The alternative doesn't bear thinking about. I know I've been difficult to live with, sweetheart, but...please, can we just get to the Abbey and sort out this Lascelles business? I promise I'll make it up to you. It's not the time to discuss something as important as our marriage.'

She knew she would forgive him. How could she do

otherwise, when he was her husband and she still loved him? But that didn't mean she would give him an easy ride to her forgiveness. Not this time. Or how would he ever learn he couldn't always twist her around his little finger? But, at least he'd said their marriage was important, and she hugged his words to her heart.

'I know it's not the time to discuss this now, Alex, but please don't imagine you can conveniently forget this conversation, avoid the subject and slip back into the same relationship.'

'Darling Janey. I promise I—'

He fell silent when the door opened and a maid entered, and curtsied.

'Breakfast is served in the dining room,' she announced and, in the hustle and bustle of breaking their fast and preparing for departure, Alex never did finish that promise.

The first snow of winter had yet to fall, but every night brought a heavy frost, and the party set off straight after breakfast, hot bricks at their feet. Alex and Jane travelled with Dominic and Liberty, plus Romeo, while Hugo and Olivia were in their own carriage, accompanied by the twins, Julius and Daisy, and Ruth, their nursemaid.

As the carriage rocked over the frozen ruts of the local lanes, Liberty yawned, saying, 'I am so tired... I feel as though I could sleep for a week. I shall never understand why sleep can elude one all night and yet overcome one once morning arrives.'

The two men were sitting with their backs to the horses, leaving Jane and Liberty facing forwards. Alex caught Jane's eye, and flicked his eyes towards Dominic. She knew in an instant what he meant. Dominic's attention was on his wife, his concern clear in his silver-grey gaze.

'Dominic, why do you not swap places with me?' Jane

shifted until she perched on the edge of the bench. 'Liberty might be able to sleep if she can lean against you.'

'Oh, no! I wasn't hinting for you to move, Jane.'

'I know you weren't—you are far too unselfish. But I don't mind facing backwards, and you need to look after yourself. A nap will do you the world of good.'

Without further ado, Jane stood and Dominic, with a murmured, 'Thank you,' swapped places with her. Within moments, Liberty was settled into his arms and both their eyes were closed.

Alex huffed a laugh. 'We are all totally talked out, are we not?'

'So it would seem.' Jane gazed at the passing countryside, glittering with frost.

'Would you care to…?'

Jane turned to see Alex had shifted position, his arms out, offering to hold her. Uncertainty glimmered in his tawny gaze, and that was enough for her to smile, and to accept by shuffling close to him until she could lean into him, her head on his chest. She breathed in his spicy, musky, unique scent and a feeling of rightness settled over her. This was where she belonged. With Alex. But the air between them still needed to be cleared.

The jolting of the carriage lessened when they reached the toll road and, within minutes, Jane's eyes drifted shut.

'We're here.'

Jane had been awake several minutes prior to Alex's announcement, conscious of the increasing tension in the arms that held her, and of the quickening beat of his heart in her ear. The familiar frontage of Cheriton Abbey filled the window, and the only sound was of the stamp of the horses' feet and the jingle of their bits. The groom opened the door, and they all descended as the Duke himself appeared at the front door, Hector by his side. His tension was clear as he waited unsmilingly for the party to troop past him into the hallway.

'Where's Grantham, Papa?' Olivia broke the silence first. 'I'm sure none of us expected you to greet us personally.'

'I sent him to the kitchen to arrange hot drinks. The rest of the men are standing watch. Here and at the stables.' His silver-grey gaze swept his visitors and paused on the nursemaid. 'Ruth, take the twins up to the nursery, if you please. You will be taken care of up there. The rest of you…' Jane saw his gaze linger for a moment on Alex '… go to the drawing room. Your stepmother is there.'

The Duchess greeted all of them with a strained smile, and a kiss to the cheek. As soon as they were all seated the Duke crossed to the fireplace and rested one arm along the mantelshelf.

'Who will start?' His gaze again settled on Alex. 'You, Alexander? Do you care to tell me why you saw fit not to warn me Lascelles was back in England?'

A muscle ticked in Alex's jaw. 'He asked me not to. He *said* he wanted to make his peace with you both in person.'

'And now you doubt that?'

Alex shrugged, his cheeks a dull red, his lips thinned to invisibility.

Tell him!

Jane exchanged a glance with Olivia and saw her own frustration mirrored on her sister-in-law's face. Old habits… Alex had reverted to the same monosyllabic man he had ever been in his father's presence, despite what they now knew. Or thought they knew. She glanced at Dominic, who was watching his father and brother with a deep frown. Of a sudden, Alex leapt to his feet.

'I should like to talk to you alone, Father.' His gaze swept over the others. 'Please.'

The Duke's eyes narrowed, but he nodded curtly. 'Very well.'

The two men left the room, and a collective sigh whispered through the drawing room as the rest of them released their pent-up breath.

Chapter Twenty-Three

Alex strode ahead of his father to the study. He crossed to the window, gazing blindly out, as Father shut the door with a snap.

'What do you have to say to me that you couldn't say in front of our family?'

He turned to face the man who, his whole life, he had wanted to love unconditionally but who he had always mistrusted. And now he knew why. The others...they thought they'd worked it all out, and Alex *hoped* they were correct. But for him to *know* it—to once and for all eradicate that eighteen-year spell of mistrust and fear—he knew he must confront his father with what he remembered. Gauge his reaction. He wanted to believe absolutely, with no room for lingering doubt.

Ironically, he must do exactly what Lascelles had been badgering him to do ever since they left Buckinghamshire. He must confront his father.

And he couldn't do that in front of his stepmother or his brother and sister. Or in front of Jane—the wariness he saw at times in her lovely brown eyes when she looked at him had wrenched at his heart. She was right not to trust him yet... He must work hard to convince her of his love and to prove himself. And he would do so. But this must come first. It had to be a private conversation, and he could only pray the answer would be the one he wanted more than life itself.

'May we sit?'

Father nodded, and they sat either side of the fire blazing in the hearth. Alex's gut churned at what he must say.

'I would appreciate it if you will hear me out before you say anything.'

Again, Father nodded.

Alex talked for what felt like hours. At one point, Father rose and poured them both a brandy. Alex kept talking. About when his mother died, what he had believed, the nightmares after his visit to the Abbey and the attack on Jane. The horror when his true memories of that day began to emerge.

His father's silver-grey gaze fixed on him unwaveringly, his expression giving nothing away until Alex spoke of his memory of walking with his mother that day, to the summer house, and of settling down to play behind the chaise longue. Only then did his expression slip, shock gleaming in his eyes, before he masked his emotions again. But, when Alex related the manner of his mother's death, the colour leached from Father's face and he surged to his feet.

'Oh, God, no! *Alex...*'

His name tore from his father's lips. Alex willed himself to sit still. He studied his father's expression…interpreting the emotions that ebbed and flowed in that normally unreadable visage. Anguish. Concern. *Guilt.*

In his younger days, he would have leapt straight to the worst possible conclusion once he recognised that guilt. But…he took his time. And he saw that the guilt could be that of a father whose child had been through hell, the guilt of not being there to prevent the nightmare, the guilt of failure to protect not only his wife, but his son. The guilt flowed towards Alex. It was not directed inwards. There was no hint of shame or of fear that he had been found out.

'I thought it was you,' Alex said.

His father's dark brows snapped together in a frown. 'Me? Who did you think was me?'

'The man I saw.'

He had never seen his all-powerful, supremely confident father at such a loss for words. His jaw slack, he stared at Alex, utterly still.

'The *killer*? You truly thought I could kill *anyone*, let alone the mother of my children?'

Alex nodded. 'When I saw him again, in those visions. In profile. He looked like you.'

Father paced then, thrusting his hand through his hair in an achingly familiar gesture. He halted before him, staring down and Alex squirmed at the desolation in his eyes.

Desolation. Not guilt. Not fear. Hope climbed. He so wanted to believe, but he was almost afraid to…afraid to risk the anguish if that hope proved false.

'Me?' His father's voice rasped. 'Why did you say nothing all these years?'

'I told you. I didn't know. Not until I started having those visions.'

Father paced away again. 'It explains, I suppose, why you have always rebelled against me.' His back to Alex, Father stared out of the window. 'Deep inside you had that memory, even if you were never consciously aware of it.'

He turned slowly, capturing Alex's gaze. 'It was not me you saw, Alex. I swear to you, on the lives of every single one of my children. It was not me.'

Alex swallowed, trust and belief battling their way out of the bleak wasteland where his feelings for his father had been trapped for as long as he could remember.

'We discussed it last night and, between us, we think we have worked out the truth. We think it was Lascelles.'

'Lasc—'

Father swayed, and Alex leapt up, hurrying to his side to catch his arm, steadying him.

'I only ever saw her murderer in profile.' The words rushed from him. 'He has the Beauchamp features we all share, but he also had black hair, like you, and black shiny boots, and…when you came…when the gardeners fetched you…your boots…'

The horror and the fear rose up to claim him and, once more, he was that small boy, shaking with terror, his gaze fixed on his father's black, shiny boots. Alex reined in those emotions…*they* were the lies. He was a grown man now, and capable of sifting facts.

'I must have seen your boots and linked them to the killer's boots. As you said, deep inside, I must have always linked *you*, specifically, with what I saw.'

He was still clutching his father's arm, standing close. He closed his eyes, hauled in a deep breath. 'I am sorry for doubting you, Papa.'

He hadn't uttered that name in eighteen long, lonely years. Emotion rose to clog his throat. Father's arm jerked out of his grip at those words and, before Alex could open his eyes, he was enveloped in a hug.

'No! You have nothing to be sorry for, Alex.' Father choked his words out. 'The fault is mine. I see it now. But… back then…I was so sure I was right. I forbade anyone to discuss that day… I simply wanted us all to forget about it. Cecily…she warned me of the dangers of allowing you to bottle it up, but you didn't speak at all for almost a year and, once that had passed, I suppose we were accustomed to avoiding the subject.'

He stepped back, clasping Alex's shoulders, and his silver-grey gaze swept across Alex's face.

'It is I who must apologise to you.'

The mood at the Abbey was sombre. The entire Lascelles business had been picked over *ad nauseam* until they were all convinced he was the murderer. Alex, however—although awash with relief at his reconciliation with his father—remained unsettled, aware of his unfinished business with Jane. Her dismay at his behaviour mirrored his own disgust. He had allowed himself to be manipulated by a killer...been fooled into trusting him, and had turned to him in his troubles instead of to his own wife. It mattered not that his thoughts had been in turmoil. It was not as if Jane was a stranger...she was his old, trusted friend... the playmate who had been by his side throughout childhood...the girl who had always defended him to the hilt.

And the woman he loved.

Somehow, it was as though a dozen veils had lifted and he could see himself and his life more clearly than ever before. And he saw a blind, stubborn fool.

'Jane?'

She looked up at him, eyebrows raised in polite enquiry, but that same caution in her lovely brown eyes pierced his heart. He had pushed a warm, loving, tender woman into becoming this guarded, cool lady. She was still his wife, and he was sure she wouldn't abandon him—the Jane he knew would not easily dismiss her marriage vows. If he took her in his arms and made love to her, he didn't doubt she would respond physically. But that was no longer enough for him. He didn't want her to stay with him simply because they were married and she had little choice in the matter. He wanted it to be the choice of her heart.

He wanted her to love him again, and to trust him with her heart and her feelings.

But her response to him told him louder than words how much grovelling he must do to banish the betrayal and the bad memories.

'Would you care to come for a walk with me?'

Fear flashed into her eyes. 'What if Lascelles is out there?'

'Father has men out keeping watch but I doubt he is fool enough to come here. You will be safe with me.'

Hugo sat the nearest to the two of them and, at Alex's words, he stood, and brushed the wrinkles from his coat sleeves.

'Dom...you suggested we might go and pay our respects to your mother. I know Livvy is keen to do so.' He fixed Alex with his dark gaze. 'Why don't we all go together? Safety in numbers, after all.'

Alex glanced around the room, realising from their expressions that his family were closing ranks around Jane. Protecting her. From him. But his spurt of anger soon fizzled out, and appreciation took its place.

His family. Protective. Always.

And now Jane was one of them, and they demonstrated their concern as they always did...by being there, as they had always been there for him even though he had given little gratitude for their support. He knew they were concerned he would either sweet-talk or coerce Jane into accepting a lightweight apology. They knew him, knew his easy charm, and they knew Jane was the essence of forgiveness and would seek to understand him first, and to make allowances for him, rather than to think of her own needs. And, in their own way, they were telling him Jane deserved better.

But he knew that. Accepted it.

He wanted better for her, too.

He nodded. He and Jane had time to put this behind them. Now he could truly be part of the Beauchamp family, and was no longer an outsider looking in, they would remain at the Abbey until Twelfth Night. He would spend that time wooing his wife—this time with his heart and mind as well as his body.

'That's a good idea,' he said. 'It is a shame there are no flowers to lay in her memory.'

'They would last no time in this cold weather.' Olivia came to Alex and smiled up at him. She nodded slightly, approval in her silver-grey eyes. 'But that is no reason not to go.'

'There's a holly bush with berries out in the copse,' Father said. 'Rosalind and I will cut a few branches before joining the rest of you.'

As diplomatic as ever. His father would allow the children time to pay their respects to their mother in private before joining them with his second wife.

Alex looked down at Jane. 'Will you accept my arm, Jane?'

She smiled, took his hand and rose to her feet. 'Thank you, yes. I expect it will be slippery in places.'

They swathed themselves in greatcoats and mantles, shawls, scarves and warm hats, gloves and muffs and fur-lined boots, and ventured outside, with Hector and Romeo. The air bit at any exposed skin and their breath condensed in the chill. They huddled together for warmth as they went out through the library on to the terrace and then hurried through the formal garden, to the path and the copse beyond, heading for the lake. Once they were in the copse, Father and Stepmother veered off to look for holly berries, Hector at their heels, and Alex, with Jane on his arm, led the way to the lake and to the weeping willow that marked the spot where their mother had lost her life.

There was no return of that dark dread that had always dogged Alex in this place, just a feeling of peace and an unwavering resolve to find Anthony Lascelles and bring him to justice. Hanging was too good for him, but Alex would be content with that.

But that reminded him…he halted. Jane looked up enquiringly.

'Will you be all right, going back to where it happened?'

'I think so.' A smile flickered around her lips, drawing his attention, heating his blood. How long since he had kissed her? He yearned to hold her in his arms, to show her as well as tell her how much he loved her. 'I must face it sometime and what better way than with my own support army?'

They continued, and soon emerged on to the lakeside path, turning towards the willow, where the summer house had once stood. At first, a thicket of hawthorn, elder and brambles masked the lake from their sight but, as it came into view—ice-covered, glittering where an occasional finger of winter sun poked through the surrounding trees, their naked branches still white with frost—Jane halted, bringing Alex to a stop. The others crowded around them.

'Look!' She pointed at the willow, at the far end of the lake. 'Is that…? Alex! It is him!'

A figure, head bowed, knelt by the willow. His silver-grey hair stood out, even at this distance.

'God's teeth!' Dominic moved to stand at Alex's shoulder. 'How *dare* he come here?'

'Hugo.' Alex glanced at his brother-in-law. 'Stay with the girls. Take care of them.'

He sprinted as fast as he could, slipping and sliding at times on the frosted grass and frozen mud, Dominic by his side. He bit back his roar of rage—no need to alert that bastard to their presence. He sucked the freezing air into his lungs, his air pipe narrowing, his breath whistling, but he kept going. They rounded another thicket of shrubs, bursting into the clearing around the willow tree and only then did Lascelles' head jerk up. He leapt to his feet, backing away, leaving his hat and gloves abandoned on the ground.

'Alex…my dear boy…' He reached out, both hands. 'It was not what you think. You gave me no chance to explain.'

Alex flung out an arm to prevent Dominic launching himself at Lascelles.

'He has a knife,' he muttered.

Alex followed Lascelles, step for step, aware Dominic was moving diagonally to his left, to cut off Lascelles' escape. He wouldn't elude them this time.

'You ran away, Lascelles. It was *you* who failed to explain.'

Satisfaction gleamed in Lascelles' eyes. He plainly imagined he could talk his way out of this, using his usual charm and manipulation. Alex smiled his own satisfaction. The bastard had no clue they now knew the truth.

'I confess I loved your mother and that we were…er… intimate. But our affair was *before* she married Cheriton, you must believe me.'

'Believe you? Why should I believe a single word that spews out of that filthy mouth of yours?'

'But Alex…my boy…it is the truth.' Lascelles halted, his face the picture of innocence. 'And you, I imagine, are here to confront your father?'

'Oh, yes,' Alex said grimly. 'It's done.'

'Oh, my poor, poor Alex! But it had to be done, my boy. Justice must be served.'

At that moment, Romeo bounced into the clearing, distracting Lascelles, giving Alex the chance to move closer. Seconds later he heard the others arrive behind him. He glanced round to see the three women approaching him, and he gestured at them to stop. They could do nothing here, and Lascelles was dangerous. Hugo, he could see, was steadily moving to Alex's right. With the lake at his back, and the three men fanned out before him, Lascelles would soon have nowhere to run.

He clearly thought himself in no danger, because he actually stepped forward, his smiling attention on the women.

'Oh! Dear Jane is here, I see. I am so pleased you two have made up your differences. Do you know…' he spoke directly to Jane now '…poor Alex was quite distraught throughout our journey. It is no wonder he completely misunderstood what I said, and flew into a rage.'

'Would that be in the same way I misunderstood seeing you try to squeeze my kitten to death?' Jane's voice was icily cold.

'You were overwrought, my dear. And who can blame you with Alex's recent behaviour…but we must hope he can put the past to rest now he has exposed his father as a murd—'

'Don't you *dare*!' Rage exploded through Alex and he strode towards his father's cousin, his fists clenched. 'We *know* you did it, Lascelles, so you can save your breath for the judge!'

Lascelles backed away. 'No. No. You have it wrong…'

'*I saw you*, you bastard! I *saw* you!'

'Your father…it was your father…'

'How did you know she was wearing yellow? I didn't tell you, so how did you know?'

'I…'

Lascelles could retreat no further with the lake at his

back. His eyes swivelled from Alex to Dominic, then swept back across to Hugo, his panic now showing.

'She only married him because she wanted to be a duchess. *I* should have been the duke, but your father took my title and stole the woman I loved. And then, when I returned to England...our passion...it was as strong as ever. We *could* have carried on. We could have been happy. But then...then...' He gulped. 'It was a moment of madness.' Tears glittered in his eyes. 'I didn't mean to. I was overcome with passion... surely you understand?' His hands reached towards them, beseechingly. 'She drove me to it...she *rejected* me...all for the chance to be a better mother...'

'And you *robbed* her of that chance,' Olivia yelled, her voice cracking. She had moved forward to stand in line with the men. 'Just like you robbed *us* of our mother! And now you'll *hang* for it!'

Lascelles's eyes widened at that. Before any of them could guess his intention, he spun on his heel and ran on to the ice.

'No! You'll not get away! You'll hang for it, you bastard!' Alex charged to the edge of the ice, dodging around Dominic as he tried to head him off.

'Alex!' Dominic's roar chased him across the frozen lake as he slid and skidded after Lascelles. 'No! Don't be a fool!'

Alex ignored him, intent on closing the gap between him and Lascelles until, with a loud crack, the ice gave way and Lascelles dropped through into the lake. Alex skidded to a halt, his heart racing. The red mist that had propelled him on to the ice dissipated as he assessed the danger. He heard Jane scream his name from the shore but the urge to bring Lascelles to justice...to see him swing on the end of a rope...was irresistible. He had cowered out of sight like a coward while Lascelles had throttled Mother...he had done nothing to save her. But here was his chance to assuage some of the guilt that had haunted him his entire life.

Lascelles resurfaced, scrabbling desperately at the jagged edges of the ice.

Alex shrugged out of his greatcoat, flinging it behind him, and unwound his neckcloth as he inched forward. It was all he had to try to reach Lascelles although he doubted the other man would have strength enough to hold on while Alex hauled him out. He edged forward, testing the ice with each foot before putting his weight on to it.

'Alex!' His heart clenched at the anguish in his father's voice as it echoed across the lake. 'Come back! Please!'

But he couldn't. Lascelles slipped below the surface a second time then rose again, trying to hold on as he gasped for breath, his face blue.

Alex took another step. His stomach dived at the slight give in the ice beneath his feet. He must lie flat…distribute his weight over a bigger surface…he glanced back at the shore. His father was on the ice, closing the distance between them.

'Father!' Alex roared, his gut churning. He must make amends for his mother, but it would all be for nothing if anything were to happen to his father. His throat tightened with fear. 'Father. Go back! It's not safe.'

'Then come back. He's not worth it. *Please*, Alex.'

A scant second later an ominous crack reached his ears. He was too late to even lie down.

Water so frigid it seized his breath as he plunged into the dark depths.

Chapter Twenty-Four

'Alex!' Jane screamed, her heart bursting. 'No!'

Hands grabbed her, hauling her away from the edge of the ice. Dominic held her tight as she struggled to free herself.

'Oh, God. Oh, dear God. Please, God. Oh, God.'

The words babbled forth as the Duke lay flat and pulled himself along the surface of the ice. Too quickly for safety. Too desperate for caution. Alex resurfaced and clutched at the edge of the ice but the Duke stopped. Mere feet away.

'A rope! Something!' Sheer desperation in the Duke's voice.

'Jane!' She tore her eyes from the drama on the ice. Dominic gripped her shoulders hard. 'Do *not* go on to the ice. Do you hear me? Let us concentrate on saving Alex.'

She nodded, one sane corner of her brain acknowledging she could only make matters worse. Dominic pushed her towards where the Duchess—her eyes huge—stared out across the lake. Liberty and Olivia stood either side of her, and they parted to let Jane back into their group.

'Hurry!' The Duke's roar resounded across the lake.

Then Hugo was among them. 'Your scarves! Quick now!'

His own neckcloth was already in his hands, and Jane

saw Dominic—his hands shaking—untying his. Hugo began to knot the lengths together. There was *something* she could do...she ran to help him, noticing he'd tied one of the neckcloths to form a loop.

'Livvy—run and get help,' ordered Hugo.

'But—'

'Now, Liv. Rope. Blankets. Men. A cart.'

Olivia turned and ran. Jane had never seen this side of the normally easy-going, fun-loving Hugo. He sounded like a general barking orders at his men.

'Hector.'

The dog loped across to Hugo, who tied the looped end of their makeshift rope to his collar. And then the Duchess was there, taking Hector to the edge of the ice.

'Find Leo, boy. Go to Leo.'

Hector's ears pricked and then he was on the ice, running, his long legs splaying out at odd angles.

'It won't be long enough, but the ice is safe enough near the edge.' Dominic stepped on to the ice as Hector reached the Duke.

'No!' Hugo stopped him. 'I'm lighter than you. Let me go first. We'll form a chain. It's the only way. If anyone else goes in, at least we'll have a chance of saving *them*.'

'I'm lighter than all of you,' said Jane. 'Let me go first.'

'You haven't the strength,' Hugo said.

Jane stood, feeling helpless and useless, her mind as numb as her body. Across the lake, Alex's head and shoulders were visible, his forearms on the ice.

Please be in time. I can't lose him. Not now.

The Duke untied the makeshift rope from Hector's collar by which time Hugo, on his belly, was already close behind him. The Duke then skimmed the loop towards Alex.

'Alex! Put both arms through the loop!'

Hugo's shout was audible from the shore and, heart in

her mouth, Jane watched as Alex—excruciatingly slowly—did as Hugo said.

Please God. Please God.

'Bend your elbows. Bring your hands to your shoulders.'

Liberty joined Jane on the shore, and hugged her.

'Don't worry, Jane. They'll get him out.'

The words and gesture freed Jane from the awful numbness gripping her. She began to shake. Her throat ached with fear, and hot tears crowded her eyes. Furious, she blinked them away. She must be able to see.

Hugo anchored the Duke's booted ankles into the crook of his elbows and Dominic was on his knees, gripping Hugo's ankles. He was tantalisingly close to the shore, but not close enough.

They began to pull. It was agonisingly slow, difficult to get any purchase on the ice, but they inched backwards and Alex slowly emerged from the hole in the ice. Dominic's muscles bulged as he pulled but his knees kept slipping from under him and he seemed as far away from the edge of the ice as ever.

Jane straightened. Wrenched away from Liberty, and ventured on to the ice.

'Jane! No!'

She ignored Liberty's scream. She hadn't ice-skated for years but, even without skates, she kept her balance. She reached Alex's discarded greatcoat, grabbed it, then slid her way back to Dominic. He glared at her, sweat beading his forehead.

'Don't waste your breath scolding me.' Jane spread the coat behind Dominic, the hem closest to him. 'Lift one knee.'

She slid the edge of the coat underneath his knee. He glanced down, then back at her, hope lighting his face. He knelt on the coat and then lifted the other knee, and Jane

quickly manoeuvred herself behind him, grabbing hold
of the sleeves of the coat, but she was still on the ice and
she knew Alex's only hope was for someone to anchor on
to the land. She lay flat, as the men had done. Luck had
played its part…she had placed the greatcoat lining side
down and she could push her arms into the sleeves up to
her elbows. Her hands alone wouldn't have the strength to
grip and pull but this would help. Hands grabbed each of
her ankles and she knew then that the Duchess and Liberty
had guessed her plan. She glanced over her shoulder. Both
of them knelt on the grass. Not the ice.

'Pull!' she screamed. 'Pull!'

She sent up another silent prayer, then gritted her teeth
against the agonising wrench as her arms felt like they
were being pulled from their sockets. But they were moving and then, of a sudden, the strain eased and Alex was
out of the water, his body sliding rapidly towards safety.
And first Jane, and then Dominic, were on solid ground,
watching as the Duke and Hugo hauled Alex unceremo-
niously over the ice and on to the shore.

Fear clawed at every inch of Jane, but she refused to
give way. Alex needed her now, and she would not fail
him. She dropped to her knees, ripped off her gloves and
began to unbutton his jacket.

'Help me,' she gasped.

Between them, they stripped Alex out of his freezing,
sodden clothes and wrapped him in hastily donated coats.
He lay still. Unresponsive. Barely breathing.

'It's not enough. He's too cold. It's not enough.'

Jane had never seen the Duke look so broken. So helpless. The Duchess, shivering in her gown and shawl, had
her arms around him, her expression bleak.

'No! There must be a way to warm him. We're not giving up!' Jane lay next to Alex, putting her arms around

him. The coats were a barrier, and she burrowed into them, nestling into him, thrusting down her despair at the iciness of his skin.

A shout sounded.

'Livvy's on her way with help.' Hugo squatted beside Jane. 'You're doing the right thing, Jane. Share your body heat. I learned that when I was a boy in Northumberland. Stay with him until we get him indoors.'

That was all the encouragement she needed. She closed her eyes and stayed tucked close as they were further wrapped in blankets and placed on a hand cart and taken back to the Abbey. Alex was then placed in a tub of warm water—*Not too hot*, Hugo ordered—and Jane sat by his side, as servants hurried in and out, dipping out buckets of cooling water and replacing them with warm for what seemed like hours.

He was breathing. His heart was beating. His skin began to regain colour. That was what she concentrated on, murmuring her love for him into his ear, begging him not to give in...to come back to her...not to die.

He'd not inhaled any water—a blessing the doctor said when he arrived. He confirmed Alex could be moved into a warmed bed, and told them they must be patient and allow Alex to wake up when he was ready.

Alex came to his senses slowly, gradually becoming aware he was in bed, in his bedchamber, with a fire in the hearth. Two figures sat at his bedside, one either side. To his right, his father. He frowned, and looked left. Relief enveloped him. Jane.

She was all he needed.

But there was something...he racked his brains...something he must say to her. Before it was too late. Something he'd regretted...something he'd wanted to say to her...when he was cold…so cold…when he was sure he'd left it too late. He shivered involuntarily, and she stirred, her eyes meeting his. Eyes filled with the love he had taken for granted until it was almost too late.

The memory shot to the surface… Lascelles…the ice… the cold…

Alex reached for Jane, and she took his hand, smiling tenderly. 'All I could think…' his voice was a hoarse whisper '…when I thought I would die…' She whimpered, and tightened her hand around his. He squeezed back. 'All I could think was I would never get the chance to tell you— and to *prove* to you—how much I love you, Janey.'

Her glorious, beloved smile was all the response he needed. He felt his eyelids droop. Everything seemed such an effort…all he wanted was to sleep again but he was loath to close his eyes, needing the reassurance Jane was with him. He was vaguely aware his father had stirred, and he wrenched his gaze from Jane.

'Welcome back, Son.' Tears shone in Father's eyes. 'We thought we'd lost you. Thank God you've lived to plague us all for a few years yet.' His smile wobbled. 'I'll say goodnight, and we'll talk in the morning.' He switched his attention to Jane. 'Thank you, Jane, for all you have done. Goodnight.'

Alex barely noticed him leave the room. He pulled the eiderdown aside. 'Come to bed, Honeybee. I need to hold you. To know I am not alone.'

She smiled again, slipped off her robe and slid into bed, wrapping her arms around him.

'Silly,' she whispered. 'You'll never be alone while you have me and your family. Now sleep.'

The following day he learned Lascelles had drowned but he found it impossible to summon up either guilt or regret. The need for revenge no longer consumed him—all he wanted, with his whole being, was to be a good husband to Jane and to share everything in his life with her. No longer would he keep parts of his life separate…he no longer needed to. He was reconciled with his father. There were no more past secrets hanging over him.

But he must talk…properly…to Jane, and set their problems to rest.

But that, frustratingly, proved almost impossible, with a houseful of people constantly asking him if he was well and wanting to share their experience of the drama with him. On doctor's orders, he was to rest and stay warm. He'd already refused to remain in bed, and compromised by agreeing to sit by the fire in the parlour but there was no privacy for what he wanted to say to his wife. She had told him, repeatedly, she was happy not to talk about it yet, but that made him more determined to clear the air. He'd spent too much of their marriage avoiding awkward conversations. It was time to put that right.

Eventually, at the end of his tether and sick of being treated as an invalid, he took action.

'Alex?' He'd taken advantage of her brief absence to order William, one of his father's footmen, to take a message to the stables to prepare his carriage. Now, Jane burst in, her eyes huge. 'William said you've ordered the carriage. Are you…are you going home?'

Her uncertainty tore at him. Still she feared the worst.

'No, sweetheart,' he said. 'I'm going nowhere without you by my side. *We* are going for a carriage ride so *I* can set your mind at rest once and for all, and without interruption from well-meaning members of my own family.'

'But you aren't strong enough, Alex. The doctor said—'

'Stuff the doctor.' Alex threw aside the rug Rosalind had insisted he wear over his legs and stood up.

'But, Alex—'

'No more "buts", Janey. I am going. Will you come with me?'

He held out his hand. Jane stared at it.

'Half an hour…that's all. I promise. We won't even leave the estate.'

Jane smiled, taking his hand. 'Very well. But you must also promise that if you start to get tired, or feel ill, or—'

'Yes, yes.' Alex laughed as he swept her into his arms and kissed her. 'I promise I will tell you. But you ought to know, my darling wife, that it will take a lot more than a dip into an icy lake to keep me down. Now, make sure you wrap up warm—I don't want you distracted by the shivers while I am eating humble pie. At least…' he captured her gaze '…not *that* sort of shivering!'

He was rewarded by her blush, and a loving smile.

He handed Jane into the carriage to find fur rugs, blankets and hot bricks already inside and he realised William must have arranged them before he relayed Alex's request to the stables.

'Thank you, William.'

William bowed. 'It would never do for Lady Jane to catch a chill, milord,' he replied, with a grin.

'Now. Janey.' Alex faced Jane as the carriage set off at a sedate walk. 'I only know to start by saying I am sorry.'

She pressed her fingers to his lips.

'I am sorry, too, Alex. If I had known what burden you were suffering under, I would never have left the way I did. I couldn't imagine *anything* so awful you couldn't share it with me. I was wrong.'

'I never meant to tell anyone about my suspicions, Jane. I certainly never intended to tell Lascelles but it somehow blurted out. Oh, Janey, I've been such a fool. You warned me how manipulative he was, but I wouldn't listen and I stepped straight into his web. All I could think of was finding out more about my mother and trying to stop the fear that my father had killed her from surfacing.'

'I still find it hard to understand how you believed it. You know your father is an honourable man—how could you ever believe he could assault and strangle his own wife?'

Alex thrust his hand through his hair. 'I didn't even know that memory was lurking in the depths of my mind. All I knew…all I have *ever* known…is that I did not dare allow my memory of that day to fully form, knowing instinctively it would spell disaster for my family. And so I kept it suppressed. I didn't even realise I'd witnessed my mother's murder. I believed what they believed, and what they told me…that I had found her body.'

He hauled in a deep breath, and took her hands in his. 'But that's not why we're here, Janey. We are here to talk about us. About our marriage. About…' and his pulse gave that little kick he felt whenever he looked deep into her beautiful eyes '…about how much I love you.'

'Do you, Alex? Truly?'

'I do,' he vowed, solemnly. 'And I shall tell you so every day. You need never doubt me again…you *may* accuse me of being a slow learner, however, for I did not realise how far you had burrowed your way into my heart until after you left.' He drew in a shuddering breath. 'I *never* want to feel that way again. Ever. I have learned my lesson.

'Darling Honeybee…' He pulled her close, and kissed her lips, but he didn't allow himself to deepen it even though his blood hummed with the need of her. He still had things to say. 'I didn't even realise how deeply I hurt you by not telling you what was in my head. It was never that I didn't trust you, please believe me. I only thought to protect you—to protect them all. And I thought I could manage it alone, as I always have. But when I found you gone…when I realised how badly I'd hurt you—only then did I realise how deeply I love you, and that I no longer want to manage *anything* alone.'

Jane smiled at him, and put one hand against his cheek. 'I love you, too, Alex. I always have, even when I was that annoying little girl for ever buzzing around and driving you mad.'

'Then I am doubly all kinds of a fool for not recognising the treasure under my nose all this time.'

His lips feathered over hers…once…twice…then he angled his head to deepen his kiss and to dip his tongue inside, tasting her sweetness as she melted in his arms.

Epilogue

The entire Beauchamp family descended on the Abbey for Christmastide. It was chaotic. And Alex loved every minute of it.

The two weeks between Alex's accident and Christmas day had been sweet beyond measure. The woman he loved was by his side—and she was happy...*he* was making her happy! And, for almost the first time in his life, he could relax enough to allow his love to shine forth.

He could finally enjoy being a member of the Beauchamp family.

His family.

His wonderful, funny, joyful family.

Dominic and Olivia and their spouses were there from the start, of course, together with Julius and Daisy. But the fun really started once Uncle Vernon and Aunt Cecily arrived with their respective families, a week before Christmas.

Remembering Aunt Cecily's reaction when she saw him still made his throat ache with emotion. Nothing, it seemed, could stem her flow of tears as she tumbled from the carriage. She'd run to Alex, hugging him as though she would never let him go...as she used to when he was a boy, until he outgrew such nonsense. Then, over the top of her head, he caught sight of first his father, his silver-grey eyes shiny, and then Uncle Vernon with his own eyes sheening and, before he could blink them away, tears rolled unchecked down Alex's cheeks.

He'd soon found himself in great demand as a fun-loving big brother to Christabel and Sebastian and as uncle to the rest of the nippers, and he discovered it wasn't only Dominic who had a natural rapport with the children. At first he hung back, expecting one of his black moods to rear up, driving him to his usual role of watching with envy as everyone else made merry. But his moods had vanished and he no longer needed to retreat behind his barriers and keep everyone at bay.

And now, the ribald comments missing from their wedding night started…teasing remarks about it being time for Alex to add to the Beauchamp clan by filling the Foxbourne nursery.

How long had it been since any of his family had ribbed him like this?

It felt good.

The only sour note had been their visit to Stowford Place. After a stultifying hour sipping tea and making polite conversation, Jane had suggested to her father that in future he might prefer to call upon them at the Abbey. He had gratefully agreed.

The six men of the family spent Christmas Eve morning collecting greenery: branches of holly, ivy, laurel and fir from the woods, rosemary and bay from the gardens, and mistletoe from the apple orchard. The women then decorated the house, adding candles and fir cones, clove-studded oranges, ribbons and silver and gold paper flowers. In the afternoon, the men then took all the children to help haul the Yule log back to the house, even George, who couldn't yet walk—Zach showing Uncle Vernon how to twist a shawl into a sling, as the Romany mothers did, to carry his baby son. The others took turns at giving shoulder rides to the younger children when they grew tired.

The log fit snugly in the huge fireplace in the drawing room, where it should burn from Christmas Eve right through to the end of Christmas night. The fire was ceremoniously lit using the remnants of last year's log, and the Christmas candle was placed on the windowsill to burn through the night.

Christmas morning dawned bright, albeit with a heavy frost. From the way the clouds were gathering—lowering and merging until the sky was uniformly white—snow looked likely by nightfall. The family attended the traditional Christmas morning church service and, on their return, were greeted by the three dogs who, with the delicious smell of roasting meat pervading the whole house, could hardly contain their excitement. Even the normally serene Hector was lolloping around, barking, tail waving like a flag, while Myrtle bounced around stiff-legged, like a barrel on springs, emitting shrill yips of excitement. Romeo hared into the drawing room and then streaked back into the hall, a slender fir branch, completed with red satin bows, trailing in his wake. He rounded the table in the middle of the hall and darted between Father's legs, evading all attempts to catch him. Liberty grew tearful, but Dominic hugged her better, reassuring her that it all added to the fun.

The family exchanged gifts. Alex immediately donned his waistcoat and Jane went all teary-eyed over the gold locket containing a lock of his hair that Alex had bought her on a quick trip to Exeter. The whole family then played riotous games of Hoodman Blind, Shoe the Wild Mare and Bob Apple—Aunt Thea proving herself almost unbeatable, much to Uncle Vernon's chagrin—until Grantham announced Christmas dinner was served and informed them it was snowing.

In accordance with Beauchamp tradition, once the meal was on the table, the servants were free to eat their own dinner in the servants' hall. That included the nursemaids, and thus all the children, even George, joined the family around the dining table…after they had all crowded at the windows to exclaim at the beauty of the familiar landscape now shrouded in white.

The snow, to Alex's mind, simply added to the magic of the occasion.

The meal was chaotic. But fun. And Susie, bless her—barely out of childhood herself at thirteen, quiet and serious and still looking much younger than her age—took charge of George, freeing Aunt Thea and Uncle Vernon to cope with Thomas and Sophie.

Finally it was over. Everyone was full of roast goose and plum pudding and the nursery maids returned to take their eight exhausted charges upstairs to get ready for bed. Susie went, too, after being begged by Thomas to read them a bedtime story, while the adults trooped out of the dining room to head for the drawing room, Alex and Jane in the rear.

Alex grabbed Jane's hand as they crossed the hall, tugging her around to face him. 'We've barely had a minute to talk all day, Janey. And I haven't kissed you since this morning.'

Jane gazed up at him, her eyes full of love. He brushed one glowing cheek with the back of his fingers and then tucked a stray tendril of silky conker-brown hair behind her ear.

'Would you have it any other way?' She tipped her head, a teasing smile on her lips. 'Is this not what you have longed for—to be happy in the bosom of your family?'

He smiled, contentment flooding him. Anchoring him. Finally he belonged.

'Yes, and it would not be half as sweet without you by my side to share it, Honeybee.' He put his arms around her slender waist and breathed in her jasmine scent. Her hands slipped up his chest to rest on his shoulders as their gazes fused. 'More importantly, have *you* enjoyed yourself?'

Words weren't even needed. The beam that lit Jane's beautiful, beloved face told him all he needed to know.

'This,' she said, 'has been the best Christmas I can ever remember. I didn't know it was possible to be so happy. I love your family, Alex. And I love you most of all.'

He lowered his lips to her ear. 'Have you seen where we're standing?'

They looked up into the forked green lobes of mistletoe, glistening with white berries.

'That is a lot of kisses.' Jane's eyes darkened.

'Better get started then.'

He gently cupped her chin. 'Merry Christmas, Janey.' He caressed her lips with his, the sweet need building inside him. He would never tire of this.

Sweet Janey. His Honeybee. His wife.

Delicate fingers slid around his nape and through his hair as a purr of pure satisfaction hummed in her throat. The blood quickened in his veins as desire rippled through him.

Footsteps on the tiled floor broke the spell.

'Don't forget to remove a berry.' Aunt Cecily indicated the mistletoe, smiling indulgently. 'But make haste. Your father sent me to hurry you along.'

Alex pressed a kiss to Jane's palm before leading her into the drawing room where the family sat on sofas and chairs grouped around the fire. Father, his arm resting along the mantelshelf, was talking to Hugo, sitting with his arm around Olivia.

Alex's stepmother smiled as Alex and Jane entered. 'Leo! Here they are.'

Father looked up. 'Splendid. Alex, pour a glass of champagne for you and Jane, would you please?'

The rest of the family already held full glasses and Alex sensed the air of expectancy in the room. As soon as Alex and Jane were settled, Father cleared his throat.

'This Christmas marks the end of a very special year for our family. We welcome both Liberty and Jane, and I, personally, should like to thank you both for making my sons the happiest of men.

'Dominic—you are to be a father yourself before long. I know you and Liberty will make wonderful parents, and Rosalind and I cannot wait to meet our next grandson or granddaughter.

'I also have Hugo and Olivia's permission to announce the happy news that the twins can expect a little brother or sister in the summer. Again, I cannot wait to meet him or her. Congratulations to you both.'

A murmur of excitement rippled around the room. Olivia blushed, and Hugo simply looked immensely proud.

'Which brings me to Alex.' Father paused, and Alex felt the full force of his penetrating silver-grey gaze. 'Welcome home, Son. For too many years you have been a stranger, but now you are back in the family fold and *nothing* could make me happier.

'Jane…' Again he paused, and when he spoke again, his voice was choked. 'Jane. Thank you. From the bottom of all our hearts, thank you. Without you, I do not believe the last few months would have had a happy ending.'

'So,' Father raised his glass high, the cut glass sparkling as it reflected the firelight, 'I now propose a toast. To us.

'To the Beauchamps.

'May we continue to go from strength to strength. From our generation,' his gaze rested in turn on Stepmother, on Uncle Vernon and Aunt Thea, and on Aunt Cecily and Zach, 'to yours,' and it was the turn of Dominic and Liberty, of Alex and Jane, and of Hugo and Olivia, 'and to the generation to follow—our beloved children upstairs, and those yet to be born.

'May they grow healthy and may they prosper and, most important of all, may they be as blessed as their elders in finding the precious gift of love.'

'To the Beauchamps.' Every voice joined in that toast.

Alex felt as though his heart might burst with joy as he looked at each member of his cherished family in turn. Finally, his gaze reached Jane and lingered, lovingly. They shared a tender smile as their glasses clinked together.

'To the most treasured gift of all,' Alex whispered. 'To love.'

* * * * *

*If you enjoyed this story
check out the other books in
The Beauchamp Heirs miniseries*

Lady Olivia and the Infamous Rake
Daring to Love the Duke's Heir

*And why not check out
The Beauchamp Betrothals miniseries?*

Cinderella and the Duke
Scandal and Miss Markham
Lady Cecily and the Mysterious Mr Gray